'I wonder where my bedchamber can be. Perhaps the landlord can show me the way.'

The corridor was very busy, and through the doorway opposite she could see that the taproom was packed with men enjoying ale and tobacco while they sheltered from the rain. Of the landlord there was no sign.

Undeterred, Evelina made her way quickly through the coffee room, trying to ignore the inquisitive stares of its patrons. She kept her eyes fixed upon the door, putting out her hand as she approached. It opened easily, but in her haste she did not see the slight step down and found herself hurtling through the doorway, off balance. She cannoned into the man nearest the door.

'Oh, I beg your pardon,' she gasped as strong arms shot out to steady her. 'I—'Her words died away as she looked up and found herself staring into the all-too-familiar face of Nick Wylder.

Evelina's breath caught in her throat, and for an instant she thought she might faint. The look of surprise on Nick's face gave way to one of wry humour. The corners of his mouth lifted.

'Oh, Lord,' he murmured. 'This was not meant to happen.'

WICKED CAPTAIN, WAYWARD WIFE

Sarah Mallory

First published in Great Britain 2010
Large Print edition 2010
Harlequin Mills & Boon Limited,
Eton House, 18-24 Paradise Road, Richmond, Surrey TW9 1SR

© Sarah Mallory 2010

ISBN: 978 0 263 21158 0

Harlequin Mills & Boon policy is to use papers that are natural, renewable and recyclable products and made from wood grown in sustainable forests. The logging and manufacturing process conform to the legal environmental regulations of the country of origin.

Printed and bound in Great Britain
by CPI Antony Rowe, Chippenham, Wiltshire

Sarah Mallory was born in Bristol, and now lives in an old farmhouse on the edge of the Pennines with her husband and family. She left grammar school at sixteen, to work in companies as varied as stockbrokers, marine engineers, insurance brokers, biscuit manufacturers and even a quarrying company. Her first book was published shortly after the birth of her daughter. She has published more than a dozen books under the pen-name of Melinda Hammond, winning the Reviewers' Choice Award in 2005 from Singletitles.com for DANCE FOR A DIAMOND, and the Historical Novel Society's Editors' Choice in November 2006 for GENTLEMEN IN QUESTION.

Previous novels by the same author:

MORE THAN A GOVERNESS
THE WICKED BARON

To the Romantic Novelists' Association,
for the unstinting friendship and support
I have found there.

Chapter One

Makerham Court, Surrey—July 1783

'Ouch!'

Evelina jumped as the rose thorn pricked her finger. How timely, she thought, staring at the tiny bead of blood. She had just been thinking that this was the most dangerous activity she undertook; cutting flowers. She sighed. These sheltered ornamental gardens at Makerham summed up her life; ordered, secure, protected. She wiped the blood from her finger and firmly suppressed the vague feeling of dissatisfaction. She had become more aware of it recently, this impression of being stifled. But she was happy, wasn't she, keeping house for her grandfather? He had promised to take care of her, to provide for her. She need not worry about anything.

Evelina picked up her basket of summer flowers and was walking back to the house when she heard the sound of hoofbeats on the drive. She looked up to see a rider approaching on a rangy black horse. At the stone bridge that gave access to the ancient, moated house she stopped, her head tilted enquiringly as he rode up. The man drew rein and jumped down. He was very tall, she noted. Strong, too, judging by the width of shoulder beneath his dark riding jacket and the powerful legs encased in buckskins and gleaming top boots. His black hair was caught back with a ribbon and there was a rakish look in his laughing blue eyes. He looked like an adventurer, she thought. Tall and dark and…

'You must be Evelina.' His voice was rich and warm as honey. 'How do you do?'

Without waiting for her reply he reached out, pulled her into his arms and kissed her. Eve was so shocked she dropped her basket. She made no effort to pull away; with his arms holding her so firmly it would have been impossible to do so, even if she had wanted to. She had never been kissed by a man before and the sensation was surprisingly pleasant, jolting her senses alive so that she was aware of the scent of his skin, the mingled smell of soap and spices and horses and…she did not know what. Man, she supposed.

He raised his head and gave her a rueful smile, although Eve thought the glint in his deep blue eyes positively wicked.

'Oh Lord,' he said, stepping back from her. 'That was not meant to happen.'

Eve stared up at him, shaken, and wondered what a well-bred young lady should do in this situation. With some deliberation she brought her hand up and dealt him a ringing slap across the face.

He flinched a little, but continued to smile down at her, mischief glinting in his blue eyes. 'I suppose I deserved that.'

It took an effort for Eve to look away from that hypnotic gaze. Her basket was lying on the floor, roses, irises and common daisies tossed on to the drive. With shaking hands she began to gather them up. The man dropped onto one knee beside her, unsettling her with his nearness.

'You do not seem very pleased to see me,' he remarked.

She concentrated on collecting up the flowers and putting them back into the basket. She said stiffly. 'I do not know you sir.'

'Oh, did your grandfather not tell you?'

Laughter trembled in his voice. 'I am Nick Wylder.' He picked up a rose and held it out to her. 'I am the man you are going to marry.'

Eve jumped to her feet. The man rose in one agile movement and looked down at her with pure amusement in his eyes. A devil-may-care man, she thought. His lean, handsome face was too attractive. Dangerous. Instinctively she drew away from him.

'Your jest lacks humour, sir.'

Those mobile black brows drew together slightly. 'Has your grandfather not told you? Then my apologies, Miss Shawcross.'

She regarded his flashing smile with suspicion. 'I see no remorse in you sir. I do not believe you know how to apologise.'

He stepped back, his smile softening into something gentler as he said contritely, 'I have truly offended you. Pray, ma'am, forgive me. I did not mean to do that.'

She was not proof against his beguiling look and found herself weakening. She made an effort to maintain her scornful attitude. 'It seems to me, sir, that there is much you do not mean to do!'

He treated her again to his devastating smile and this time she noticed the dimple in his cheek. It was so very distracting.

'Aha, you are not so angry after all. I see the twinkle in your eye, Miss Shawcross. You would laugh, if you were not determined to put me in my place! Am I forgiven, ma'am?'

She turned away that he would not see her smile. 'That depends upon your future conduct Mr... Wylder. Am I to understand that you have come to see my grandfather?'

'I have indeed, ma'am, if he is well enough to receive me. I sent my man over this morning to advise you of my arrival.'

She inclined her head. 'I have not seen Grandpapa since we broke our fast together, so I know nothing of your message. However, that does not mean you are unwelcome. Pray come in, sir, and I will ascertain if he can see you.'

She left the visitor in the great hall with its walls lined with armour. Shields, swords and halberds battled for place between the long windows, a reminder of the turbulent period when the hall was built. As she ran up the stairs she glanced back at him. He was standing before the huge fireplace, studying the crest carved into the overmantel. His head was thrown back and she was treated to an excellent view of his profile with its straight nose and strong jaw-line. Powerful. Confident.

She thought how well he would fit into those unsettled times.

As soon as she was out of sight at the top of the stairs she stopped and leaned against the wall. Her heart was thudding uncomfortably in her chest. So it had happened; her grandfather had always promised her that one day he would bring home a husband for her. He had told her to trust him to find a suitable gentleman, one who would look after her as he had always done. One who would make her happy. She pressed her hands to her cheeks. She had expected Grandfather to bring home someone like Squire Amos from Makerham village, someone solid and respectable. There was no doubt that the gentleman now standing in the great hall was solid—when he had crushed her to him he had felt very solid indeed—but she doubted very much that he was respectable. Eve was aware that she had led a very sheltered life, but she knew that respectable gentlemen did not kiss young ladies before they had even been introduced! And respectable young ladies did not stay to exchange banter with such scoundrels. Eve wondered why she had not run away when the man released her. Somewhat to her surprise she realised that he had not frightened her. She had been shocked, yes, and outraged, but never afraid. She took a deep breath and smoothed her hands down over her gown. If only it was as easy to smooth her disordered nerves. If Grandpapa discovered the cause of her agitation he would be alarmed; he might even send his visitor away. With a little jolt of surprise she realised that she really did not want that to happen.

Eve found her grandfather in the morning room. His winged chair had been moved to the window and he was sitting now with a blanket across his knees, gazing out over the park.

'Grandpapa?'

Sir Benjamin Shawcross had been a good-looking man in his youth, but ill health had aged him prematurely and although he was not much more than sixty, his skin had grown sallow and the flesh hung loosely on his large frame.

However, despite the great effort it cost him every morning, he insisted that his valet, Rooney, should help him out of bed and dress him in his velvet coat and fresh linen. His sparse grey hair was hidden by a curly wig in the old style and there was always a twinkle in his faded blue eyes. It was in evidence now as he looked at his granddaughter.

'Eve, my dear, come in. Rooney has made me

comfortable here, you see, where I can look out of the window. I have a visitor, you know.'

'Yes, sir, I do know.' Eve put down her basket and slipped across the room to his side.

As she bent to drop a kiss on his forehead she glanced out of the window. The room looked out over the front drive, but thankfully any view of the little stone bridge was blocked by the bulk of the Gate House tower. Her grandfather would not have seen her first encounter with his guest. She dropped down to sit on the footstool beside his chair and gathered his gnarled old hands between her own. 'Mr Wylder is even now in the hall, Grandpapa.'

'Captain, my love; he is Captain Wylder. He sailed with Admiral Howe against the French and acquitted himself well, by all accounts.'

'That may be so, sir, but before he is brought up I want you to tell me just why he is here.'

'A pretty thing, child, if I must answer to you for inviting a guest to my own house!'

Eve was not deceived by his blustering tone. She saw the consternation in his faded eyes, but she was not to be swayed from her course. 'Please, Grandfather, tell me.'

'I have known the family for years. Nick Wylder

is the younger brother of the Earl of Darrington. Of course we are not well acquainted, for he is so much younger than I am and he has spent most of his time at sea. He resigned with Howe in '78, you know. Neither of them thought very much of the government's handling of the American War but before they could return to England they were caught up in the defence of Rhode Island. Clever bit o' work, that.' Sir Benjamin chuckled. 'Outwitted the French all right and tight, and young Nicholas in the thick of it. Commended for his bravery, mentioned in the newspapers. You may remember it—'

'That was five years ago, Grandpapa,' Eve interrupted him quietly but firmly. 'And I do not remember you ever drawing my attention to a Captain Wylder.'

'No, well, perhaps not. In fact I did not recall much about it myself, until young Nicholas sought me out at Tunbridge Wells last month. It was Percy Anderton told me his history. Percy lost his son in the action, you see, and Captain Wylder came to see him as soon as he returned to England, to pay his respects. Percy was very impressed. Captain Wylder has friends in the government, too it appears—young Pitt and Lord North—'

'But you said Captain Wylder sought you out, Grandpapa,' Eve persisted, frowning. 'Why should he do that?'

'Why should he not? Old family friend, after all.'

'Yes, but why should he wait until now to look you up?'

'I have no idea, but I am very glad he did. A fine young man, Eve, and very attentive to me. I invited him to call upon us…'

'But you have not said a word about him to me, Grandpapa.'

Sir Benjamin stirred uncomfortably in his chair. 'No, well, the time did not seem propitious, and after all, I did not know if he would really come.'

'Have you brought him here as a husband for me?' she asked in her direct way.

'He did mention to me that he was looking for a wife, and…'

'And you want me to take a husband.'

'Only if you are inclined to do so, Evelina.'

'I have told you, Grandfather, I have no wish for a husband yet.'

'But you will need someone to look after you when I am gone.'

'Grandpapa!'

'Do not frown at me, Eve. We both know that I am

failing. Doctor Scott has warned us that my heart is very weak now; the end cannot be far away—'

'You must not say such things,' she said fiercely.

'Ignoring the inevitable will not prevent it, my love. If Nick Wylder wants to wed you I recommend you to accept him. I shall not insist, of course, but I would ask that you consider the matter very carefully.' He squeezed her fingers and released them. 'Now, we must not keep our guest waiting any longer. Have Captain Wylder fetched up, Evelina.'

'But, sir—'

He waved his hand impatiently. 'Would you have me thought uncivil, gel? Tell Green to show him up.'

The order was given, and Eve went back to stand beside her grandfather. He reached for her hand.

'Trust me on this, love; I am thinking only of you. Ah…' He turned towards the door as the butler announced his visitor. 'My dear sir, you are very welcome! Forgive me for not getting up to meet you, but my legs are very weak today. The baths at Tunbridge did not help me overmuch on this occasion.'

'I am sorry to hear it, Sir Benjamin.'

Evelina watched Captain Nick Wylder stride into the room, his healthy vigour even more in evidence

when contrasted with her grandfather's feeble-
ness. He came forwards and bowed to his host,
exuding energy. Sir Benjamin smiled and nodded.

'You have met my granddaughter, Evelina?'

Eve found those blue eyes fixed upon her. She
had the strange impression that he could read her
innermost thoughts. She put up her chin and
returned his look defiantly.

'Yes indeed.' Nick Wylder turned and made a
fine leg to her. 'That is, we introduced ourselves,
but I am glad of this opportunity to be more
formally presented, sir.' His eyes laughed at her.
'I fear Miss Shawcross disapproves of me.'

She sank into a curtsy, her cheeks burning. How
was it possible to want to laugh and be cross at
the same time? She had no experience of gentlemen like Captain Wylder, but instinct told her to
beware of him.

Eve determined she would not talk to the captain
but her resolve was unnecessary. By the time she
had risen out of her curtsy, he had engaged Sir
Benjamin in conversation, discussing with ease
such diverse subjects as the efficacy of hot baths,
the pleasures of hunting and the grand tour. There
was nothing for her to do but to arrange her
flowers in the vase Green had provided for her.

She was out of reason cross that she could not deliver a snub to the laughing gentleman.

'I saw you ride in, Captain,' said Sir Benjamin. 'I take it your baggage follows you?'

'Yes, sir. Richard Granby, my valet, accompanies it in my travelling carriage.'

'You are staying?' Eve blurted out.

Once more those disturbingly blue eyes rested upon her.

'I am afraid so. Will that inconvenience you?'

'N-no...' she faltered. 'That is, you are staying no more than the one night, I hope.'

Sir Benjamin chuckled. 'Take no notice of my granddaughter, Captain Wylder. She is a great one for jesting.'

'So I have noticed, Sir Benjamin.' He smiled across at her in a way that made Eve want to hit him.

'Captain Wylder is making a prolonged visit with us,' explained Sir Benjamin.

'Really?' Eve pinned on a brittle, sugar-sweet smile.

'I am greatly indebted to your grandfather for allowing me to stay with you,' Nick bowed to her. 'I shall have plenty of time to grow used to your funning.'

Eve turned back to her flower arrangement. Her

angry, jerky movements broke one of the stems and she was obliged to breathe deeply and calm herself before she continued. The butler came in with a decanter and two glasses and after that the gentlemen paid her no attention, engrossed in their discussions of hunters and bloodlines, so, as soon as she had finished, Eve muttered her excuses and made her escape.

Nick watched her leave the room, her little heels kicking up her skirts as she crossed the floor. A slight cough from Sir Benjamin made him turn and he found his host was holding out his empty glass, indicating with the lift of an eyebrow that it should be refilled. Nick hesitated and the older man winked at him. 'Come along, my boy. My butler and my granddaughter might argue that brandy is not good for me, but *you* have not heard my doctor say so. Life is for living, sir, and I mean to enjoy what little time I have left.'

'I cannot fault that philosophy, Sir Benjamin.' Nick grinned and carried both glasses over to the decanter. 'Miss Shawcross seems a little agitated,' he remarked. 'I do hope my visit is not inopportune…'

Sir Benjamin chuckled. 'Her feathers are ruffled because I omitted to tell her you were coming.'

'I gathered that much.' Nick smiled to himself as he recalled his first meeting with Evelina Shawcross. 'I am afraid I might have ruffled her feathers even more.'

'No matter, she'll come round.' Sir Benjamin sipped his brandy. 'She's a good gel, my grand-daughter. Level-headed and with as sweet a nature as any man could wish. She's not the flighty sort, never shown any desire to go off exploring.' The old man sighed a little. 'Her mother was quite the opposite. Never happier than when she was travelling the world. Took my son off all over the place when they was married. But Eve's different, a quiet gel. She needs a husband who can give her all the comforts she has enjoyed here at Makerham. A man who will look after her properly. Can you do that, Captain?'

Nick suddenly found himself fixed with a fierce stare from those faded eyes. He returned the look steadily.

'You know my circumstances, Sir Benjamin. I believe I can keep a wife in tolerable comfort.'

'Yes, yes, but will you make her happy?'

Nick fought down a smile.

'I have never had any complaints yet, sir.'

'That's what worries me, a good-looking dog

like you. I saw the women at Tunbridge making eyes at you, throwing out lures—and some of 'em old enough to know better!'

'But what you didn't see was my responding to any of their—er—lures,' replied Nick evenly. 'Let us be clear, Sir Benjamin. I am not a monk; there have been plenty of women in my life, but none of 'em more than a flirtation. If I take a wife, she will have nothing to fear on that score.'

'I'm glad to hear it. Well, sir, if you are wishful to marry my granddaughter, then go to it. But mind you; it must be her decision. I'll not have her coerced into anything.'

Nick raised his glass.

'From the little I have seen of the lady, sir, I think she will make up her own mind.'

When Eve went to her room to change for dinner, her maid Martha was laying out her new gown.

'My blue silk?' she exclaimed. 'Is that not a little grand for a family dinner?'

'We must make you look your best for your visitor, miss.'

'I am not sure the occasion warrants such a display,' Eve objected mildly, but Martha was not to be deterred.

'Captain Wylder is a fine gentleman, miss. Son of an earl, his man says.'

'I know that, Martha.'

'Ah, but did you also know that he is a hero? In the Americas he was, fighting the rebels. Captain *Wyldfire* they called him.' She spread out the petticoats for Eve to step into them.

'Martha, what have I told you about repeating servants' gossip?'

'This is not gossip, miss,' Martha corrected her; 'It is *information*. He was a bold and fearless captain, Mr Granby told me, always to be found where the fighting was thickest. That's where he got the name Wyldfire, they say, because he blazed his way through the enemy lines.'

'And who says so? His own servants, I don't doubt.'

'Aye, well, Mr Granby told me some of it, but William the coachman also had it from his groom, who has been with the family for ever.'

Eve gave a little huff of disbelief. 'I believe they are all besotted with their master. I shall write to my old schoolfriend Maria Scott—Lady Gryfford as she is now. Her letters are always full of society gossip so I am sure she will be able to furnish me with a true account of our guest.'

'I am sure she will, miss,' replied Martha comfortably. 'And I am sure it will bear out all that has been said. Well, you only have to look at him, so tall and handsome as he is. A real hero, is Captain Wyldfire.'

'Well there will be no need for him to be a hero in this house,' retorted Eve crossly. She glanced at the red leather box on the dressing table. 'What is that?'

'Your sainted mother's sapphires.' replied Martha. 'Sir Benjamin ordered them to be sent up to you. He wants you to wear them tonight.'

Eve put a hand up to her bare neck. 'G-Grandpapa sent them?'

'Why, yes, miss. Most insistent he was.'

She stared at the box. At last she said quietly, 'Then, of course, I must wear them.'

Nick stood by the fireplace in the little parlour and looked down at the flames leaping merrily in the hearth. One of the logs had fallen forward; he resisted the temptation to push it back into place with his toe. Richard had worked hard to coax him into his dark blue frock-coat and the knee breeches that were the required mode of evening dress for a formal dinner and he knew his trusty servant would think his efforts wasted if he was to end up with wood ash on his soft leather shoes or, even worse, spattered on his white silk stockings. Instead he picked up the tongs and rearranged the logs until the flames were licking hungrily around them. He straightened as the door opened and Miss Shawcross entered. After their encounter on the drive he thought he had himself well under control, but it was an effort to prevent his jaw from dropping as he looked at her. She was a vision in cobalt blue and silver lace, her glorious hair piled on her head and one glossy black curl falling on to her shoulder. Nick smiled to himself; he had come to Makerham determined to court Evelina Shawcross, even if she had been hunchbacked and with a squint. This glorious creature was like a gift from the gods. She aroused in him all that was good—and bad! There was a troubled look on her face as she came into the room and he said hurriedly,

'I understood this is where you meet before dinner…'

'You are perfectly correct, sir. I am only sorry that there was no one here to greet you.'

He smiled.

'You are here now, that is all that matters.' He walked forwards to give her his arm. The sapphires around her neck twinkled, enhancing the beauty of that slender column. He longed to put up a hand and touch the creamy skin, but she was like a wild animal, tense and ready for flight. He must go carefully.

'Miss Shawcross, you are not happy with me here.'

'Oh—no, I—'

Her hand fluttered on his arm and he covered her fingers with his own. She was trembling.

'Please,' he murmured, 'while we are alone let me say this. If you would prefer me to leave, I will make my excuses to Sir Benjamin—'

She stopped, her eyes downcast, the long lashes black against her pale cheeks. Nick watched the play of emotion on her countenance; saw the resolute set of her mouth.

'You are my grandfather's guest, sir. It is his will that you should stay, and to me his will is paramount.'

'But I shall be guided by your wishes, lady. Tell me what you want me to do.' He continued softly, 'We made a wretched beginning. Forgive me for that, Miss Shawcross, and allow me to show you that I can be a gentleman.'

He saw the delicate blush tinge her cheeks, read the uncertainty in her eyes when she looked at him, then his gentleness was rewarded with a shy smile.

'Very well, Captain Wylder, I am ready to be persuaded.'

There was a twinkle in those soft brown eyes, a hint of mischief. The temptation to steal another kiss was very strong, but he resisted. That would *not* be the action of a gentleman! Instead he escorted her to a sofa. He intended to sit down beside her, but as she sank down she spread out her blue skirts, completely covering the seat. With a wry grin he moved to a chair on the opposite side of the fireplace. It would be slow work to win her round, but he found himself warming to the challenge.

Evelina was aware of an irrational disappointment. She had been convinced that he was going to kiss her again, and her heart leapt into her throat at the thought of it. The man had about him an air of danger, a delicious sense of the unknown that set her pulse racing. But now he was determined to be the gentleman. She was glad of it, of course. She flounced down upon the sofa, her silken petticoats billowing around her.

'Your grandfather explained to me that you and he live here alone,' remarked the captain, lowering his long frame into a chair. 'He told me your parents died when you were a child. I am very sorry.'

'Thank you, but you do not need to pity me; it was more than ten years ago. My parents liked to travel a great deal and I was left at home with Grandpapa, so I never knew them that well; I think they were a very restless couple.' His sympathetic silence encouraged her to say more. 'It was a fever; they were on the Continent when they were struck down.' She paused briefly then forced a smile. 'But I am very happy living here with Grandpapa, I want for nothing.'

'But you are very secluded here; do you not find it a little…lonely?'

'Grandpapa is companion enough for me,' she responded quickly. 'I have no wish for female company—and I am beyond the age of needing a chaperon.'

The corners of his mouth lifted fractionally. 'Remembering our first encounter, I beg to disagree with you on that last point, Miss Shawcross.'

Eve blushed hotly. She was relieved that her grandfather's entrance created a timely diversion.

Sir Benjamin came in, leaning heavily on his stick and declaring that they should go directly into the dining room.

'If I sit down here I shan't be able to get up again,'

he explained with a chuckle. 'No, no, my dear, I do not need your arm; let Wylder escort you.'

They processed slowly to the dining room, where Eve found herself sitting opposite Nick Wylder.

'I told Green to rearrange the table,' said Sir Benjamin, correctly interpreting her look of surprise. 'Silly for you to be sitting at the far end and Wylder here, halfway between the two of us. Much better to have you near me, where I can see you both. Just a snug little dinner, Wylder,' he continued. 'We do not stand upon any ceremony here. It's plain cooked fare, but you won't find better in the county, and you have Evelina to thank for it.'

'Grandpapa!' She shook her head at him.

'No need for this modesty, miss! It is only right that our guest knows what a treasure you are. She has been mistress here since she finished her schooling.' Sir Benjamin laughed. 'Just seventeen years old, she was then, Wylder. I wanted her to go off and stay with her young friends, to enjoy herself, but she would have none of it. She insisted upon coming home to live with me. Not that she needed to, for we have a very capable housekeeper in Mrs Harding, but Evelina was determined that she would look after me. And she has done so, magnificently.'

'I do not doubt it,' returned Captain Wylder. 'And how many years has that been, sir?'

'Seven,' responded Sir Benjamin instantly.

While her grandfather turned his attention to his plate, Eve glared across the table at Nick Wylder. He met her look with a glinting smile.

'Four-and-twenty,' he murmured. 'Far too old for a chaperon.'

'Positively on the shelf!' she retorted. Eve signalled to the footman to refill the glasses. 'So, Captain, you were at Tunbridge Wells. Were you taking the waters?' She added sweetly, 'A touch of gout, perhaps?'

His eyes acknowledged the hit, but he said merely, 'No, I was there on business.'

'Oh? And is your business now concluded, that you have time for a *prolonged* stay here at Makerham?'

Again that wicked glint flashed in his deep blue eyes. 'I hope to conclude my business while I am here.'

'And just what is your business, sir?' Eve picked up her wine glass.

'Marriage.'

She choked.

'Oh dear, dear,' muttered Sir Benjamin. He bent

a reproving look upon his guest. 'I had not planned to broach this delicate subject for a day or so, sir.'

'Then I apologise, Sir Benjamin, but given your granddaughter's advanced years I did not wish to waste time.'

Evelina, still recovering from her choking fit, could only gasp. Sir Benjamin's mouth fell open, then his face creased into a smile.

'Ah, you are funning, sir! Giving my girl her own again, what? Eve, my dear, I think you have met your match, here. Captain Wylder is as big a jokesmith as yourself!'

Evelina forced her lips into a smile, but the look she threw at Nick Wylder promised dire retribution.

Nick turned his attention to his dinner. Damme, but he was enjoying himself, and far more than he had anticipated. Sir Benjamin was a considerate host and although he was confined to the house by his poor health he was remarkably knowledgeable and the conversation did not flag. Then there was Miss Shawcross. She was a mixture of spirit and adorable innocence; an unforeseen bonus to his plans. Nick realised with a little jolt of surprise that he wanted to know more about her.

* * *

Eve excused herself after dinner and went to her room to dash off a letter to her old school friend.

I understand Captain Wylder to be something of a hero, she wrote at the end her letter. *But however highly he is regarded as a sailor, I hope you can furnish me with some information as to his character as a man.* 'There,' she said to herself as she applied her seal. 'If I know anything of Maria, she will be only too delighted to find out everything there is to know about Captain Nick Wylder.'

Sir Benjamin did not keep late hours at Makerham, so it was not until the following morning that she saw their guest again. It was her custom, upon summer mornings such as these to take a stroll through the ornamental gardens that surrounded Makerham. Sheltered and secluded at the bottom of a wooded dell, the moated manor house was always inviting, but looked at its best in summer. She loved the way the old stone seemed to glow and the golden sunlight twinkled in the leaded windows; it gave the old house a fairy-tale quality. She was wandering through the lavender-lined paths when she heard footsteps on the gravel behind her. She turned to find Captain Wylder approaching.

'Good morning, Miss Shawcross. You are an early riser.'

'Yes. I often take a walk at this time; the gardens are at their best with the dew still on the flowers.'

'Then I will join you, if I may?'

After a brief hesitation Eve nodded. She would not take his arm, but walked along beside him, keeping a safe distance between them. At Nick's request she pointed out the more unusual flowers and described to him the history of the building. When they reached the end of the ornamental gardens they stopped and turned, looking back at the old house.

'It's beautiful,' said Nick. 'It is clear that you love Makerham.'

'It is my home.'

'But it is entailed.' At his words she glanced up at him and he spread his hands. 'Your grandfather told me.'

'Yes. When Grandfather dies the estate will pass to my cousin, Bernard Shawcross.'

'And you will have to leave.'

Evelina thought of her cousin with his clammy hands and air of ownership. He seemed to assume that she was included in his inheritance. Eve knew she would do everything in her power to avoid that fate.

'Yes,' she said quietly. 'I will have to leave.' The chiming of the bell in the clock tower brought her head up. 'It is time I went indoors. Grandfather will be coming downstairs shortly.'

Nick accompanied her back to the house, but any plans for furthering his suit were dashed when she announced that they would meet again at dinner.

'But you will be breaking your fast now, Miss Shawcross?'

She shook her head. 'Breakfast will be served to you and Grandpapa very shortly, Captain. I have arranged to walk into Makerham.'

'Will you not wait for me? I should like to escort you.'

Again a little shake of the head. Nick was convinced there was a mischievous twinkle in her eyes.

'I go to take a little food to the poor in the village. They would not thank me for bringing a stranger into their homes. Grandpapa will be very pleased to have your company for the day,' she added with a sunny smile. 'And I shall be happy to know that he is entertained.'

Nick watched her walk away, a little smile

playing around his own mouth. Out-manoeuvred, by Gad. Miss Evelina Shawcross might be an innocent, but she was not unintelligent. To win her over would be a challenge. Nick's smile grew.

He could never resist a challenge.

Chapter Two

'Evelina, my love, you are being quite tiresome!'

Sir Benjamin's mild reproof brought his grand-daughter's wide-eyed gaze to his face. They were sitting together in the morning room where Rooney had helped Sir Benjamin to his favourite chair and was tenderly placing a rug over his legs. Eve waited until the valet had finished and was making his way out of the room before she answered.

'Grandpapa, I have no idea what you mean.'

'What game is this you are playing, Eve? I bring Captain Wylder here as a suitor and you seem bent on avoiding him.'

'No, no, Grandpapa, I have been most attentive!'

'You have presided over my dinner table and served him tea in the drawing room after,' retorted Sir Benjamin. 'Hardly effusive behaviour, my love. I understand from Rooney that you are gone from the house before breakfast every day and do not return until late in the afternoon. Are there suddenly so many distressed families in Makerham that require your attendance?'

'The summer has brought on a deal of sickness and ague, sir.'

'Then you must send Martha with a basket of food, child. I will not have you neglect our guest.'

Eve cast down her eyes. 'Yes Grandpapa.' She stole a glance at Sir Benjamin and saw he was frowning at her. She put out her hands. 'Oh, sir, pray do not be angry with me. It is such a novelty to have any man save yourself in the house and it is taking me a little time to grow accustomed.'

She might have added that she found her grandfather's guest far too attractive for her comfort, but decided against it.

'Well I consider four days is long enough for you to *grow accustomed*, as you put it. I don't say that the captain isn't excellent company, but it's not me that he has come here to see. If you continue to absent yourself, he will think you do not like him.'

'It is not that, Grandpapa—'

'My dear child, I know this is very sudden for you. When I took you to Tunbridge Wells a few years ago I had hoped that you might form an alliance, but none of the gentlemen took your fancy, and you could not be persuaded to stay with your friends in London—'

'I could not leave you, Grandpapa,' she said quickly. 'You were ill and I wanted to look after you.'

He patted her hands. 'Your heart is too kind, Eve my love, but I should have made you go; imprisoned here with me, you have no opportunity to meet eligible gentlemen.'

'But I have not been unhappy, sir.'

'That is not the point, Evelina,' Sir Benjamin leaned forwards, saying urgently, 'I am growing weaker, my love. When I am gone there will be no one to protect you. Your cousin inherits Makerham, there is nothing to be done about that, but I do not like him. I have seen the way he looks at you when he is here. I would not have you left to his care.'

She shivered at the thought. 'You are right, Grandpapa, I do not think I should like that.'

'So you will consider Captain Wylder's suit?'

'Yes, Grandpapa. If he should offer for me, I will consider his suit.' Eve smiled. She had made up her mind that she would not relax her guard until she had received word from London about Captain Wylder. Now, with her friend Maria's letter nestling in her pocket, she had decided upon a course of action. 'I am sorry if I have not been as attentive to our guest as you would like, Grandpapa. I promise you I am now quite ready to entertain Captain Wylder. In fact,' she added with a twinkle, 'I will start this very day!'

Nick looked up from the letter he was reading as Richard Granby came into the room.

'Bad news, Captain?'

Nick shook his head.

'No news at all,' he said. 'Our quarry has gone to ground.'

'I'm sorry to hear that.' Granby hesitated and then said delicately, 'And, if I might enquire, how are your plans progressing with the young lady?'

Nick tossed the letter aside. 'They are not,' he said shortly. 'I am wondering if we should weigh anchor and try another tack. The admiralty wants answers and there are other leads to follow...' his lips twitched '...though none so attractive.'

A knock at the door interrupted them. Nick hurriedly took up his letter and put it away while Granby answered the door. He heard a murmur of voices and turned to see his valet approaching, a folded paper in his hand.

'A note for you, Captain.'

'Well.' A slow grin appeared as he read the missive. 'Perhaps all is not lost. Miss Shawcross wants to see me. In the garden.'

Nick strode along the gravelled paths until he reached the yew walk. At the far end was a small clearing where a statue of Pan nestled against the surrounding hedge. On either side white-painted benches had been placed for those who wished to rest for a while in this sheltered retreat. Evelina was sitting on one of the benches, reading a letter. As Nick approached she looked up and gave a slight smile. He bowed.

'You wished to talk to me, Miss Shawcross?'

She gestured towards the opposite bench and Nick sat down.

'I did indeed, sir.' Her soft brown eyes rested upon him. 'You said at our very first meeting that you came here to marry me. Is that truly your intention?'

'A direct attack,' he said approvingly. 'I like that.'

'You have not answered my question, Captain.'

'Then, yes. It is indeed my intention, Misss Shawcross.'

Her gaze did not falter. 'Why?'

Nick's brows rose. This was blunt indeed. 'It is time I settled down. My family has been nagging me to do so ever since I came home from sea.'

'But you know nothing about me.'

He smiled at her. 'You are beautiful, witty, accomplished—and Sir Benjamin assures me you are an excellent housekeeper. Is that not enough?'

She dropped her gaze, a delicate flush mantling her cheek. 'But you knew nothing about me when you sought out my grandfather at Tunbridge Wells.'

She raised her eyes again and Nick hesitated. How much should he tell her?

'I did go to Tunbridge in search of Sir Benjamin,' he admitted. 'I planned merely to renew my family's acquaintance with him. It soon became clear to me that Sir Benjamin was looking for a husband for you.' A smile tugged at his lips. 'He seemed to think I might be a suitable candidate.'

'Do you mean that *he* suggested it?' She looked shocked. 'And you agreed to…to…'

He spread his hands, saying apologetically, 'This seemed an opportunity not to be missed. I am glad now that I came.'

For a moment she looked delightfully flustered, but she soon recovered. 'Very well, sir.' She settled herself more comfortably on the bench and glanced at the papers in her hand. 'Grandpapa may consider you suitable, but you have yet to convince *me*! I would like to ask you a few questions.'

Nick leaned back and crossed one booted leg over the other. 'I am at your disposal, ma'am.'

'We have already established that you are a sailor, and, one cannot deny it, a brave one.'

'Thank you,' he said meekly.

'But you have something of a reputation in town, Captain.' She stared down at the letter. 'Last year your name was linked with a Mrs Stringham.'

He blinked. The chit had been checking up on him!

'We were…friends for a few months, yes.'

'I understand she is a lady with a somewhat tarnished reputation.' She shrugged. 'No doubt much more interesting for you than an ingénue.'

He choked, but she did not seem to notice and was again peering at her list.

'Then there was Lady Alton.'

'What of her?' he asked warily.

'She was your mistress, was she not? You look shocked, Captain Wylder. I thought you liked the direct attack.'

Nick sat up. By heaven, the wench was teasing

him! 'May I ask how you came by this information, Miss Shawcross?'

She held the letter to her breast. 'You may ask, but I shall not divulge my sources.'

He leaned forward. 'And what else do your… sources…say of me?'

She studied the sheets of paper again. 'Well, there was Miss Brierley from Rochester, many people thought you might offer for her.'

'What, because I took her driving in the park?'

'Apparently so,' she murmured, not raising her eyes from her letter. 'And Dorothy Chate, the actress, not to mention the opera dancers—'

'I would much rather we did *not* mention the opera dancers!'

She regarded him sternly. 'Since quitting the navy, your life seems to have been one of dissipation, sir.'

He tried to look remorseful. 'Alas, I am very much in need of a wife to keep me in order.'

'I am not at all sure that anyone could keep you in order, Captain Wylder. Are you saying that if we were to marry you would give up your dissolute ways?'

'I would try.'

He gave her a soulful look and noted with satisfaction the smile tugging at the corners of her mouth. She was having difficulty keeping her countenance.

'I am not at all sure that I believe you.'

'I fear I am in need of an occupation.'

She turned the page. 'My correspondent tells me that you *have* an occupation.'

Nick froze. Now how the devil did she know that?

'Or you *should* have one; you should be managing your properties in the north, Captain Wylder, not wasting your time in idle pursuits.'

He breathed again. 'I would not call looking for a wife an idle pursuit.'

'Captain Wylder,' she said seriously, 'I am not at all sure I am the wife for you.'

'Miss Shawcross, the more I know of you the more I am convinced that you are the *perfect* wife for me!'

'But I am not at all worldly. What I mean is…' She blushed again, looking so adorable that he wanted to cross the space between them and take her in his arms. 'What would happen when you grew tired of me?' When he did not respond she said quietly, 'I am not quite as naïve as you might think, Captain. I know my parents' marriage was unusual; they were so much in love they did everything together, as equals.' She gave a sad little smile. 'They even died together. I do not expect that, but…'

Nick half-rose from his seat, then sank back down again. He knew that any attempt to comfort her was more likely to frighten her away. 'But what, Miss Shawcross?'

The colour flared in her cheeks, but she was determined on her course. Her words were almost inaudible. 'I w-would not want to share you with a mistress.'

Nick took a deep breath. By heaven, he admired her bravery. Now he must honour it with an honest reply. 'Miss Shawcross, whatever else you may have heard about me, pray believe that I am a gentleman. If we were to marry, I give you my word you would always be treated with respect, and I would do my best to make you happy. I can promise you that I have no mistress hidden away.' He laughed suddenly. 'Now what is that look, do you not believe me?'

She glared at him. 'I do not think you understand, sir.'

'Then perhaps you can explain.'

He sat back, as she threw him another scorching look. He felt more sure of his ground when she was angry with him.

'I have always expected Grandpapa to arrange my marriage for me, but I thought it would be a local gentleman. Someone…'

'Someone safe and staid and boring,' he put in helpfully.

'Well…yes.'

He spread his hands. 'Even the most upright country gentlemen take mistresses, you know.'

'But they are less likely to have women falling at their feet,' she retorted. She brandished her letter. 'My correspondent tells me the ladies in town find you fatally attractive.'

'Does she indeed?'

'How do you know it is a woman?'

'I have an instinct for these things. Does your correspondent find me fatally attractive, too?'

'Captain Wylder I do not think you are taking this seriously.'

'But I am! And your grandfather has already spoken to me of this.'

'He—he has?'

'Yes.' Her consternation made him smile. 'It is a question that would occur to any loving guardian. I have already assured him that, if I take a wife, she will have nothing to fear on that score.' He paused. 'Sir Benjamin approves of me, you know. Will you not at least consider my suit?'

She held his eyes for a moment, then folded her papers and put them into her reticule. 'Yes,

Captain Wylder, I will consider it,' she said quietly. 'But it is not a decision to be taken lightly.'

'No, of course not.'

'Thank you for being so frank with me, Captain.'

As she rose he jumped up and reached for her hand, carrying her fingers to his lips.

'I hope we understand one another now, Miss Shawcross.'

'I am not sure.' She regarded him with a tiny crease between her brows. 'I still do not understand why you should want to marry me, but we will let that pass, for now.' She withdrew her fingers and, with a slight, regal nod of her head, she turned and walked away from him.

Eve returned to her room, her mind going over and over her interview with Captain Wylder. He had not denied any of the liaisons Maria Gryfford had detailed in her letter, but he had looked wary. Were there even more lovers that she did not know of? Eve realised she did not care how many lovers he might have had in the past; only the present and the future concerned her. A line from Lady Gryfford's letter flitted through her mind; *If the dashing Captain Wyldfire has made you an offer, then snap him up immediately, my dearest Eve. We are all mad for him!* But why should he want to marry her? He did not look like the sort of man who would marry merely to please his family. But then, she had been brought up to believe she would marry to please her grandfather. Were they so very different? She put her arms around herself. It was a big decision, to leave the safety of the only home she had ever known and put herself under the protection of Nick Wylder. After all, what did she know of him? Did she trust him?

'Yes,' she said aloud. 'Yes, I do. Perhaps I should not, but I do.'

'Your pardon, Miss Eve, did you say something?'

Martha came bustling into the room.

'What? Oh, no, no. I was merely talking to myself. Is it time to dress for dinner already? I think I will wear my blue gown again tonight, Martha.'

'Ah, you want to look your best for the captain, is that it?'

'Do not be so impertinent!'

Eve frowned at her handmaiden, but Martha had been part of her household since Eve had been a baby and was not so easily snubbed.

'Well, what else is one to think, when you and he have been in the garden together this afternoon?'

'Who told you that?'

Martha shrugged. 'Mr Granby mentioned it…'

'How dare you gossip about me!'

'Lord love you, Miss Eve, we wasn't gossiping. Mr Granby just happened to mention it in passing. Heavens, miss, how you do take one up. And what does it matter anyway, since you are going to wed him—'

'Martha! Who says so?'

The maid stared at her. 'Well, is it not so?'

'No. Yes—that is…' She dropped down on the bed, crying, 'Oh, Martha I do not know what to do!'

'Don't you *want* to marry the captain?'

Eve spread her hands. 'I must marry someone.'

'And the captain *is* very handsome, miss.'

Eve felt herself blushing. 'Yes he is. Very handsome.'

And exciting, and witty: Eve had never felt so attracted to any man before. Not that she had much experience, one short visit to Tunbridge Wells being the nearest she had ever been to entering society, but she had read lots of books. She knew exactly what a hero should be like, and although the gentlemen she had met at Tunbridge had all fallen well short of her expectations, she was forced to admit that Nick Wylder was the embodiment of her secret dreams. The thought was a little frightening.

'Well, if you'll be guided by me, you will listen to Sir Benjamin and do as he bids you, miss,' Martha advised her. 'He has never let you down yet.'

'I know, Martha, but this is…marriage.' She whispered the word, suddenly nervous of it and the thoughts it conjured.

'Lord love you, that is just the time to be advised by your grandpapa,' said Martha cheerfully. 'If Sir Benjamin thinks the captain is the right man for you, then so it is, and a sight better catch than your cousin Bernard,' she added, suddenly serious. 'And that's who you'll end up with if the master dies and leaves you alone. I've seen 'im sniffing round you when he's been here on a visit.'

'Stop it, Martha.' Eve shuddered. 'Besides, I have heard that my cousin is hanging out for a rich wife.'

'Aye, well, maybe he is,' opined Martha darkly. 'But that won't stop him trying to get you between the sheets, with or without a wedding ring!'

With this dire warning she went off to fetch Eve's gown, leaving her mistress to stare after her.

By the time she went down to dinner Eve was no closer to making a decision, but she was too well-bred to let her inner turmoil show and she greeted Sir Benjamin and the captain with her usual calm smile. Despite her assured performance in the garden that afternoon she was a little nervous of meeting Nick again, but his polite, gentle friend-liness soon put her at her ease. However, Sir Benjamin's suggestion after dinner that the young people should take a stroll in the garden while it was still light threw her into a panic.

'An excellent idea,' murmured Nick, his eyes glinting, but not unkindly. 'Come, Miss Shawcross, indulge me in a little walk.' He leaned closer and murmured. 'It need be nothing more, I promise you.'

Feeling the hot blood in her cheeks, she hurried away to fetch her wrap and returned to find only Nick waiting for her in the hall.

'Sir Benjamin has retired,' he informed her as she came down the stairs towards him. 'He asked that you go up to see him when we come back in.' He held out his arm to her. 'Shall we walk? You need not worry,' he added, seeing her hesitation. 'We shall talk of the most unexceptional subjects, if you like.'

His understanding calmed her jangled nerves. She put her hand on his arm and allowed him to lead her out of the house.

At first they discussed the weather, then books and music, but when they had strolled past the parterre and into the shrubbery, Nick said suddenly, 'I think, Miss Shawcross, that I owe you an apology.' She glanced up at him and he continued, 'It seems Sir Benjamin truly did not prepare you for my visit.'

She flushed. 'This is not the unexceptional topic you promised me, Captain.'

'I know, but you are very reserved with me tonight. You are trying to make up your mind whether or not to marry me, is that not so?'

'Of course not!' she exclaimed, startled. 'It is…' She trailed off. 'To be truthful with you, yes,' she admitted.

He stopped and turned to her, catching at her hands. 'And what is so difficult about that decision, Miss Shawcross?'

He lifted her hand to his lips and began to kiss her fingers, one by one. She watched, transfixed. 'I, um…'

He lifted her other hand and, when he had finished with her fingers, his lips moved on to her wrist, sending a fiery shock the length of her arm.

'I cannot think,' she confessed.

He raised his head and smiled at her. Eve's fingers were still tingling and she found herself staring at his mouth, wondering at the havoc his lips could cause. The smile in his eyes deepened. He cupped her chin.

'Sometimes it is best not to think,' he murmured and gently brought his mouth down upon hers.

It was the lightest of kisses, a mere brushing of lips, but it sent Eve's senses reeling and as Nick pulled away her face remained upturned, inviting him to kiss her again. He gazed down at her.

'A young lady should not allow a gentleman to kiss her unless she means to marry him,' he murmured.

'Then perhaps you have made my decision for me,' she replied.

He laughed, pulled her hand back on to his arm and they resumed their stroll.

'I shall not coerce you into this, Miss Shawcross; it must be your decision.'

'It is in truth my grandfather's decision,' she told him. 'Or at least, his wish. But your assumption was correct, Captain. He did not mention you were coming. I should not be surprised by it, however. He always said that one day he would bring home a husband for me.' She sighed. 'I never really believed him.'

'Surely he has not kept you locked away here all these years?' He sounded slightly shocked and she gave a little gurgle of laughter.

'Like a princess in a fairy-tale? No, of course not. I have attended assemblies in Makerham village upon occasion. And I went to Tunbridge a few years ago.'

'Then of course you know all you need to know about the world!'

'I know enough to realise that I am very happy to remain here at Makerham. Everything I want is here.'

'Is it? Do you never long to know what is going on outside these walls?'

'There are the news sheets—'

'That is not the same! There are towns and cities—whole countries waiting to be explored. Does that thought not fill you with excitement?'

The thought filled Evelina with dread. She stepped away from him to cup a particularly lovely rose between her fingers, breathing in its fragrance while she formulated her answer. Apart from one or two early memories of life with her parents and a few brief years at school, Makerham was the only world she had ever known. Outside was alien and full of danger, like the infection that had carried off her parents. Her life here at Makerham was safe, secure; the thought of her cousin taking possession was something she did not want to consider.

'I am very happy here,' she said again.

Nick strolled along beside Evelina, his hands clasped firmly behind his back to prevent them reaching out and pulling her into his arms. He had never known such a glorious summer's evening; bees hummed around the plants and the scent of lavender filled the air. Then there was Evelina herself; she was beautiful, but there was an air of calm about her, serenity. It was like finding a safe harbour after stormy weeks at sea. When he had sought out Sir Benjamin at Tunbridge Wells he had already formulated his plans; if he needed to marry to obtain his ends, then he was prepared to do his duty, but never had he expected *duty* to be quite so pleasurable.

He stopped and gently turned her to face him. 'I understand how much you love Makerham, but could you consider living elsewhere?'

'I think I must, sir, since the house will pass to my cousin when Grandpapa dies.'

'That is not quite what I meant. Sir Benjamin brought me here as a prospective husband for you. I am not sure what he has told you about me…'

'Only that your father was an earl: that is looking pretty high for a baronet's daughter.' Her lilting smile jolted his senses. It took all his willpower not to drag her into his arms and cover her face with kisses, but he needed to talk to her.

'Evelina—Eve, from our discussions this afternoon you know I have not led a blameless life, but I told you that will change when I take a wife. I have a comfortable income and two estates in the north. I can afford to give you a Season in town every year, should you wish it. You will have your own carriage and we could buy a property nearer Makerham, closer to your grandfather, if that is what you want.'

'Captain Wylder, this is too soon!'

He put a finger against her lips. 'Perhaps, but I do everything in a hurry, my dear; as soon as I saw you I knew that I wanted to wed you.' He saw the confusion in her face and stopped. He drew away a little, took a breath and said gently, 'You need not answer immediately. I merely want you to understand what I am offering you.'

There was a slight shadow in her eyes as she looked up at him. 'That is all very well, Captain, but I do not understand what *I* can offer *you*.'

He hesitated, then said lightly, 'I believe that you bring with you your mother's property at Monkhurst.'

She laughed. 'A rundown house on the edge of

Romney Marsh! I love it, and spent some happy times there as a child, but no one has lived there since Mama and Papa died. It is a poor dowry, Captain Wylder. I fear I will get the best of this bargain, sir!'

His spirit soared. She was almost his, he could read it in her eyes. A dizzying happiness shook him. He ran his hands down her arms and caught her fingers.

'No, Eve, I think I will have a great deal more than I bargained for!'

Eve stared at the dark head bent over her hands. This could not be happening to her; when she was at school she had read novels of handsome knights carrying off damsels in distress, but that was fantasy. Besides, she was not in distress. Or was she? She was twenty-four years old and she had never found anyone she would like to marry, nor was she likely to meet anyone while she lived in such seclusion. Her grandfather was much weaker than he had been even a few months ago. If he should die while she was still unmarried, then what would become of her? The vision of her cousin filled her mind. She had never liked Bernard, sensing in his nature a cruel streak that made her a little afraid of him. And now here was this handsome, dashing sea captain offering her his hand and he came with her grandfather's blessing. There really was no choice.

Eve realised Nick was looking at her with a steady, unsettling gaze. She needed to say something. 'How soon do you wish to be married, Captain Wylder?'

Goodness, how matter of fact she sounded.

'By the end of the month.'

'The end of the—!'

'Why, yes, I see no reason to rush into this with a special licence. We have time for the banns to be read in church. We shall be married here, of course. I have no doubt that is what you would like—'

'But I haven't agreed to it yet!'

With a laugh he pulled her into his arms. 'No, but you will.'

He was grinning down at her. Eve found it difficult to concentrate, her thoughts seemed to centre on the dimple in his left cheek.

'Wh-what will Grandpapa say to such a hasty marriage?'

'Oh I think he will agree.' He kissed her, a sizzling, burning kiss that sent shockwaves tingling right down to her toes. 'What say you, Eve, will you be my wife?'

'But—' She tried to collect her wayward thoughts. 'We have only just met!'

'And we have more than three weeks until the wedding to get to know one another.' He kissed her again. 'Well?'

She struggled out of his arms. 'No, no. It is out of the question,' she said crossly. 'You appear out of nowhere, big and brash and—and totally over-whelming, and you expect me to agree to be your wife! No, sir, I will not do it!'

He dropped to his knees before her, throwing his arms wide. 'Evelina, don't you *want* to marry me?'

She clapped her hands over her mouth to stifle a giggle. 'Get up, sir, before someone sees you!'

'Not until you answer my question.'

Evelina stared at him. His blue eyes twinkled and that irrepressible dimple cut into his cheek. Heavens, was the man never serious?

'Well, Evelina; will you give me your answer?'

A stillness settled over the garden. The birds were silent, not a breath of wind stirred the bushes; the whole world was hushed, waiting for her reply. Suddenly she knew that there was nothing she wanted more than to be married to Nick Wylder.

'Very well,' she said quietly. 'I will marry you.'

Chapter Three

'Oh heavens, what have I done?'

Evelina paced about her bedroom, her clasped hands pressed to her mouth. The arrival at Makerham of a prospective husband should not have come as a surprise, her grandfather had told her often that he would find her a suitor and she had told him that she would abide by his judgement. But she had not expected that gentleman to be so dazzlingly attractive as Captain Wylder, nor had she foreseen that he would propose to her upon such short acquaintance. Even more extraordinary was the fact that she had accepted him!

Eve paused by the window. The last remnants of daylight had disappeared and the glass reflected her image like a dark mirror. She had always considered herself a sensible, level-headed young woman, so what madness had possessed her, standing in the garden with the heady scent of summer roses in the air, to accept his proposal?

'No, no, it will not do,' she said aloud, resuming her perambulations. 'Tomorrow I must tell him I have changed my mind—*not* changed my mind,' she amended. 'Merely that I want a little more time to think over his proposal.'

She climbed into bed and snuffed out her candle, satisfied that she had resolved upon a very sensible course of action.

'Hell and damnation we're in the suds now.' Nick shrugged himself out of his coat and tossed it to his valet. 'I had not planned this, Richard!'

'I thought the whole point of coming here was to propose to the young lady,' murmured Granby, folding the coat and laying it tenderly over a chair.

'Yes, of course, but I behaved like a veritable mooncalf!'

'But I understand Miss Shawcross has accepted your offer, Captain.'

'Aye, she has.' Nick slumped down into a chair and gave a heavy sigh.

'Then I wish you happy, sir.'

'Damn your impudence! This wasn't meant to

happen—or only as a last resort.' A wry smile tugged at one side of his mouth. 'The truth of it is she's bowled me over, Dick. She floored me with the very first glance from those great brown eyes and I haven't recovered since.'

'Her maid tells me Miss Shawcross is a very accomplished young lady.'

'Aye, so she is. The wonder is that she wasn't snapped up years ago.'

'Martha—that's her maid, Captain—Martha says that she's lived here very quietly since she finished her schooling. Sir Benjamin's health being so poor they have never been in the habit of entertaining.'

Nick gave a short laugh. 'So she's been waiting here all these years, like a Sleeping Beauty! But the devil of it is I'm no Prince Charming.'

A ghost of a smile flitted across Richard Granby's impassive features. 'If you'll pardon me, sir, I think there's plenty of ladies would disagree with you there.'

Nick waved his hand impatiently. 'What if she finds out why I am really here?'

'Perhaps you should tell her.'

'Damn it all, Richard, what would she think of me, marrying her to get control of her property?

No, I'll keep my own counsel. After all, another few weeks and this business will be finished, so there's no reason for Miss Evelina Shawcross to know anything about it.' Nick ran a hand through his hair. 'But I do not like the idea of rushing her into this marriage. Mayhap we will merely go through the ceremony. After all, I shall need to get back to the coast almost as soon as the wedding is over. That way, if she finds she really cannot stomach me—'

'If you'll forgive me saying so, Captain, whenever your *liaisons* have finished it's rarely been the lady's choice to end it.'

'Aye, but Miss Shawcross is different.' He pushed himself out of the chair and stretched. 'Look out my nightgown, if you please, Richard. It must be well after midnight by now and time I—' He broke off, frowning. 'Now what the devil is the matter?'

From the corridor outside his room came the sound of urgent whispers and hurrying footsteps. Nick strode over to the door and flung it open. Sir Benjamin's valet was making his way along the passage and by the glow of the lamp he was holding aloft Nick observed that his coat was un-buttoned and his hair tousled, as if he had been roused untimely from his bed. Nick stepped out into his path.

'Well, Rooney, what's amiss?' he demanded.

'It's the master sir. He's had one of his turns.'

'Can I be of help—can Granby ride for a doctor?'

'Thank you, Captain, but no. I've already despatched a groom to fetch Dr Scott. If you will excuse me, sir, I must get back to Sir Benjamin. Miss Eve is with him, but I do not like to be away for too long.'

'Of course.' Nick stepped aside and, after watching the valet hurry out of sight, went back into his room.

'Is it the old gentleman sir?' asked Granby. 'I heard he was very down pin.'

'Yes, he is. Go along and see if there is anything we can do, Richard. Sir Benjamin's man is reluctant to trouble *me*, but he may be more forthcoming to you.'

Having despatched his man, Nick found himself alone. Silence settled around him but it did nothing to relieve his anxiety. He was a guest in the house, but it was unthinkable that he would sleep while Eve was sitting up with her grandfather. He snatched up his coat. There must be something he could do.

* * *

When Eve left Sir Benjamin's room her eyes were gritty with lack of sleep. She held aloft a bedroom candlestick to light her way through the dark passages and down the stairs. The arch leading to the great hall glowed with a welcoming light and as she moved forwards she could see that the fire had been built up and several candles burned brightly in the wall sconces. Nick Wylder was bending over the fire, stirring a large black pan that seemed to be balanced precariously amongst the flames. He straightened and turned as he heard her approaching footsteps.

'I was told that you were here, Captain.' She nodded towards the fireplace. 'I doubt anyone has cooked upon that fire for generations.'

'Punch,' he said, smiling. 'Nothing like it for restoring the spirits in the middle of the night.'

'I am sorry if we woke you.'

'No need, I was not asleep.' He reached out for her hand and led her to the settle on one side of the hearth. 'How is Sir Benjamin?'

'Quieter now. Grandfather panics when an attack comes on and he cannot get his breath, but Dr Scott always calms him.'

She sat for a moment, staring into the flames.

'I hope you do not mind, I built up the fire. It is summer, I know, but somehow a good blaze always seems more comforting at times like these.'

'It does, thank you, but you should not have had to do that.'

He waved his hand dismissively.

'Your servants are busy with their master. I would not add to their load.' He turned back to the cooking pot and ladled some of its contents into a cup. 'Here, try this.'

She curled her fingers around the warm cup. She had not realised how cold she had become. A sweet, pungent aroma rose from the liquid and her eyes widened.

'Rum.' Nick grinned. 'Try it.'

Cautiously she took a sip. It was warm and sweet with a fiery bite that made her cough, but it was strangely comforting. Nick was watching her and she managed a small smile.

'Thank you. That is just what I need. Perhaps we should offer some to Dr Scott before he leaves.'

'Of course. Are these attacks a regular occurrence?'

'They have been more frequent in recent months.'

'I did not realise Sir Benjamin was so ill.'

'He hides it well. He does not like people to

fuss over him.' She read the question in his eyes and her gaze dropped to the cup clutched between her hands. 'The attacks weaken his heart. The doctor says we must be prepared…' She did not trust her voice to continue so she sipped at the punch. When she looked up again Nick was watching her, such kind concern in his face that she found herself smiling at him. 'Perhaps now you understand why Grandpapa is so eager to see me settled,' she said, handing him back the empty cup. 'He worries so about what is to become of me when he is gone.'

He sat down beside her on the settle. 'Then at least I can relieve his mind on that account, and perhaps on another.' He reached for her hands. 'When we are married we need not remove to Yorkshire immediately. I think you would prefer to remain near your grandfather.'

His words allayed her barely acknowledged anxiety. She fixed her eyes on his face.

'Truly, you would not mind if we lived here for a little while?'

'Truly. I have an excellent steward who has managed my affairs for a good many years; he will cope for a little while longer.'

'Thank you.' Her relief and gratitude were

palpable. Without thinking she leaned towards him and he enfolded her in his arms. It is, she thought, nestling her head contentedly against his shoulder, like coming home after a long and tiring journey.

Nick rested his cheek against her hair, breathing in the sweet, flowery fragrance. She felt so fragile, so delicate within his arms that he was afraid to hold her too tightly lest she should fracture. His heart ached. He wanted not only to possess this dainty creature but to protect her. It was an unfamiliar feeling, and not altogether comfortable.

They remained locked together in companionable silence for several minutes while the long case clock ticked steadily and logs crackled in the fireplace. He wondered if now was the time to talk to her, to take her into his confidence. He held his peace. It was government business, not his to share. She was so fragile that he did not want to add more worries to her slender shoulders. Besides, in a few more weeks it would all be settled.

Chapter Four

'Dearly beloved, we are gathered here…'

The little church at Makerham was packed. Evelina stood, eyes modestly lowered, and wondered how she had come to this. A month ago there had been no thought of marriage in her head, then Nick Wylder had ridden into her life and changed it for ever. A month ago she had not known of his existence; now she could not imagine life without him.

With the exception of a few days when he had been obliged to go to town on business, Nick had been her constant companion at Makerham Court. They rode through sun-dappled lanes, walked in the gardens and in the evenings they played cards with Sir Benjamin, or Eve would sit in the corner with her embroidery while the two men talked or played backgammon together. Nick's energetic presence filled the house. Eve woke every morning with a little thrill of anticipation, knowing he would be waiting for her. They talked for hours, although she had little recollection of what they talked *about*. Occasionally they would argue, and it would end with Nick pulling her into his arms and kissing her. She had never known such happiness. It was especially gratifying to see her grandfather's approval of her future husband and not even the business of the marriage contract upset this happy state of affairs; Sir Benjamin talked to Eve with smug satisfaction about jointures and settlements and Eve did not press him for details: it was enough for her that he was happy.

And now they were in Makerham church, standing side by side, exchanging marriage vows. A fairy-tale. Some might say it was too good to be true. Eve had to keep pinching herself to believe in her good fortune. Nick's brother, the Earl of Darrington, came to act as his groomsman. Eve thought he looked rather disapproving, but his greeting was kindly enough and he even kissed her hand when she came out of the church on her husband's arm. Her husband. A *frisson* of excitement trembled through her.

'So, you are my sister now.' The earl smiled, lightening his rather sombre expression and all at once looking much more like Nick. 'Welcome to the family, my dear Evelina. I look forward to the day when I can welcome you to Wylderbeck Hall. It is a long way north, but Nick will tell you it is well worth the journey. I wish it was not necessary for me to leave immediately after the wedding breakfast, but so it is; if Nick had given us more notice of your nuptials we would have had time to become acquainted—'

'And have you cut me out, brother?' put in Nick. 'I wanted to make sure of my lady first!'

The earl's smile was a little strained.

'Take care of her, Nick. And bring her north very soon, that she may meet the rest of the clan.'

'I should like that, my lord.' Eve cast a questioning look at Nick.

'I will bring her to you as soon as I can, brother. Our plans are a little uncertain for the moment; we will be staying at Makerham for a few weeks yet.'

'My grandfather's health is not good,' explained Eve. 'The wedding has been a great effort for him, although he was determined it should be held here.'

Nick put his hand over hers. 'I said I would not

take you away from Makerham until he is better. You have my word on that.'

She nodded and leaned against him, drawing comfort from his presence at her side. They both knew there was little chance of her grandfather growing stronger. She did not wish to consider the more likely outcome, but it was there, unspoken, and Nick understood. The message was in his eyes now as he looked at her. They would not leave Makerham while Sir Benjamin had need of her.

'I am only sorry that more of your family could not be present,' she said later, when they were standing at the entrance to Makerham Court, ready to receive their guests at the wedding breakfast.

'Do not be,' laughed Nick. 'They would have turned our little celebration into a riotous occasion! Darrington is the serious one, the rest of them are rakes and rabble-rousers, as you will see when I take you to Yorkshire to meet them!'

'I am sure they are not as bad as you make out. Indeed, there are some from my own family that I would as lief not see here,' she murmured, directing his attention to a tall, heavy-browed gentleman who was approaching them. She raised her head, saying more loudly, 'Captain, may I introduce to you my cousin, Mr Bernard Shawcross?'

Mr Shawcross swept off his hat and made such a deep bow that his nose almost touched his knees.

'We have met in town, Cousin. Let me tell you, Captain Wylder, that you have stolen the march on me, it was always my desire to wed my lovely Cousin Evelina.'

She gave him a honey-sweet smile. 'A pity then that you did not apprise me of the fact, Cousin.'

'Ah, but I did not wish to deprive Sir Benjamin of his most devoted companion,' came the smooth reply.

'Oh?' she murmured, 'from the number of times I have read your name in the society columns of the London newspapers I thought you were far too busy chasing heiresses to think of *me*. A pity that you have been unsuccessful thus far, Bernard.' His mouth tightened in displeasure and her smile widened.

'Mere gossip, Evelina,' he replied shortly. 'I am surprised you should take note of such tittle tattle.'

'And have you come directly from town today, sir?' asked Nick.

Bernard Shawcross shook his head. 'I am currently staying with friends near the coast. I regret, Cousin, that I have engagements there I cannot break and will be returning to Sussex in the morning. I shall leave you my direction, in case you need me.'

'Thank you, Bernard, but I can't think that we shall ever *need* you,' she murmured wickedly. 'However, let us not quarrel; I bid you welcome, Cousin. We are delighted that you have graced our wedding with your presence.'

'It was the very least I could do, Evelina, even though the event has taken place with—er—indecent haste.'

Her smile widened at his obvious annoyance.

'We are merely following Grandpa's wishes,' she returned, coolly. 'Have you spoken to him yet? No? Then perhaps you should do so now, while he is free.' She added quietly, as he turned on his heel and stalked away, 'It would do you no harm to play the dutiful heir once in a while.'

Nick drew his breath in with a hiss. 'Remind me never to get on the wrong side of you, madam wife,' he murmured.

'At one time Bernard was forever calling at Makerham, asking Grandpapa to advance him loans against his inheritance. Thankfully he has not called at all for the past year, so I can only suppose that he has learned to live within his means.'

'That, or he has found an additional source of income,' observed Nick. 'You will note that his coat is of the very finest cut: such tailoring only comes at a price.'

'I do not care how he comes by his money as long as he stays away from Makerham.' Eve shuddered. 'I cannot like him, his manner towards me has always been…possessive, and I dislike the way he fawns over Grandpapa, as though his well-being is his only concern, yet when he leaves he never writes to enquire after Grandpapa's health—but perhaps I refine too much upon it.'

'You need not concern yourself with your cousin any longer, sweetheart. I will not let him trouble you.' Nick squeezed her fingers. 'Come, my dear, our guests have all arrived now, I think we may take our places at table.'

They feasted in the great hall, which had been decorated for the occasion with garlands of summer flowers. Even though she was the bride, Eve was also the hostess and it was her duty to announce the wines for the diners and to direct their attention to the cold meat dishes and salads available on the sideboard. She also had to watch the servants to make sure no guest was neglected. With so much to do it there was little time for reflection. It was not until the meal was ending that she allowed herself to think about the coming night.

Her wedding night.

'That went off very well, I think,' declared Sir Benjamin as the last of the carriages drove away. 'I do wish, however, that we had invited at least some of our people to stay here.'

Eve came to stand beside his chair.

'You know we would not have been able to accommodate more than a few of our guests—and we should have been obliged to offer Bernard a room; you know how much you would dislike that.'

'You are very right, my love. They will be a deal more comfortable at the White Hart. Ah, and here is Rooney come to take me to my room. Goodnight, my dear, Captain Wylder. Such a tiring day, I shall sleep well, I think.'

As she watched her grandfather leave the room, leaning heavily upon his valet's arm, Eve knew a moment of panic. For the first time that day she was alone with her husband. There had been no awkwardness on previous evenings; she had merely bade him goodnight and they had gone their separate ways, but tonight she knew that the oriel bedroom had been prepared for them. It was the principal bedchamber in the house and legend had it that Henry VIII had slept there. On Sir Benjamin's instructions it had been cleaned and the huge tester bed furnished with new bed linen. Eve had a sudden, wild fancy to ask Nick if he would like to play a game of backgammon.

'We should retire,' he said gently. 'Your maid will be waiting to put you to bed and Richard will be looking out for me also; we must not disappoint them.' He took her hands and lifted them one after the other to his lips. Even that small gesture made her knees grow weak. 'Off you go, my dear. Send word when you are ready for me.'

She found Martha bustling around the oriel bedroom. Her new linen nightgown was laid out on the bed. It looked pale and insignificant against the blood-red velvet of the bedhangings. Eve shivered.

'Martha, I don't know what to do,' she whispered, desperately.

Her maid chuckled. 'With the two of you smelling of April and May ever since Captain Wylder arrived? You will have no problems, Mistress. Leave it all to the captain. Now then, Miss Eve, let me help you out of your gown.'

Send word when you are ready, Nick had said.

Perhaps she need not send for him at all. She thought wildly that she would lock the doors and spend the night alone, but she knew that would not do. In the event it was not her decision. Once Martha had put her into her nightgown and arranged her hair becomingly around her shoulders, she gathered up her clothes.

'There. You look as pretty as a picture, mistress. I will send word to the captain that you await him. Shall I light the candles before I leave you?'

'No.' The summer night was drawing in, but it was not yet dark. 'Leave them.'

Outside the open window Eve could hear a night bird singing. Her nerves were on edge and every sound seemed louder, sharper.

I'm not ready for this, she thought suddenly. *Nick Wylder is a stranger.* She wrapped her arms about her, closing her eyes to conjure his face in her mind. She pictured him smiling at her with that warm, understanding look in his eyes and her panic subsided. Nick was no stranger. In her heart she had always known him.

Nick stood in the doorway and regarded the little figure by the window. She had her back to him, and her head was bowed as if in prayer.

'Eve?' He spoke her name quietly.

She jumped and turned. The light from the window provided a gleaming halo for her hair as it flowed down over her shoulders. He could see every curve of her body through the gossamer-thin nightgown. The sight inflamed him, rousing the desire he had kept under control for the past four weeks. His breath caught in his throat. By heaven, how he wanted her! As he crossed the room he saw how nervous she was. He felt a desperate desire to tell her everything, but he dare not. Not yet. He must control himself, play for time. As long as they did not consummate the marriage then he could set her free, when it was all over and the danger was past. He would explain why it had been necessary to marry her in such haste and then, if she still wanted to be his wife, so be it, but it must be her choice. He owed her that much. He reached out and placed his hands gently on her shoulders. Her eyes, dark and luminous in her pale face, looked towards him for reassurance. His mouth was dry; suddenly *he* was anxious. What if he broke her heart?

'Eve, we do not have to do this tonight…'

She put her fingers against his mouth. 'I want to, Nick. I want to, very much,' she murmured, then with her hands on his shoulders she reached up and kissed him.

Nick felt the touch of her lips and he was lost.

Evelina marvelled at her temerity, yet when she had seen the concern in Nick's eyes her own doubts had fled and she had desperately wanted to comfort him. She felt his arms around her and her own crept about his neck. As Nick kissed her back with increasing urgency her lips parted and his tongue explored her mouth, flickering and teasing and stirring up the hot fire that burned deep in her belly. He was wearing a brightly patterned dressing robe, but through the heavy silk she could feel his body, hard against hers and she experienced a heady, exhilarating sensation of power even as he swept her up and carried her to the bed. She kept her eyes on his face, marking every line and shadow, the purposeful curve of his lips and the deepening colour of his eyes—they were almost black as they looked at her now and she trembled at the passion in their depths. He laid her on the covers and she reached up for him, wanting to kiss him again, but he resisted while he untied the belt of his robe. Eve's eyes widened as he shed the heavy satin. She had expected him to be wearing a nightshirt and the sight of his naked body surprised her. Nervously she ran her tongue over her lips. Nick lowered himself gently on to the bed beside her, measuring his length against hers, propping himself upon one arm while he ran his free hand gently across her cheek.

'You are so beautiful,' he murmured. 'More than I ever imagined.'

Eve swallowed hard. 'So, too, are you,' she managed to say with a shy, tremulous smile.

He bent his head, capturing her lips again while his hands moved over her, caressing her body through the thin nightdress. Eve's own hands were exploring too, running over Nick's arms, stroking his shoulders, tracing his spine. His body was smooth and firm beneath her fingers, the muscles rippling beneath the skin. His kisses deepened and her own desire mounted. She wanted to be closer to him; even the thin muslin of her nightgown between them was too much. She broke away and sat up, scrabbling to drag off the last scrap of fabric that separated her from Nick. After a heartbeat's hesitation he helped her, his breathing as ragged as her own. As she raised her arms to drag the gown over her head she felt his hands capturing her nakedness. Collecting up her breasts, he buried his face in their softness. Gasping, she freed herself from the flimsy material and they fell together on to the covers in a tangle of limbs.

Nick's lips moved back up her body, slid over her mouth, his kiss urgent and demanding while his hands on her skin caused her body to writhe out of her control. She threw back her head, shuddering with surprise and delight as his hand moved between her thighs, gently easing them apart. She arched beneath his questing fingers, moving against them, not knowing why, only aware of the ache in her groin and the pleasurable sensations he was arousing deep, deep within her. He kissed her neck; she felt his lips briefly on her collar-bone, then they fastened over one erect nipple and she gasped. The pleasure was so heady and intense that she thought she might faint. She was soaring, flying and falling all at the same time. Her hands gripped him, fingers digging into his shoulders as the first spasm shook her, then a second. She knew a moment's panic as those pleasuring fingers eased away and Nick rolled over and entered her. She gave a little cry and he froze. Desperately Eve pushed against him.

'No, no, do not stop,' she gasped.

She heard him give a shaky laugh. 'I don't think I could, even if I wanted to.'

The blood was pounding in her ears, singing through her body as they moved together. The wave of pleasure had receded, but it was building within her again. She matched her movements to Nick's, running her hands over his muscled back, keeping pace with him as the tempo increased, the heady wave building and building until at last, when she thought she might die of pleasure, it crested and broke. She heard a cry, but did not know if it came from her or Nick. He tensed and tensed again before they subsided together, shuddering and gasping for breath.

They lay side by side on the silken bedcovers, fingers entwined. The daylight had gone now, replaced by a fine silvery moonlight that cast a magical gleam over their naked bodies.

'Nick?' Eve raised herself upon one elbow and looked at him. Her heart lurched. Could this handsome man really be her husband? Was it possible that he could love her, that she could satisfy him? She gently brushed her hand across the scattering of crisp black hairs that grew on his chest. 'Was—was that how it is meant to be? Was it, I mean, was I—?'

His hand came up to trap hers against his chest.

He grinned at her. 'You were magnificent, Eve. I am a very lucky man.'

She flushed with delight. He reached up, hooked his fingers around her neck and began to pull her down to him. 'In fact,' he whispered, 'I think we should try that again, just to be sure…'

Chapter Five

Eve awoke the next morning to the sound of birdsong outside her window. As her sleepiness disappeared and memories of the previous night returned, a delicious feeling of well-being spread through her body. She reached out, expecting to feel Nick next to her, but she was alone in the bed. Eve opened her eyes.

Nick was standing by the window. With the early-morning sun behind him she could not see his face but she knew that he was watching her.

'Nick?'

As he came towards the bed she noted that he was dressed for riding, already booted and spurred.

'I did not want to wake you. You looked so peaceful.'

'You are going out? Will you not wait for me and I will go with you—'

'That is not possible,' he murmured, sitting on the edge of the bed and taking her hand. 'I have to go away for a few days. The messenger came this very morning from Hastings. Business, I am afraid, my love, that requires my urgent attention.'

Eve sat up. 'Hastings! What business can be so important it takes you away so soon after the wedding?' she demanded.

'That I cannot tell you.'

'Oh, but—' He put a finger on her lips and shook his head at her.

'Hush, my dear. You must trust me on this.'

He was still smiling at her, but there was something in his blue eyes that gave her pause, made her bite back the host of questions she wanted to ask him. He leaned forwards and kissed her, very gently. 'Only the most urgent business could tear me away from you at this time,' he said. 'Can you believe that?'

She nodded, suddenly feeling sick with misery. This was nothing unusual, she told herself. Gentlemen did not discuss business affairs with their wives. She shivered, suddenly aware of her nakedness. Nick walked across the room to fetch her wrap of apricot silk. She slipped out of bed and scrambled into it, giving her attention to fastening the ties so that she did not have to look up. He reached out for her.

'I am sorry, sweetheart.'

As he hugged her to him, Eve leaned her head against his chest, willing herself not to cry.

'How soon will you be back?'

His arms tightened around her. 'I do not know. A week, if all goes well. Longer, if not.'

'And—you cannot tell me what is this business that takes you away from me?' Eve knew he would not tell her, even as she asked the question. He put his fingers under her chin and tilted her head up. She looked up into his eyes, blinking to clear her own of the tears that threatened to spill over.

'I must ask you to trust me, my love.'

'I do,' she said passionately.

He kissed her. 'Then stay here, keep yourself safe for when I return.'

She shuddered suddenly and had a vague premonition of danger. 'Promise me you *will* return!'

He laughed down at her, the light glinting in his blue eyes. 'You adorable little goose, of course I shall return!' He kissed her soundly and she leaned into him, returning his kisses and hoping he would sweep her up and carry her back to the bed for one final act of lovemaking before he left. Her disappointment as he gently put her aside was so strong it almost made her weep. 'I must get on, my sweet.'

'Can you not give me ten minutes to dress? I would like to come downstairs and take my leave of you.' She noted his hesitation and added quietly, 'Please, Nick.'

He relented. 'Very well. Ten minutes.'

Nick watched her walk out of the room, her head held high. A wave of tenderness welled up in him. She did not understand why he must go yet there were no tears, no tantrums. He had asked her to trust him and she did. He put out his hand, opened his mouth to call out to her, but something held him back. The moment was lost; the door had closed behind her.

'Just as well,' he told himself. 'The less she knows of this affair, the better.'

A little over ten minutes later, Eve accompanied Nick out of the house, trying not to cling too tightly to his arm.

'Will you be able to write to me, sir?' She tried to keep her voice light.

'I shall try, but it may not be possible if I am very busy.' He lifted her hand to his lips. 'Be strong for me, my love, until I return.'

Looking up into his laughing face, she remembered her first impression of him; an adventurer, a man who courted danger. Her fingers suddenly clenched on his hand. 'You will be careful?'

He gave a merry laugh. 'Sweetheart I am always careful!' With a squeeze of her fingers he turned away and mounted nimbly upon his black horse.

'Granby will be following me with the carriage in an hour or so.' He grinned down at her, his eyes glinting. 'I do not want to hear that you have gone into a decline, madam.'

She dragged up a smile. 'I am not such a poor creature, sir. I shall keep myself busy until your return.' His warm look turned her heart over.

'Good girl. Come up, Admiral!' He raised his whip in a salute as he turned and galloped away down the drive.

Eve watched from the little bridge until Nick was out of sight, then with a sigh she went back into the house. There was an aching void in her chest and she had a desperate desire to burst into tears. She glanced at the clock in the great hall; it was still very early. She had been married for less than twenty-four hours and already her husband had given her both more pleasure, and more pain, than she had ever known before.

* * *

When Eve joined Sir Benjamin in the morning room some time later, he held out his hand to her. 'Rooney told me Nick has been called away, my love. That is a great pity. But it means I have you to myself again.'

She smiled as she grasped his outstretched fingers. 'Indeed you do, Grandpapa.'

'And are you happy with the husband I have found for you, my love?'

She smiled down at him. 'Can you doubt it, sir?'

'No, love. You have been glowing with happiness these past few weeks.' Sir Benjamin sighed. 'But we shall miss him. He is a very lively fellow, Nick Wylder—Wyldfire, they called him, when he was at sea.' He chuckled. 'He certainly sets the house alight with his energy! And he has entertained us royally, has he not, my dear?'

'Yes, sir, and while he is gone we must entertain each other,' said Eve bracingly. 'It is a beautiful day, Grandpapa, will you not take a stroll with me through the garden? I should like you to see the flowerbeds; the roses are particularly fragrant just now. Rooney will give you his arm…'

'I think not, my love. My legs do not feel so very strong today.'

'Then let me bring the backgammon board into the morning room. I know Nick's skill is superior to mine, but I can acquit myself creditably, I think.'

Sir Benjamin patted her hand. 'Not just now, Evelina. I am very tired. I think I should like to rest here quietly in the sunshine for a little while.'

'Of course, Grandpapa.' She bent to kiss his cheek. 'There is plenty for me to do. I fear I have neglected my household duties recently.'

Poor Grandpapa, she thought as she went out. *He will miss Nick almost as much as I do.*

Evelina kept herself busy. She threw herself back into the life of Makerham, for she was still its mistress, and would remain so until Nick came back and carried her away to run his own houses in the north. During the long, lonely nights in the big tester bed she stifled her longings with thoughts of her new life so far from the only home she had ever known. She would be sad to leave Grandpapa, of course, but the thought of moving away did not frighten her: with Nick at her side she knew she need not fear anything.

A week had gone by and there was no letter from Nick, only a hastily scribbled note, telling her that if she had need of him she could leave word at the Ship in Hastings. Eve was philosophical about this; her grandfather had been a very poor correspondent when she had been at school, sometimes a month would pass without a letter and then when it came it would be little more than a few lines dashed off in haste. She folded Nick's note and placed it under her pillow; she would not worry. Besides, she had a much more pressing concern. Sir Benjamin's health was failing rapidly. She sent for the doctor, and came hurrying downstairs to meet him as soon as he arrived.

'Thank you for coming so promptly, Dr Scott.'

'It is no trouble at all, Miss Eve—I mean, Mrs Wylder,' responded the doctor, a twinkle in his kind eyes. 'Now tell me, what is the matter with my patient? Is it his legs again?'

Eve nodded. 'He is complaining of pains in his chest, too. Since the wedding he has not been out of the house,' she said as she escorted him up to her grandfather's room. 'I thought at first he was a little tired from all the celebrations, but this past week he has kept to his bed. And he is eating so little.'

'Well, take me to him, Mrs Wylder, and I'll see what I can do.'

* * *

Eve was busy arranging a bowl of roses in the great hall when the doctor came in search of her.

'I thought I would take these up to Grandpapa,' she said, as he descended the stairs. 'He is so fond of flowers and the perfume from these is delightful.' Her smile faltered as she looked at him. 'It is not good news, I fear, Dr Scott.'

'You must remember he is an old man,' said the doctor gently. 'And a very sick one.'

'I do,' she murmured. 'I am very grateful that he has been with me for so long…'

'I have often thought that he was determined to keep going for your sake. Now that you are married—'

'Oh, pray do not say that!' cried Eve, distressed.

'No, well, perhaps not.' Dr Scott patted her shoulder. 'Go to him, my dear. Take him your flowers. I will call again tomorrow.'

'Grandpapa, I have brought you some roses. Since you cannot go to the garden, the garden must come to you. I shall put them here, near the window where you can see them. There, are they not beautiful?'

Sir Benjamin smiled a little. He was propped up

on a bank of plump pillows, but his eyes were shut. He looked gaunt and grey and very frail in his nightcap and gown.

Eve went over to the bed and took his hand. 'Will you not look at the roses, Grandfather?'

His eyes opened a fraction. 'Very pretty,' he murmured. 'You must excuse me, my love. I cannot seem to get my breath.'

'Then do not waste it on words,' she whispered. 'I shall sit here beside you: we need not talk.'

By the time Dr Scott returned the next morning it was all over. Evelina met him with a black shawl wrapped around her shoulders. Her eyes, she knew, were red and swollen from crying, but she made no excuses.

'Oh, my dear.' He took her hands.

Evelina lifted her head a little higher. 'It was very peaceful,' she said, 'Rooney and I were with him.'

'I'm glad, the two people who loved him most in the world. He would like that. But what will you do now? You should not be here alone.'

'Why not? I am accustomed to that.'

'But not in these circumstances. There are arrangements to be made,' said Dr Scott. 'The funeral, for instance…'

'I shall instruct Grandpapa's lawyers today; they will know what is to be done. And I shall write to my husband.' A new burst of sadness clogged her throat making it difficult to speak. She missed Nick so badly. 'He is away for the moment.'

'Then I wish him God speed to return to you, Mrs Wylder.'

Evelina wished it, too, but she could not allow Nick's continued absence to fill her thoughts, there was too much to do. Letters had to be written, lawyers consulted and funeral arrangements to be put in place. Evelina left the running of Makerham to Mrs Harding while she busied herself with the rituals of bereavement. She sent off her note express to Hastings and wondered how soon she could expect a reply.

Two days later she was in one of the attic rooms, searching through trunks of her mother's clothes for anything that might be altered and used as a mourning gown when from the open window she heard the sounds of a carriage on the drive. Her heart began to thud painfully at the thought that Nick had returned. She hurtled down the stairs, arriving in the great hall just as the door opened.

'Oh I knew you would come! I—'

She broke off, fighting back a wave of anger and disappointment when she saw Bernard Shawcross stepping through the doorway.

'I am delighted to think I have not disappointed you, Cousin,' he said smoothly. As he straightened from his bow he put his hand to his neck. 'You see, I have adopted a black cravat. Thought it fitting.'

'Y-yes, thank you,' she stammered. 'You received my letter.'

He inclined his head. 'I came immediately. I thought you would need me. This is a very distressing time for you. You have my deepest sympathy, dear Cousin. Such a shock for you.'

'Shock? No…no. Grandpapa's health has been of concern for some time. That is why we did not remove to my husband's home in the north country. But you must think me very rag-mannered. Pray sit down, Bernard; you must be wondering why Captain Wylder is not here to greet you. He is away, you see. On business.'

'Ah.' His close-set eyes under their heavy brows were fixed upon her. 'So you have not heard from him?'

'N-no, not yet. It is my hope that he is even now on his way to Makerham.'

Bernard's mouth stretched into a smile. 'Let us

hope so, indeed. But in the meantime I am here to support you. If you would ask Mrs Harding to prepare a room for me…' He waved one hand. 'I know, by rights it should be the master's room, but perhaps it is a little soon.'

She knew a little spurt of anger at his presumption. 'Far too soon,' she retorted. 'Grandfather's bedchamber is still as he left it—' She broke off, gathered herself and said more calmly, 'One of the guest rooms shall be prepared for you.'

Eve was glad of the excuse to leave her cousin and she hurried away to consult the housekeeper. Mrs Harding's reaction to his arrival was typically forthright.

'So he's turned up, has he? Like a bad penny, that one.'

'He is the master here now, Mrs Harding,' Eve reminded her gently. She ignored the housekeeper's scornful look. 'I must clear Grandpapa's room for him, but not yet.'

'No of course not yet, Miss Eve! Why, the master ain't even in his grave. We'll strip the room out completely after the funeral, miss, and we'll do it together. It's not a job for a young lady to take on alone.'

'And…' Eve bit her lip '…and will you join us for

dinner, Mrs Harding?' She could not explain her uneasiness, but the older woman nodded immediately.

'Of course, miss, and I'll be in the drawing room of an evening, too. You shouldn't be left alone with that man.'

'Oh, I am sure there is nothing…'

'You cannot be sure of anything with that one,' retorted Mrs Harding grimly. 'He's trouble, you mark my words. I just wish the captain was here, he would know how to look after you.'

Eve forced a smile. How easily the staff had taken to Nick.

'Perhaps we shall have news of him tomorrow.'

Chapter Six

It was not until the day of Sir Benjamin's funeral that they received word of Nick and when it came, the news was shattering. Evelina was in the morning room with her cousin, waiting for the carriage to take them to Makerham church when Green announced that Captain Wylder's valet had arrived and wished to speak to her.

'At last!' She gave a brief look of apology to her cousin as she hurried away to the great hall where Richard Granby was waiting for her.

'Well,' she greeted him, 'what news have you from your master?' She heard footsteps on the stairs behind her and knew a moment's irritation that her cousin should follow her, but it was forgotten as she observed the grave look upon Granby's face. 'What is it?' she said sharply. 'Tell me.'

'There has been an…accident, ma'am.'

Evelina stared at him. Bernard put his arm about her and guided her to a chair.

'You had best sit down, Cousin,' he murmured.

She kept her eyes fixed upon the valet. 'An accident? Is he badly hurt?'

Granby shifted uncomfortably and Eve put her hands to her cheeks as a shocking idea forced its way into her head.

'Not—?'

Bernard's hand clenched on her shoulder. 'Is he dead?' he said harshly. 'Out with it, man.'

'Yes, sir.'

Eve could only stare at him. The world was shifting, unbalanced. She was having difficulty thinking. She heard Bernard asking what had happened and tried to concentrate upon Granby's answer.

'Drowned. Fell overboard from the yacht. On Saturday last.'

'Perhaps he survived,' suggested Bernard. 'Might there not be some hope?'

Granby shook his head. 'No sir. They were somewhere beyond the Rocks of Nore, too far out for an injured man to swim. But we did check the beaches…'

'Yacht?' Eve frowned. 'But he went to Hastings on business. What was he doing on a *yacht*?'

Granby looked even more uncomfortable.

Bernard patted Eve's shoulder. 'There will be time for such questions later, my dear. For now I think you should lie down.' His calm assumption of authority put new spirit into Eve.

Impatiently she shook off his hand. 'I have no intention of lying down. I am not ill, Cousin, and I shall not fall into hysterics because my husband is—' She could not bring herself to say the word. She knew her composure could shatter at any moment and she would not let that happen. She must stay strong. Eve took a deep, steadying breath. 'You must have ridden half the night to reach here so early, Mr Granby. Thank you for that. I suggest you rest now.'

'Yes, ma'am. I am very sorry, Mrs Wylder.'

'Mrs Wylder,' she murmured. 'No one calls me that here.' She looked up. 'One more thing, Mr Granby. My husband's body…?'

The valet hesitated. He avoided her eyes as he murmured, 'Lost, ma'am.'

'It might still be recovered,' put in Bernard.

'The news was spread along the coast.' Granby nodded. 'They have promised to send word if he is…found.'

'They?' said Bernard. 'Who would that be?'

'The master's business acquaintances.'

In spite of the numbness that had settled over her, Eve almost smiled. The valet's haughty tone and the look that accompanied his words said very clearly that Nick Wylder's business was his own affair, certainly not to be shared with Bernard Shawcross. She rose.

'We will talk later, Mr Granby.' She turned to her cousin, 'Perhaps you would escort me to the carriage, Bernard.'

'My dear cousin, it is not necessary—indeed, it is not usual—for females to attend a funeral.' Eve stared at him and he continued gently, 'I have no doubt you would prefer to go to your room. Shall I send your maid to you?'

'No, Cousin. I will go to the church. I need to be active.'

'But surely—'

She put up a hand. Her voice, when she spoke, was barely under control. 'I wish, Cousin, you would stop trying to order my life. I shall go on much better if I am allowed to keep busy. Please let me have my way in this.'

'My dear Evelina, I am head of the family now—'

Granby coughed. 'Beggin' your pardon, sir, but Mrs Wylder is part of Lord Darrington's family now.'

Eve felt a flicker of gratitude for Richard Granby. Bernard scowled, but as he opened his mouth to retort she forestalled him.

'Yes, thank you, Mr Granby. That is all for now. You may go.' She reached up to her bonnet and pulled the veil down over her face. 'Cousin, our carriage is at the door.'

Sir Benjamin had been an important figure in Makerham and the little village church was packed with those wishing to pay their last respects. The sight of Evelina in her flowing black robes and leaning heavily on her cousin's arm caused more than one stolid parishioner to blink away a tear. When the coffin was carried out of the church and Miss Shawcross fainted clean away, there were many that said it was a blessing she should be spared the sight of her beloved grand-father's body being consigned to the earth.

Martha accompanied her mistress back to the house and half-carried her up to her room, but it was not until her maid had tucked her up in her bed and departed that Eve allowed her pent-up grief to spill over. Tears burned her eyes and huge, gasping sobs racked her body as she mourned for the loss of her grandfather and her husband. She curled herself into a ball and sank her teeth into her fist to prevent herself screaming with rage and grief and pain. Sir Benjamin's death had long been anticipated, but Nick's loss was unbearable; she was not prepared for the agony and in some strange way she felt betrayed. He had ridden into her life and she had tumbled headlong into love with him. She had trusted him with her heart and now he was gone, as quickly as he had come. She dragged the covers over her head and allowed the tears to fall, crying for her grandfather, for Nick, for herself. Finally, as exhaustion set in, she buried her face in her damp pillow, praying that the expensive feather-and-down filling would deprive her lungs of air and suffocate her.

When Eve awoke to the grey dawn, her first conscious thought was disappointment. Disappointment that she was still alive. The silence in the house told her it was very early. She threw back the covers and crawled out of bed; there was a heaviness to her limbs that made every movement a struggle. She dragged herself over to the window and looked out. The garden was grey and colourless in the half-light. Very fitting, she thought. A house in mourning. She crossed her arms over her chest and tried to make sense of her grief. She had been prepared to lose her grandfather; they had said their goodbyes and she was comforted by the thought that he was no longer suffering from pain or ill-health. She was saddened by his death, but not bereft. But Nick— Nick with his dazzling smile and laughing blue eyes. He had ridden into her sheltered world and given her a glimpse of a much more exciting one. She had known him for such a short time, but now she missed him so much it was a physical pain inside her.

She gazed out at the horizon, where a watery sun was climbing through the clouds. Soon the house would be awake and Martha would come in with her hot chocolate. Life would go on and she was expected to do her duty. With a sigh she turned away from the window. The day stretched interminably before her. She had no idea how she would bear this misery.

Her fairy-tale had turned to a nightmare.

'Ah, Cousin, here you are.'

Evelina schooled her features as Bernard

Shawcross came into the morning room. To smile at him was impossible, but she must not glower.

'So I have found you alone at last.' He laughed gently. 'I was beginning to think you were avoiding me.'

And with good reason, thought Eve. Aloud, she said, 'I have been very busy. Since the funeral there have been so many visitors wishing to offer their condolences, then there are all the legal matters to attend to as well as the household duties to be done…'

'At least with that I may assist you,' he said, sitting down near her. 'After all, Makerham is my home now, so I can remove that worry from your pretty shoulders.'

She repressed a shudder. 'Makerham was never a worry, Cousin,' she replied coolly.

'Green tells me that you have been closeted with your lawyer this morning. Is there any news of your husband?'

She shook her head. 'Mr Didcot urges caution. Without a—' she swallowed hard '—without a b-body he is loathe to pronounce me a widow. Both he and Granby advise me to go to Yorkshire and place myself under the protection of my husband's family.'

'Yorkshire is a wild, uncivilised country, Cousin. You would not like it.'

She raised her brows. 'You cannot call York and Harrogate uncivilised. Really, Bernard, you are quite Gothic at times.'

'Perhaps, but you have always lived in the south, always at Makerham. We are the last of the Shawcross family, Cousin. It is only right that I should want to take care of you.'

He reached out as he spoke and put his hand on her knee. Eve froze.

'Please, Cousin. I am a married woman.'

'You are a *widow*, my dear.'

'You are very certain of that.'

'I would not have you keep false hopes alive.' The hand on her knee tightened. 'And now that you have experienced a man's touch—'

She jumped up. 'Pray stop. It is far too soon for such a conversation, Bernard! Please, excuse me!'

She turned away but his hand shot out and caught her arm.

'Think, Evelina. What do you know of Wylder's family? You must not go north. You would be far from everything you have ever known, ever loved. Consider what I can offer you.' He was standing behind her now, his breath hot on her neck. 'He was a hellraiser, that husband of yours. Did you know that? Did you think you could reform him? Impossible, madam: you cannot tame a tiger, only cage him. If he was truly changed, how could he leave you so soon after your marriage?'

She shook her head. 'No,' she protested. 'I shall not listen to you!'

'But you must! He tricked you, Eve. He never really loved you. Had he done so, he could not have left you. How could any man leave you?' He pulled her back against him and murmured in her ear, 'You love Makerham, and you need never leave it. You can stay here, run it as you have always done. We will marry, of course, as soon as that is possible, but until then, we can be… discreet.'

Eve fought down her growing panic. His grip on her arms was like iron, biting into her flesh. She knew she could not free herself by force. She must stay calm if she was to escape. She said in a low voice, 'Please, Cousin. This is all so, so unexpected. My thoughts are in turmoil.'

'Of course. I should not have spoken yet.' She felt his lips on the back of her neck. 'Off you go, my dear. We will talk more of this later.'

Eve forced herself to walk slowly out of the room, her back rigid with fear, as though there were some wild animal behind her, ready to pounce. As soon as she reached the hall she picked up her skirts and fled to her room, trying to blot out the memory of Bernard's mouth upon her skin.

Eve changed her gown and at the dinner hour she made her way down to the drawing room with some trepidation. She was relieved to find only the housekeeper awaiting her. 'Mrs Harding, I must get away from Makerham.'

'Away from the new master, you mean.'

The blunt statement made Eve smile.

'His intentions are—ultimately—honourable.'

Mrs Harding gave a scornful laugh. 'Aye. He'll have to marry you if he is to get Monkhurst.'

'I beg your pardon?'

'I heard him talking to Lawyer Didcot when he came to read the will.' The housekeeper flushed slightly. 'I needed to pick some rosemary from the bush outside the study window, so I couldn't help but overhear, mistress. He questioned Mr Didcot very closely, he did, about who would get Monkhurst now you was married. Mr Didcot said of course he wasn't at liberty to discuss the marriage settlement, but he *could* tell him that Monkhurst was secured on you and your heirs.

Unless you died without issue,' she continued, her brow furrowed in concentration. 'Then of course it would go directly to your husband. It seems Bernard was hoping it might revert to the family, but as Lawyer Didcot explained to him, it belonged to your mama's family, the Winghams, and was never part of the entail.'

'But why should he want Monkhurst? The house has been shut up for years, since Mama died, in fact.'

Mrs Harding spread her hands. 'Mayhap 'tis greed, Miss Eve. He wants everything.'

'Well he shall not have it,' declared Eve. 'Any more than he shall have me!'

Mrs Harding put up her hand. 'Hush now, dearie, I hear his step in the hall. And you need not look so anxious, I am not about to leave you alone with that man.'

The housekeeper was as good as her word, and after an uncomfortable dinner Eve made her excuses to retire to her room. There she was careful to make sure her door was locked securely. She crept into her bed and lay rigidly beneath the covers.

It was little more than a week since she had tried to cheat sleep and stay awake each night to think about Nick Wylder, to go over their conversations, relive their moments together. Since the news of Nick's death, when her whole being ached for the oblivion of sleep, it would not come. But at least now, following Bernard's sudden declaration, she could spend the long, sleepless night making her plans.

Early the next day she summoned Granby to the morning room, and when he came in she began without preamble. 'Granby, I am leaving Makerham.'

'Ah. We go to Yorkshire, ma'am?'

'No. I plan to go to Monkhurst.'

'Monkhurst! But, that's impossible!'

'It is very possible,' she replied crisply. 'The marriage settlement is quite clear; Monkhurst remains my own.'

'But surely it would be better for you to be under the protection of the master's family.'

'No, why should it? My grandfather provided for me very well in his will, and Mr Didcot assures me that it will not be affected by my—my widowhood. I am dependent upon no one, Mr Granby.'

'Of course, ma'am. But—'

'My mind is made up.'

The valet stared at her, his usually impassive countenance betraying his consternation. 'I pray you, mistress, reconsider. You said yourself Monkhurst has not been lived in for the past ten years! It—it could be derelict. Allow me to escort you to Yorkshire. You will be made very welcome, and—'

'Now why should you be so horrified at the thought of Monkhurst?' she asked him. 'It is my own property, after all. I lived there with Mama and Papa for the first few years of my life. And as for being derelict, no such thing! I was used to help Grandpapa with the accounts and I know he is still paying the housekeeper and her husband to look after the house. I shall feel more comfortable amongst my own people, under the present circumstances.'

'Of course, ma'am, but surely—'

'Yes?' There was a touch of impatience in her voice now.

The valet bowed his head. 'I am sorry, madam, if you think I speak out of turn, but the master would want you to go to his family.'

'But the master is not here.' She was not able to keep the tremor from her voice.

'No, ma'am, but—'

'Enough, Mr Granby. My mind is made up. Since you returned from Hastings in the travelling carriage I should like to use it to go to Monkhurst. You may use the baggage wagon to take Captain Wylder's trunks on to Yorkshire. I shall ensure you have sufficient funds for the journey.'

'No, ma'am.'

'I beg your pardon?'

Granby tilted up his head, his chin jutting obstinately. 'I cannot leave you, Mrs Wylder. The master would never forgive me. I mean,' he added hastily, 'if you are going to Monkhurst, then I should like to come with you, mistress. I could be useful to you. As a courier, perhaps, or a steward at Monkhurst.'

'A steward! Do you know anything about such matters?'

'I sailed with the captain for years, madam, and only became his valet when he left the sea. I know a great deal more than how to dress a gentleman, and I cannot like the idea of you and Martha travelling so far without a man.'

Eve regarded his solid figure. 'I confess it would be a comfort to have a manservant with me.'

A look of relief flashed in his eyes. He bowed. 'Then it is settled. Mrs Wylder. I shall go and pack.'

'Hurry, then, for I wish to be away from here by noon.'

* * *

It was not to be expected that Bernard would take Eve's decision calmly, but in the presence of Mrs Harding and the servants he could not argue too strongly and Eve was careful not to give him the opportunity to speak to her alone. By noon the carriage was packed and ready to depart.

'I fear you will find the house in a dreadful state,' Bernard warned her as he helped her into the carriage.

'Perhaps, but I sent a messenger off at dawn to advise the staff there of my arrival.'

'The devil you did! You planned this and never a word to me!'

'Come, Bernard, do not scowl so. Let us part as friends.'

After a slight hesitation he took her hand and bowed over it. 'Very well. But I cannot like it.' He kissed her fingers. 'Remember, Evelina, you will always be welcome here at Makerham.'

It was shortly after noon when Eve left Makerham. She dare not look back at the house that had been her home for so many years, nor at the churchyard where Sir Benjamin's remains now rested. Instead she kept her gaze fixed upon Granby, who was riding alongside the carriage. It reminded her of her first sight of Nick Wylder, when he came cantering towards her on his magnificent black horse. The memory brought a lump to her throat. She could not yet believe that she would never see Nick again. Eve wondered what had become of Admiral. She must ask Mr Granby. If the animal was still at Hastings then he must be fetched, even if he had to be sold. Yes, he most definitely would have to be sold, she thought, trying to be practical. But not yet. Not until she was settled in her new life.

The day dragged on. Even the thought of seeing Monkhurst again, a house Eve had not visited for a decade, did not have the power to excite her. Her grandfather's loss had not been unexpected and although she grieved for him she was not overcome. It was Nick who filled her thoughts. Nick with his devastating smile and that twinkle in his blue eyes, his energy and enthusiasm for life. She remembered the night they had shared, a single night that had transformed her from a girl into a woman. Nick had made her feel alive, he had aroused emotions in her such as she had never known—and now would never know again. Eve closed her eyes and turned her head towards the window so that Martha should not see her tears.

Their progress had been slow through the lanes around Makerham, but once they reached Guildford the roads improved and they made good time. Eve had given instructions that they were to press on as quickly as possible, but even though their stops to change horses were brief, and Eve had alighted only once at Tenterden to partake a hurried dinner, it was nearly ten o'clock when they arrived at their destination. As the carriage pulled up at the closed gates Eve let down the window.

'I can smell the sea on the breeze,' she murmured. 'I had forgotten how the winds carry the salt air inland.'

'There's no lights in the house,' muttered Martha, peering out of the window towards the shadowy building, outlined against the darkening sky. 'We're locked out.'

'Nonsense,' Eve replied. 'There is a light in the window of the Gate House. Mr Granby is even now knocking on the door.'

A few minutes later the valet approached the carriage followed by a large, ambling figure. 'This is Silas Brattee, Mrs Wylder, the gatekeeper. He says your message never arrived.'

'But I sent it express!'

Granby shrugged. 'I will follow that up tomorrow, madam.'

Eve waved him aside and peered at the figure behind him. 'You are Aggie's husband, are you not?' she said. 'You will not know me, for you were at sea when I lived here as a child.'

'Aye, I was, mistress. Went off to sea about the time that you was born, I'm thinking. The mistress was dead by the time I came home for good, but Sir Benjamin kept me an' Aggie on here to look after the place.' Silas was shifting from foot to foot as he spoke to her. 'If we'd known you was comin' ma'am, we'd've spruced up the house. As it is, the place ain't fit…'

'Well, it will have to do,' replied Eve. 'Unlock the gates, please.'

'Mebbe the Bell would suit, or the Woolpack,' suggested Silas hopefully.

'That is only a mile or so back,' added Granby. 'They will have rooms for the night.'

'Nonsense. I took the precaution of bringing my own linen. It will not take a moment to prepare beds for us.'

'Nay, mistress,' said Silas. 'You'd be much more comfortable in the village, miss, believe me.'

Eve peered through the darkness at him. 'I am beginning to wonder if you received my message, but decided to ignore it,' she declared. 'Let me in now, Mr Brattee.'

'The house has not been lived in,' Granby warned her. 'It may well be damp.'

'I do not care if the roof is falling in,' retorted Eve. 'I will stay in my own house tonight.'

Her fierce glare had its effect. Granby nodded and muttered to Silas to unlock the gates.

'Well,' sighed Eve as they clattered onto the grass-covered drive and drove up to the front door. 'This is a poor beginning.'

'Mrs Brattee is going to bring coffee and some food up to the house later,' said Granby as he helped Eve to alight. 'However, I fear you will not be very comfortable.'

'I am so exhausted now I think that as long as I can lie down I shall be happy,' she said, following him into the dark entrance hall. She stood for a few moments, pulling off her gloves while the valet moved around the walls, lighting candles. As the feeble glow strengthened, the outline of the large panelled hall could be seen. It was furnished with a large table that filled the centre of the room and a number of solid chairs and heavy dark chests pushed against the walls.

Martha gave a gusty sigh. 'Ooh, miss, this reminds me of the last time we was here, when your sainted mother was alive. I was nobbut a girl then, o' course, like yourself. My first post away from home, but I remember your mama saying how glad she always was to come back here after her travels.'

'I am sure she never had to come to an unprepared house!' retorted Eve with asperity.

'No, miss, but she wouldn't have worried about it. A very spirited lady was your mother and one who loved adventure, God rest her soul.'

'Well, *I* want nothing more than a quiet life!' Eve sighed. 'Let us see what we can do, Martha. Fetch a candlestick and we will go upstairs. I had best take the main bedroom; if my memory serves, there is a maid's room adjoining. Ask Dan Coachman to bring up the trunks and we will search out the sheets.'

'You are never going to be making up beds, miss!' Martha was shocked. 'Rich—I mean, Mr Granby can help me with that.'

'Well, if you think I am going to sit alone down

here like a great lady while you are labouring away you are very much mistaken,' replied Eve, amused. 'I am just as capable as you of putting sheets on a bed—well, almost—and we shall have it done in a trice. Mr Granby would be better employed in the kitchen, helping Mrs Brattee to prepare our supper!'

Eve was thankful that the main bedchamber was still furnished and once they had removed the dust sheets she declared herself very well satisfied. She gave a cry of delight when she found her mother's portrait propped against the elegant little writing desk and immediately charged Martha to assist her in hanging it on the empty hook above the fireplace.

'There,' she said, bringing the candles closer. 'Now I feel much more at home.'

'She was a beauty, Miss Eve, and no mistake,' remarked Martha. 'And you have the look of her, too.'

'Do I?' Eve gazed up at the painting. She saw an elegant woman in a gold sack-backed gown standing very erect with one hand resting on a large atlas. Eve recognised some similarities, the thick, luxuriant dark hair, straight little nose and smiling mouth, but there was a confidence about her mother that she had never felt in herself: those dark eyes seemed to look out upon the world with such self-assurance.

'This was painted just before her marriage,' she murmured. 'Even then she yearned to travel the world, whereas I—I have always been content to live quietly at home. What a disappointment I would be to her.' She stared at the portrait for a few moments longer, then gave her head a little shake, as if to throw off some unwelcome thought. 'Well, such musings will do no good! Open those trunks and find our sheets, Martha, we must prepare for bed.'

There were no hangings on the tester bed, but the mattress was in place beneath its protective cover and it did not feel damp. Martha grumbled as she pulled the sheets from the trunk, but Eve was glad to be active, it helped her forget her unhappiness for a while.

That night Eve dreamed Nick was still alive. In those darkest hours just before dawn, when dreams are at their most vivid, she saw him clearly, heard his ringing laugh and knew in her very core that he was near her. The disappointment, when she opened her eyes and memory returned, made her feel physically sick. Eve looked around at the unfamiliar furnishings and knew a moment's panic. This was not Makerham, neither was it the warm sunny place of her dream, the place where Nick was. She closed her eyes again, trying to bring the dream back, but it was impossible. All that was left was a vague, half-remembered happiness and she clung to it, holding on to it like a talisman, to be touched and rekindled when the demands of the day grew too great.

As Eve made her way downstairs she thought that Monkhurst looked much more welcoming with the morning sunshine flooding in. She found Mrs Brattee waiting to escort her to the small parlour where breakfast was laid out for her.

'Aggie!' Eve smiled fondly upon the housekeeper. 'I am so sorry I missed you last night. Martha insisted that I take supper in my room, and to tell you the truth, by the time we had finished making the beds I was ready to fall asleep! You have not changed a bit, yet it must be all of ten years since I was last here!'

'Aye, ma'am, that it is,' replied Aggie, her harsh features softening a little. 'And you a grown lady now. I'm that sorry for last night, Mrs Wylder. If only we'd known…'

'It cannot be helped. We shall soon make everything comfortable.'

'You are planning to stay here?'

Eve observed the look of horror upon the housekeeper's face and knew a strong desire to laugh. 'Why, yes,' she said, taking her seat at the breakfast table. 'Granby is very keen for me to go to Yorkshire, to his master's house, but I would rather stay here, for now.'

'But it's not fit for you, mistress. It's been empty for years.'

Eve sipped at her coffee. 'I made a quick inspection before coming downstairs, the house is in much better order than I dared expect. One would never believe it has been ten years since it was occupied. In fact...' Eve fixed her eyes upon the housekeeper '...one of the rooms—the one I used to know as the blue room—has every appearance of having been used recently.'

'Well, mistress, how that can be I cannot say, I'm sure,' replied Mrs Brattee, bustling about the parlour.

'Can you not? Grandpapa always said Mama's family had links with the free traders. I thought perhaps they might have been here.'

There was a loud crash as the dish the housekeeper had been holding dropped to the floor and shattered. Eve raised her brows.

'Oh? Am I correct, then?'

'No, mistress. I swear there was no smugglers sleeping in the house!' declared Aggie, looking thoroughly alarmed.

'Well, who?' Eve said gently, 'I do think I have a right to know who has been sleeping in my house.' She waited, fixing her eyes upon the housekeeper, who shifted uncomfortably. 'Tell me,' she commanded.

'I can't, mistress. I promised I wouldn't say.'

'I think you must.'

The old woman eyed her doubtfully and Evelina tried again.

'Come,' she coaxed her gently. 'Tell me who it was. Well?'

The housekeeper twisted her apron between her hands. 'It was the master,' she blurted out.

'Grandpapa? But he has not been near the place for years.'

'No, no, the *young* master,' replied Mrs Brattee. 'Captain Wylder.'

Chapter Seven

Evelina stared at her housekeeper. She began to tremble and clasped her hands together, digging the nails into her palms to fight down her panic.

'When was this?'

'About a week since.'

'Then you saw him just before he, before—'

'Aye, miss.' Aggie nodded. 'He—he came down to talk to Silas, said that now he was wed to you it would be quite proper for him to stay at Monkhurst. Showed Silas the marriage papers, he did. Everything looked to be in order so Silas let him in. Didn't think there'd be any harm in it…'

Eve jumped to her feet. 'No harm! Richard Granby knew of this, and he did not tell me! Where *is* Granby?'

'He's taken the old gig to the village, ma'am. Said

he would fetch me some provisions, to tide us over until Silas can take me to Appledore in the cart.'

'Then he will be gone for hours.' Eve sank down again, her brow furrowed with thought. 'Nick, stayed here?' she mused. 'But why?'

'That I can't say, mistress, but Silas was never one to refuse the captain—'

'Wait.' Evelina put her hand to her head, trying to make sense of what she was hearing. 'Did—did my husband *know* Silas?'

'He did, ma'am. They sailed together, years ago. Silas was always talking about Captain Wyldfire and he was that pleased when the captain came looking for him, but he wouldn't let him into the house, ma'am, not until it was all legal, like.'

'Do you mean that…that C-Captain Wylder came here *before* we were married?'

'Oh, yes, ma'am.' It seemed that now Mrs Brattee had made her confession she was happy to talk. 'Back in the spring he fetched up here. Silas was so surprised—'

'But what did he want?' The closed look returned and Eve said impatiently, 'You have told me this much, Aggie I do not think you can stop now.'

'He…he was asking about the free trading.'

'Is Silas—I mean—does he know about such things?'

The housekeeper gave her a pitying look. 'There's not a family hereabouts that doesn't, miss.'

'But I don't understand. Why should Nick come *here*?'

'That I couldn't say, mistress. He stayed in the village for a week or more, went out with Silas and the boys—do you remember my sons, ma'am, Sam and Nathanial? You wouldn't recognise 'em, they're strapping men now. Both married; my Nathanial has twins and Sam has a babe on the way.'

Eve smiled reminiscently. 'We used to play together on the Marsh, did we not? I know you did not always approve of my running wild with the boys, but Mama did not mind, and we were very young. It all changed when I was sent away to school.'

'You had to learn to be a lady, Miss Eve.'

'I suppose I did.' Eve sighed. 'But we digress. You were telling me about Captain Wylder's visit.'

'Ah, yes. As I was saying, Silas keeps a galley on the Marsh, you see, and Captain Nick went out with them—'

'Wait, wait, wait!' Eve interrupted her again.

'Are you saying Captain Wylder helped them to *smuggle* goods into the country?'

'Silas prefers to call it free trading,' said Mrs Brattee, affronted. 'They brings in a few barrels of brandy, sometimes a bit of Brussels lace—it's not as though anyone hereabouts could afford to buy it, if they had to pay the duty, so it ain't doing any harm.'

Evelina realised it would be useless to argue and turned her mind to her main anxiety. 'But why Nick? What interest did he have in such things?'

'There's many a seafaring man turns to free trading to repair his fortunes, mistress.'

Eve shook her head. 'Nick Wylder was not in need of money. I know that because Grandpapa discussed the marriage settlements with me. Not only did my husband have property, there is also a great deal of prize money invested in the Funds. So why should he come to Monkhurst?'

'The captain was very interested in the house, but Silas was adamant. Apart from the odd visit from your grandpapa, Monkhurst has been shut up since your parents died.' Aggie gave a noisy sigh. 'Very attached to your mama, was Silas. Apple of his eye, she was, so he wasn't about to let anyone into her house. Even when your cousin, Mr Bernard Shawcross, came down here a couple o' years ago. Silas turned him away, sayin' he'd had his orders from your grandpapa to shut the house up and shut it would remain.' She snorted. 'And your cousin didn't take it anything like as well as Cap'n Wyldfire. Raged at Silas, he did; said he was family and entitled to be let in, but Silas said if that was the case he should go and get permission from your grandfather.'

'Yes, but what of Captain Wylder?' Eve prompted her gently.

'The cap'n went off. Back to London, we thought. Then, next thing we knows, he comes back to tell us he's wed—and to our own Miss Shawcross!'

'But why did he not tell *me* he had been to Monkhurst, or that he was coming back here?'

The housekeeper's blank look was genuine, and Eve forbore to press her further. However, the question continued to plague Eve. She played with the gold band on her finger, turning it round and round as an answer lodged itself in her brain. Nick had not trusted her.

Only because he did not know me, she told herself fiercely. *He would have learned to trust me, in time.* If only… A little scream of frustration forced its way up through her. She banged her fist into her palm. 'Ooooh, I hate that man!' she hissed. 'How could he do this to me? I hate him, I *hate* him!'

Tears welled up again but she fought them down. She would be strong. And she would get to the bottom of this mystery.

However, an interview with Silas proved even less rewarding, for the old man merely shook his head, saying he had no idea why Captain Nick had come looking for him.

'But you took him out in your boat with you when he was here in the spring.' She added quickly, 'Come now, Silas, I know all about your…activities.'

'The captain ain't concerned with the piddlin' little bits we bring in,' he said. 'He's after bigger fish, that much I do know. But he was impressed with the galley that we uses to go in and out to the sea. Deal-made, she is, and fast in the water. Me brother Ephraim 'as another just such a one over at Dimchurch and I told the cap'n how in the old days we used her to row across to Boulogne. Can't beat Kentish oarsman, mistress, although these days when there's a drop we just meets the lugger off shore and brings in what we need through Jury's Cut.'

'I am sure you do, but it is still illegal, Silas, and I cannot have it.' She regarded him steadily. 'You must promise me to give up the trade, Silas. I will find work for you, and for Nat and Samuel, but you must not take part in any further smuggling.'

It was not to be expected that Silas would capitulate immediately, but Eve was adamant and eventually she wrested from him a grudging promise that he would cease his illegal activities. Satisfied on this point, Eve could once more give her attention to finding out why Nick had come to Monkhurst.

'What did Captain Wylder want here, Silas? How long did he stay in the house?'

'No more'n a couple o' nights. We took a dinghy out on the Monkhurst Drain, Miss Eve, that leads down to Jury's Cut and the sea, and I showed 'im the boathouse, but that ain't been used for years.' Silas twisted his cap in his hands and looked at Eve anxiously. 'I didn't think there was any harm in it, mistress, knowing the cap'n, and him now being family…'

'And you trusted him, Silas?' she said, a little wistfully.

'With my life, mistress. The cap'n knew I'd follow him anywhere,' he ended proudly. 'When we was fighting the rebels in the American War he was never happier than when he was kicking up a dust. Unpredictable, see, like his nickname, Wyldfire. He was here one minute, then the next, he's up and gone to Hastings.' Silas frowned, shaking his head. 'Not but what that was a mistake, God rest his soul.'

There was nothing more to be learned from the old man. Evelina dismissed him, but the problem nagged at her throughout the morning while she worked her way through the house, trying to decide what was required to make it a comfortable home. The early morning sun had given way to heavy storm-clouds and a blustery wind whistled through the passages, signalling a change from the dry, sunny weather of the past few weeks.

It was noon before Eve heard the sounds of the gig returning. A glance out of the window showed her that it was raining heavily and she felt a certain grim satisfaction when she saw that Granby had omitted to take a greatcoat with him, and was soaked through. She hurried to the kitchens and found the valet drying himself off before the kitchen fire. Paying no heed to Mrs Brattee, who was busy unpacking the baskets Granby had brought in for her, Eve went straight into the attack.

'Why did you not tell me my husband stayed here?'

Granby swung round and she saw the flash of surprise before he schooled his countenance to its usual inscrutable mask. 'I thought it might distress you, ma'am.'

'I am more distressed to think you lied to me. What else have you omitted to tell me?' she demanded. 'What was Captain Wylder doing here?'

'I believe he wished to renew his acquaintance with Mr Brattee and his family,' said Granby, smoothly.

'But he had already done that, he had visited Silas before he made Grandpapa's acquaintance at Tunbridge Wells.'

The valet bowed. 'As you say, madam.'

Eve watched him closely. 'Captain Wylder told me he had business in Sussex.'

The valet inclined his head. 'That is true ma'am. The master stayed here only a few nights before going on to Hastings.'

'And this…business: did it involve smuggling?'

Granby looked shocked. 'Captain Wylder's acquaintances in Hastings are most respectable people, ma'am.'

'I do hope so, Mr Granby.'

He smiled a little and spread his hands. 'You have my word upon it, Mrs Wylder.'

'I shall have more than that.'

'Ma'am?'

Eve put her hands on her hips and looked at him. 'Go and change into dry clothes, Mr Granby. And order my carriage. We are going to Hastings.'

Granby's smile vanished. 'Hastings! Now?'

'Yes, now. As soon as we are packed.'

'But, madam, there is not the least need—'

'There is every need,' she flung at him. 'I am anxious to know that I am not the widow of a common villain!'

'Mrs Wylder, I beg of you, at least postpone your journey until this storm has eased.'

Richard Granby stood beside Eve in the doorway, looking out with dismay at the rain that lashed the house while the coachman packed the trunks securely, water running from the brim of his hat and his oiled coat.

'I am determined to reach Hastings today,' she retorted. 'You may ride in the carriage with Martha and me, if you do not wish to get another soaking.'

The valet declined the offer, and clambered miserably up beside Dan Coachman.

'He is afraid I shall interrogate him further,' remarked Eve cheerfully as she climbed into the carriage.

Her maid sniffed as she settled herself beside her mistress. 'Mr Granby was only trying to save you unnecessary worry, Miss Eve.'

'Is that what he has told you, Martha?'

'No, madam, but I know he's a good man.'

'Is he?' Eve looked closely at her maid. 'You seem to be uncommon friendly with Richard Granby.'

Martha flushed, but she said stiffly, 'Given his position and mine, it is only natural that we should talk.'

Eve forbore to tease her. 'Of course it is,' she said, turning her mind back to her own worries. 'And if Mr Granby has passed on anything concerning my husband's death, I would like you to tell me, Martha. I shall not be easy until I know what sort of business it was that took my husband away from Makerham in such haste. I hope we may find some answers at Hastings.' She leaned back against the thickly padded seat. 'And I confess I want to see where Nick spent his last days,' she murmured to herself.

The wind howled around them, rocking the carriage while the heavy rain drummed on the roof and pattered against the windows. The pace was necessarily slow. The storm grew worse as they neared the coast and it was a relief to drive through Rye, for although the cobbles shook the coach until Eve's teeth rattled in her head, at least the houses gave them some shelter from the buffeting winds. The carriage slowed to a stop and Eve leaned forwards to peer out of the window. A horseman had stopped beside them and was shouting something at the coachman.

Eve let down the window. 'What is it, is there a problem?'

The rider turned to look at her, touching his hand to his sodden hat.

'Aye, ma'am. The Winchelsea road is closed. They wanted to take advantage of the dry weather to repair the road, but the dam—dashed fools didn't start it until yesterday. Now the grass verge is too wet to take the weight of a carriage and there's only room for a horse to squeeze by.'

'Is there another route?' asked Eve.

The rider nodded. 'Aye, you can go via Broad Oak Cross and then south through Battle.'

Granby leaned down from the box, shaking his head at her. 'That's a long journey, Mrs Wylder.

Dan says he must proceed slowly if we are not to be overturned by the high winds on the open road.'

'Then that is what we shall do,' said Eve decisively. 'Tell him to drive on!'

'Very well, madam.'

Martha sniffed. 'The poor man will very likely catch his death sitting up on the box in this weather.'

'Very likely,' replied Eve, unmoved.

'We should turn back,' said her forthright handmaiden. 'No good can come of this, Miss Eve, you mark my words. What do you want to go traipsing all the way to Hasting for? What if you hears things you didn't want to know about the master?'

Eve did not answer. Martha had voiced the fear that had been nagging at her, that Nick was involved in some villainous activity, but it was no good. She had to know the truth, however bad. Besides, illogical as it was, she wanted to visit the place where he had died.

To say goodbye.

Tears filled her eyes again and she blinked them away, angry at herself. Why should she feel such sorrow for a man she had known for less than a month? Yet the tug of attraction had been so strong, she could not resist it. He still haunted her dreams.

Nick had wound his way so effectively into her heart that now his loss threatened to break it.

'You are a fool, Evelina,' she told herself angrily. 'You let yourself believe that Grandpapa had brought you a knight in shining armour!'

The sudden stopping of the carriage dragged her away from her depressing thoughts.

'Oh, Heavens, what is it now?' cried Martha.

The cab rocked as someone climbed down from the box and Eve pressed her nose to the window, trying to see out. It was impossible; inside, the glass misted with her breath and outside the raindrops distorted her view. She let down the window and immediately the driving rain slapped at her face. There was another carriage stopped in front of them, and Granby was talking in earnest conversation with the driver, one hand clamped over his hat to prevent the wind from whipping it away.

'There is some sort of hold up,' she said to her maid as she put up the window once more. 'Granby is looking into it now.'

Moments later the valet yanked open the door. Even though he was standing on the most sheltered side of the carriage the wind swirled around and threatened to drag the coach door out of his hands.

'The road is under water, ma'am. A culvert has

collapsed. One wagon has already tried to drive through and has broken an axle. No one is hurt,' he hastened to assure them, 'but we must turn back.'

Reluctantly Eve agreed. She glanced past him at the rain, still sheeting down. The thought of spending another couple of hours returning to Monkhurst was not a pleasant one.

'Very well, Granby. Tell Dan to drive back to the nearest village. We will put up for the night.'

But when they drove into Udimore, Eve took one look at the rundown hostelry and quickly changed her mind. She ordered Dan to drive back to Rye.

'What I saw of the slatternly maids and greasy landlord convinced me we should not be comfortable there,' she said to her maid as the carriage set off once more. 'Granby tells me we passed several well-appointed inns at Rye. We shall do better there.'

'I do hope so, madam,' replied Martha in a failing voice. 'I fear if I don't get out o' this jarring, jolting cab soon I shall have to ask you for your smelling salts!'

Eve laughed. 'Then I would have to disappoint you, Martha, for I do not carry such a thing!

'Well then, it's a good job I put a bottle of Glass's Magnesia in your dressing case! With your permission, Miss Eve, I shall take some as soon as I can lay my hands on it.'

'You would be better advised to take a little walk and get some fresh air,' replied Eve, 'but as you wish.'

She looked out of the window. The rain had eased a little and looking up she saw the squat tower of Rye church, secure on its hill, a black outline against the lowering sky. The clatter of hooves on the cobbles told Eve that they had reached the town and she knew a few moments' anxiety when they pulled up at the George, only to be told that every available room had been taken, but minutes later the carriage turned into the yard of the Mermaid, another busy coaching inn, and Granby was holding open the door for her to alight. Evelina had the impression of overhanging eves and a half-timbered building surrounding the yard as she hurried across to the entrance. She was immediately shown into a small private parlour filled with gleaming brassware and polished panelling.

'This is very much more the thing!' she exclaimed. 'A warm, clean room and the most appetising smell from the kitchens. I vow I am quite famished. Granby must bespeak dinner for us as soon as maybe.'

Her maid groaned. 'I feel as sick as a cat, miss.'

'Poor Martha. Sit you down then and rest until the landlord brings us coffee. Or should I ask him for some tea?'

'Just as you like, miss. I wants nothing more than to sit quiet for a bit.'

'Then you shall do just that. Granby is organising our rooms for us and will see that our bags are taken upstairs. I never realised before how useful it is to have a man to do these things for one. Perhaps I shall keep him on, after all, as my major-domo.' A glance at the pale figure sitting beside the fire showed her that Martha was not listening, so she busied herself instead with making them both comfortable. She helped her maid to remove her bonnet and cloak and put them with her own over a chair. A rosy-cheeked maid brought in her coffee, apologising for the delay.

'We've been that busy, what with the storm and everything. Every table's took.' She looked around, smiled and bobbed a curtsy. 'You'm lucky to have this parlour, madam. You'll be comfy enough in here.'

As the maid went out, Martha opened one eye. 'Will you not sit down, miss? You must be exhausted, all that travelling—'

'Not a bit of it! I did not like being bounced all over the road, but I am more excited than tired. You know how little I have travelled. My last real journey was to go to Tunbridge with Grandpapa two years ago and the pace was so slow and decorous I think we would have moved quicker had we walked!' She went over to the window and looked out. 'If it would only stop raining, we could take a walk now and see the town.'

Her handmaiden groaned again and Eve turned back to her.

'Poor Martha, here am I, chattering on when you are feeling so poorly. You do look very pale, you poor thing. Perhaps a little Magnesia would settle your stomach. I wonder where Granby can be. He will have taken the dressing case to my bedchamber. Well, perhaps the landlord can show me the way.'

She went to the door and looked out. The corridor was very busy and through the doorway opposite she could see that the taproom was packed with men enjoying a mug of ale and pipe of tobacco while they sheltered from the rain. To her right was a much more ordered scene, for the corridor opened on to the coffee room where travellers were seated at small tables and were served refreshments by a number of harassed-looking waiters. Of the landlord or the cheerful maid there was no sign. Undeterred, Eve stepped out of the room to go in search of her host. The ancient building was large and irregular, and for a moment Eve could not decide on the best way to go. She had seen a number of people using a door on the far side of the coffee room and surmised that it would lead to an inner hall where she might find an obliging chambermaid who would take her upstairs. Eve made her way quickly through the coffee room, trying to ignore the inquisitive stares of its patrons. She kept her eyes fixed upon the door, putting out her hand as she approached. It opened easily, swinging away from her and she spotted Granby in the corridor beyond, talking with a group of ragged-looking men. In her haste she did not see the slight step down and she found herself hurtling through the doorway, off balance. She cannoned off the man nearest the door.

'Oh, I beg your pardon,' she gasped as strong arms shot out to steady her. 'I—'

Her words died away as she looked up and found herself staring up into the all-too-familiar face of Nick Wylder.

Chapter Eight

Evelina's breath caught in her throat and for an instant she thought she might faint. The look of surprise on Nick's face gave way to one of wry humour. The corners of his mouth lifted.

'Oh, lord,' he murmured. 'This was not meant to happen.'

Eve regained her balance and pushed away from him. Something was wrong. It was her husband, but it was not the fashionable beau she had married. The superbly tailored frock-coat and snow-white linen were replaced with a worn frieze jacket and a coloured shirt, while his raven-black hair was no longer neatly confined by a ribbon and one black lock hung rakishly over his eyes. The blood was drumming in her ears as she sought to make sense of the situation.

'You are alive.' She could not take her eyes from his face. 'But how, why—?'

One of the other men shook his head and said warningly, 'Cap'n…'

Nick put up his hand. 'I cannot explain now, sweetheart, but you must not been seen with me. Richard shall take you back to your room.'

'No—I—'

Nick reached out and caught her arms. 'I will explain it all later.' He gave her a little shake. 'Go back inside, Eve. You must act as if you have not seen me, do you understand?'

Eve swallowed hard. She understood nothing and wanted to argue.

'Eve.' He held her eyes. 'I need you to do this for me.'

'Y-you'll come to me?' she whispered, her hands still clutching at his coat.

'You have my word.' He looked down at her, then in one sudden movement he pulled her to him and kissed her once, hard, on the mouth. 'I'll join you in your room, very soon. Now go.' He turned her away from him and gave her a little push.

Richard Granby took her arm and walked her back to the private parlour. There was so much conjecture in her head that this time she did not notice the diners in the coffee room or the raucous laughter as they passed the taproom.

Granby ushered her into the private parlour. Martha, who had been dozing in her chair, uttered a shriek and jumped to her feet.

'In Heaven's name, Richard, what have you done to her?'

Granby guided Eve to a chair and gently pressed her down. 'She has had a shock. Can you fetch a glass of wine?'

Eve raised one hand. 'No,' she said, her voice unsteady. 'I want nothing, only to know what is happening.'

'It will all be explained later, ma'am. For the moment you must stay here and say nothing.'

'May I not tell Martha?'

'Tell me what?' demanded her maid, looking bewildered.

Granby gave her a reassuring smile. 'Oh, I think there would be no harm in that, as long as it goes no further. I shall return in a little while and escort you to your room.'

He bowed and retired in his usual unhurried style, leaving Martha almost hopping with impatience.

'What is it, Miss Eve, what are you to tell me?'

Eve stared at her anxious face. 'I have just seen Captain Wylder. He is alive.'

Martha's reaction was as noisy as Eve's had been controlled. She screamed and fell back on her chair, drumming her heels on the floor. It was unfortunate that the tavern-maid chose that moment to come in with a fresh pot of coffee. Remembering Nick's words, Eve knew it was imperative that Martha did not blurt out her secret, so she immediately took her by the shoulders and shook her.

'Stop it, stop it this instant!' Her sharp treatment had its effect; Martha stopped shrieking and subsided into noisy sobs. Eve dismissed the round-eyed tavern-maid and waited patiently until Martha had stopped crying and mopped her eyes. With no more than the occasional hiccup she apologised for her outburst and quietly requested her mistress to tell her everything. Eve obliged, but she found that relating her meeting with Nick only added to her frustration, for Martha kept asking her questions she could not answer.

Eve wanted nothing more than to sit quietly and consider her own feelings. The first shock of finding herself face to face with her husband had been followed by a surge of elation, but that had been replaced almost immediately with consternation. Why had he wanted her to believe he was dead? Answers crowded in upon her, none of them satisfactory, most too painful to contemplate, so she resolutely pushed them aside, determined to remain calm and to await Nick's explanation. Martha's reaction to the news was much more straightforward. The master was alive, and she was glad of it. Eve wished she could be so easily satisfied. She was relieved when at last Granby came in the room and announced that the landlord was waiting to escort her to her room.

'It is our finest apartment, madam,' their host told her as he led the way through a winding corridor and up the stairs. 'It has been said that good Queen Bess herself slept there. I am sure you will find it very comfortable.' At the end of a dim corridor he threw open the door and stood back for her to enter. 'There, is it not a handsome apartment?'

Eve had to agree with him. It was a large, square room with an ornate plaster ceiling and richly carved panelling on every wall. Candles glowed from the wall sconces, illuminating the rich scarlet-and-gold hangings that decorated the huge tester-bed and the matching curtains pulled across the window to blot out the gloomy rain-sodden sky. A large chest of drawers and a sofa covered in wine-red damask occupied the far corner of the room and the only other items of furniture were two chairs and a small gate-legged table set before the stone fireplace, where a merry blaze crackled. The table was already laden with dishes and it was set with two places. Eve's eyes flew to the landlord. He beamed at her and tapped his nose.

'Mr Granby suggested a collation, so you need have no servants interrupting you. There's meats, bread, pastries, fruit—everything you could wish.' He pointed to a little door in the corner of the room. 'That is a private stair, madam. Leads up to your maid's room and down to the back hall, so even she can come and go to the kitchen for her dinner without disturbing you.' He gave her a knowing wink and Eve felt her cheeks grow hot.

'Thank you.'

With another beaming smile the landlord bowed himself out and shut the door carefully behind him. Martha was already bustling around, inspecting the room.

'Very comfortable, Miss Eve. Everything just as it should be. And very clean, not a speck of dust. Shall I unpack your trunk, ma'am? Seems such a lot of work for just one night.'

'Yes. No. That is, no.' Eve tried to think of practical matters, but her brain did not want to work.

'Then I'll lay out your nightgown—'

'No! No, leave it where it is, Martha. Go now. I shall call you if I need you again. Oh, Martha—' she pulled a small bottle from her dressing case and handed it to the maid. 'You never did dose your self with Glass's Magnesia.'

'No, ma'am, I'll take it now, if you don't mind. Thank you. That is, if you don't want it yourself?'

Eve looked towards the table, where a decanter and two glasses stood in readiness for the coming meal. She felt in need of something more than medicine. 'No, but you may pour me a glass of wine before you go.'

Eve watched the maid fill up one glass with blood-red wine before making her way to her own room. The little door closed behind her with a click and Eve was alone. But it was not the peace of the old room that enveloped Eve: it was a brittle, ice-cold fury.

'I will not see him!' she said aloud. 'He has treated me abominably. I shall not see him.'

She walked over to the main door and bolted it. There was a wooden peg on the door to the servants' stairs and she used it to secure the latch.

She gave a long, deep sigh. There, it was done. Slowly she removed her pelisse, folded it neatly and placed it upon her trunk before returning to the table and picking up her glass of wine. The storm had passed and there was a stillness about the room. No noise filtered through to her from below and the air seemed to settle around her, calm and tranquil, in complete contrast to her own nerves, which were stretched tight as a bowstring. Let him knock. Let him hammer on the door, she would not admit him.

She stood in the middle of the room, facing the door, straining to hear the slightest sound. Clutching at her wineglass, she silently berated herself for her anxiety. No one could surprise her, the room was secure. Or was it? The scrape of wood on wood made her spin around in time to see one of the panels beside the fireplace swing open and Nick Wylder step into the room. He still wore the frieze coat, but instead of the tattered coloured shirt he now wore a fresh white one, fastened with a froth of white lace at his throat, and a black ribbon at the nape of his neck confined his black hair, glossy as a raven's wing. The baggy sailor's trousers and worn shoes had been replaced by buckskins and topboots. With the skirts of his coat swinging around him the inconsequential thought came to her that he looked every inch a pirate. Nick gestured towards the panel.

'The stair leads up directly from the alley. You need not be alarmed; I have bolted the door at the foot of the stairs; no one else can come in that way.'

He stood, feet slightly apart, hands at his sides, watching her. Like a cat, she thought. Alert, wary. Eve's heart had misssed a beat but now it was thudding painfully against her ribs. She did not know whether she was going to laugh or cry, to be thankful or furious.

'You did not drown,' she said at last.

'No. Sweetheart, I am so sorry I was not there to help you when Sir Benjamin died.'

'You lied to me.'

'Evelina, I—'

A red mist descended over Eve, blotting out reason. The wineglass flew from her hand, its contents leaving a dark trail across the floor. Nick side-stepped neatly and the glass sailed past him to smash against the wall.

'How dare you!'

'Sweetheart, listen to me—' He ducked as she snatched up the second glass and hurled it towards him. 'Eve, I am sorry. Let me explain—'

His words were lost as the glass shattered on the panelling and fell in tinkling shards to the floor. With a shriek of rage Eve picked up the carving knife and advanced upon him.

'I hate you, Nick Wylder!'

As she hurled herself at him he caught her arm, holding the lethal blade away.

'Eve, I had no choice.'

Unable to plunge the knife into his heart, Eve brought up her other hand, her fingers curled ready to scratch his eyes out. With an oath Nick caught at her arm, easily overpowering her.

'I know you are angry, my love, but I am not going to let you kill me.' His fingers tightened on her wrist; her grip loosened and the knife clattered harmlessly to the floor. 'That's better.' He grinned and released her. 'No wonder my father said never trust the carving to a woman!'

'Are you *never* serious?' She gave a sob of frustration and began to beat at his chest with her fists.

Nick reached out and put his arms about her, pulling her closer. 'I know,' he said quietly as she continued to pound him. 'I know I was a monster for doing this to you.'

She hammered her fists against his hard, unyielding body until there was no strength left in her arms. Then, as her anger evaporated, it was replaced by tears. She found herself crying; huge, gulping sobs that could not be controlled. She did not resist as Nick pulled her closer, stroking her head and murmuring softly. He continued to hold her while she cried herself out and at last she collapsed against him, taking deep, shuddering breaths. He reached into one of the capacious pockets of the old coat and pulled out a clean handkerchief.

'I thought this might be needed,' he murmured, pressing it into her hand. 'I had no idea my wife had such a temper.'

'Nor I,' mumbled Eve from beneath the handkerchief.

He touched his lips to her hair. 'Now will you listen to me? Will you let me try to explain?' He guided her across to the sofa and they sat down together, Nick keeping one arm firmly around her shoulders. 'I did not plan this, Eve. Believe me.'

'Why should I believe you?' Angrily she shrugged off his arm and sat up very straight while she wiped her eyes. 'You have lied to me from the beginning. You married me to gain control of Monkhurst, did you not?'

'Richard told me you had gone there. Yes, it is

true that I wanted access to Monkhurst. Marrying you was one way to get that.'

Misery clutched at her heart. 'You are despicable!'

He sighed. 'Perhaps I am, but I never meant to hurt you. I admit I went to Tunbridge Wells in search of your grandfather, knowing he owned Monkhurst. I soon learned that the property was part of your marriage settlement and that Sir Benjamin was looking for a husband for you.' The irrepressible smile tugged at his mouth. 'It all fitted neatly with my plan—and my family have been nagging me for years to settle down so I knew I would be pleasing them, too. So I accepted Sir Benjamin's invitation to visit you at Makerham. What I had *not* anticipated was finding such an adorable young lady waiting to meet me.'

Evelina stifled the traitorous surge of pleasure she felt at his words. She dare not consider them or her brittle self-control might shatter. She injected a touch of impatience into her voice. 'And just what were your plans? *Why* did you need Monkhurst?'

'I suspected Monkhurst was being used by smugglers.'

'Very likely.' She shrugged. 'Nearly every house in the area would be the same.'

'Yes, I know that, but—I think I should go back to the beginning.' He paused and Eve waited, pulling his handkerchief through her restless fingers. 'My—ah—adventurous career in the navy brought me to the attention of the Admiralty, and since returning to England I have been working for them, investigating certain… activities.'

'Smuggling. You have said that.'

'Yes, but not the innocuous practice carried out by Silas and his friends, a few barrels of French brandy and bundles of Brussels lace. The villains I seek are involved in a much bigger enterprise. Not only are they depriving the government of duty— and before you interrupt me let me say that I have heard all the arguments that the duty is too high! The people I seek are flooding the country with a tea that is, at best, illegal and at worst, poisonous.

'They call it smouch. It is made from leaves gathered from the English hedgerows and mixed with chamber-lye, green vitriol and other choice in-gredients, including, very often, sheep's dung. Then it is baked and rubbed to a black dust. Quite,' he said, observing her look of horror. 'I traced the most recent consignments to this coast. It is being shipped to Boulogne, then sold to our—er—freetraders.'

'But they wouldn't,' she exclaimed. 'Silas would never carry such a cargo.'

'Not knowingly, but he has been duped into bringing it ashore. Did you not think it odd that Mrs Brattee had no tea in her store cupboard when you arrived at Monkhurst? Now Silas knows the truth he will not trust any tea coming from the Continent.'

Eve's eyes darkened. 'It is some horrid French plot to poison us!'

Nick shook his head. 'I wish I could say that was it; the evidence points to it being made in this country, and in this area.'

'And you suspected Monkhurst? My house?'

'One of the cargoes we intercepted contained a fragment of a letter. Monkhurst was mentioned in it. Silas swore there was no connection, but I wanted to see for myself.'

'So you married me to gain access to my house.'

'Yes.'

She threw him another savage look. 'You do not apologise for it.'

He smiled. 'I am not sorry I married you, Evelina. I never could be.'

Her skin tingled when saw the glint in his blue eyes. It was difficult to remain angry when he smiled at her like that. She reminded herself that his smiles meant nothing. They were as worthless as his honeyed words. She looked away, scowling. 'Go on.'

'Once Silas was persuaded to let me into the house we searched it thoroughly. There are extensive cellars, and a very interesting underground passage leading to the boathouse on Monkhurst Drain, but no sign that it has been used in recent years.'

'Well there is nothing secret about that! Mama showed me the tunnel when I was a child. She told me her grandfather had built it so that the family need not get wet walking to the boathouse on rainy days, but if that was the case why does it come up into the kitchen? And why is the entrance hidden behind the panelling at the back of the boathouse? From the outside the tunnel is well hidden; it appears that the boathouse is built into the bank.' Eve shook her head. 'I always believed it was built for smuggling goods into the house, but Mama would never admit it.' She forgot her anger as a half-forgotten memory surfaced. 'I remember having nightmares about people stealing into the house through the tunnel, so Papa took me down there. He showed me the iron grating at the far end. It had a big lock and the key was kept on a hook in the tunnel, so that anyone from the house could get *out*, but no one could get in.'

'That is still the case, Eve, so you may still rest easy. But the boathouse is in a sad state of repair.'

'When Mama and Papa died the boats were sold. Grandpapa kept the house in order, but we only visited Monkhurst once or twice after that.'

Nick had stretched his arm along the back of the sofa. His fingers were playing with one of the curls at her neck. It was a great temptation to turn her head and rest her cheek against his hand, but she resisted it.

'And what about you, Eve?' he said softly. 'Do you dislike the house?'

'Oh, no, it holds only good memories for me. We lived there until I was about nine, you see, then I went to stay with Grandpapa while my parents went abroad and…they never came back. They died in Italy.'

His fingers left the curl and squeezed her shoulder. 'I know, you told me they caught a fever. I am sorry.'

'So, too, am I, but it was a long time ago.'

'I am sorry, too, about your grandfather, and even sorrier that I could not be with you.'

She drew herself up, not prepared to accept his

sympathy. She hunched her shoulder to shake off his hand, yet was disappointed when he removed it. She said gruffly, 'We are straying from the point, sir. Why did you leave Makerham so suddenly?'

'My enquiries had led me to suspect that Lord Chelston was involved in this business. He owns a sizeable property near Northiam and keeps a yacht at Hastings. I have had people watching him for some time now, but he is very elusive. On the morning after our wedding I received word that a rendezvous had been arranged. After so many months of work I could not leave my men to deal with it alone, so I had to come here to the coast.'

'But you have not arrested Lord Chelston?

'He is a powerful man. We need hard evidence before we make our suspicions known. Besides, I want to catch *all* the main players and close down the whole operation. If we move too soon they will merely go underground, move production to a new location.

'These people are clever; they have a warehouse in Boulogne. The French are not averse to helping anyone who is working against England. You said yourself, smuggling is a way of life in these parts; the local gangs are trusted by their regular customers who believe they are purchasing good Black

Bohea.' He leaned forwards, resting his elbows on his knees. 'There were reports that a consignment of smouch was ready to be shipped out of Hastings on a brigantine and transferred to a French lugger cruising off this coast. We thought it would be possible to catch Chelston's men red-handed with the goods; with their evidence we could convict him. Captain George has a cutter at his disposal, the *Argos*, but on the night of the rendezvous some of us were in disguise on a small fishing smack, hoping to get close enough to the brigantine to board and overpower the crew, but they discovered the plot.'

'What happened?' asked Eve, enthralled in spite of herself.

'In the fighting I was shot and toppled into the water.'

'Shot!'

'A flesh wound, just below the ribs. Nothing serious, but it carried me over the side. Thankfully I managed to swim to the *Argos*, but having been lost overboard it was decided it would be to our advantage to let everyone else think I had perished.'

Eve kept her eyes on his profile, noting the fine laughter lines etched at the corner of his eye and at the side of his fine, curving lips. It would be so easy to lose her heart to him all over again. She squared her shoulders, determined to resist the temptation.

'I understand that you would not want these villains to know you were alive, but what of me?' she said quietly. 'Why did you send Granby to tell me you were dead?'

He turned his head to look at her and for once there was no smile in his blue eyes. 'I never intended to tell you. I thought we could wrap up this matter quickly and there would be no need for you to know. Then I received your note, saying your grandfather had died, and I knew I would have to send Granby to you.'

'But why? I do not understand.'

'Because the man who shot me was your cousin, Bernard Shawcross.'

Chapter Nine

'Either the world has gone mad or I have lost my wits!' Eve put her hands to her cheeks. 'Confess you are joking me.'

'It is no joke, Eve,' Nick said quietly. 'When you wrote to tell me of Sir Benjamin's death, I knew Shawcross would go to Makerham. When your note reached me I was too weak to leave my bed or I promise you I would have found some way to get to you. Instead I had to send Richard to protect you.' With a sudden, impulsive move he slid from the sofa to kneel on the floor before her, taking her hands and looking up earnestly into her face. 'I never meant to cause you such pain, Evelina; we had known each other less than a month, only one night married—I did not think you could care for me so very much.'

'Well, you were wrong,' she muttered, pulling

her hands away. She rose and walked about the room, trying to make sense of all he had told her.

Nick sat back down on the sofa, watching her. At last he said, 'You are looking very pale, love. Are you hungry? When did you last eat?'

She stopped her pacing, frowning as if she did not understand his words. 'At breakfast.'

'Then we must dine.' He jumped up. 'But first, my little termagant, we need to call your maid.'

Martha was quickly summoned and came into the room, dipping a slight curtsey towards Nick as she did so.

'I am very pleased to see you looking so well, Captain Wylder.'

'Thank you, Martha,' he responded cheerfully. 'Would you be good enough to bring up some fresh glasses? We had a—er—little accident with the others. But mind, not a word to anyone that I am here.'

She nodded solemnly. 'No sir, I'll keep mum, my word on it.'

Nick smiled at her and Eve noted with a stab of irritation how her usually stern-faced maidservant softened under the force of his charm.

'And I'll fetch a brush to clear up the glass in the corner, too, Cap'n.'

When she had gone Nick shrugged off his coat and tossed it aside. 'I hope you do not object to me dining in my shirtsleeves, sweetheart, but this is a very rough, workaday garment, not at all suitable for sitting down to dinner with a lady.'

He was not wearing a waistcoat, and the linen shirt fell softly over his powerful shoulders. Eve observed the contrast between the billowing white shirt and tight-fitting buckskins that hugged his narrow hips and powerful thighs. Memories of that strong, athletic body pressed against hers made her tremble and she resolutely pushed them aside. As Nick came to the table she realised that he was not walking with his usual grace.

'Your wound,' she said. 'Is it very painful?'

'Only if I move too quickly.' The corners of his mouth lifted. 'Or if I have to fight off an angry lady.'

She ignored that. 'May I see it?'

'There is little to see,' he said, pulling his shirt away from the waistband of his buckskins. 'It is almost healed.'

'Then why is it still bandaged?'

'Protection,' he told her. 'The wound still bleeds occasionally.' He lifted his shirt away and Eve gazed down at the white linen strips that were bound around his body. 'Well,' he said, 'do you want me to remove the bandages, so that you may see I am telling the truth?'

Eve flushed. 'I believe you.' She waved her hand at him. 'Pray, tuck in your shirt.'

He unbuttoned the waistband of his buckskins and she could not resist the temptation to look at the exposed skin on his stomach and abdomen, smooth and taut with a shadow of crisp black hairs, a shadow that continued on down towards—

Eve dragged her eyes away. She must not think of such things because it made the excitement stir deep inside and her knees grew weak. She sat down abruptly at the table, her hands clasped tightly in her lap while he finished tidying his clothes. Nick Wylder was a scoundrel. She must not think of him as anything else.

Martha bustled back into the room and while she busied herself sweeping up the broken glass, Eve tried to concentrate upon Nick's story, and not upon his body. The mere thought of dining together made her mouth dry; the little table was so small their knees would almost be touching beneath it. She watched Nick follow the maid to the door and lock it after her. She was not sure if that made her feel more or less safe; might as well be locked in with a tiger, she thought as he prowled back towards her.

'I cannot believe Bernard is involved in smuggling.' Nerves made her voice sharper than she intended. 'He is an odious little toad, but I cannot think so ill of him.'

Nick poured wine into her glass. 'Can you not? It is a very lucrative trade.'

Eve was silent. After a moment she said slowly, 'I think I told you that at one time he was always calling upon Grandpapa, asking him for money, coming to Makerham to hide from his creditors.'

'But not recently?'

'No. You saw him at the wedding; a modish new coat and his own carriage.' She paused while he carved a slice of ham and put it on her plate. 'He asked Mr Didcot about Monkhurst. He thought it was part of Grandpapa's estate.' She clasped her hands together, her fingers tightening until the knuckles showed white. 'He began to—to hint that I should marry him, now that you were—that I was…'

'Now that you were a widow.'

'Yes.' She did not look at him. 'That was why I left Makerham. I feared he might…compromise me.'

'For that alone I would thrash him,' he muttered savagely.

She smiled slightly. 'Thank you. But you cannot

blame him; he believes you are dead. Is that not what you wanted, to catch the villains unawares?'

'Yes, but it wasn't only that; I thought it would protect you. Once Chelston knew I was on to him, I feared that he might try to get to me through you. Making Chelston think I was out of the way removed that threat. However, when Sir Benjamin died I knew your cousin would be swift to claim his inheritance and if he suspected news of my death was a ruse then you would be in even greater danger. That is why I asked Richard to take you to my family in the north. I could be sure you would be safe there.' His eyes softened. 'I did not know then what a stubborn little minx I had married.'

'If Mr Granby had told me the truth—'

'Poor Richard was merely following my orders.' Nick hesitated. 'I did not know—I did not know if I could trust you.'

She shrugged, the core of misery hardening in her heart. She had thought as much. 'And now?' She looked up. His eyes were midnight blue in the candle-glow. Inscrutable.

'Now I have no choice.' He reached across the table for her hand. 'I cannot be sorry that you know the truth, Eve, but this is a dangerous game; you would be advised to let Granby escort you to

Yorkshire, to the protection of my family. I will join you there when I have finished my work here.'

'But you could still be killed.'

He laughed. 'Faith, sweetheart. I have faced greater dangers than Chelston and his cronies!'

Nick was holding her hand, his grasp warm and comforting and he was smiling at her in that reckless, devil-may-care fashion that invited her to enjoy the adventure. She swallowed.

'Let me stay.' She heard the words come out of her own mouth. 'Let me stay and play my part in this.' Suddenly *she* felt reckless, no longer afraid of the world. She put up her chin. 'If you are going to get yourself killed, I want to be on hand to know of it!'

He was staring at her intently. 'Are you sure, Evelina?'

She met his gaze steadily. The weeks since he had left Makerham had been the most miserable of her life; Grandpapa was at peace, there was nothing more to be done for him, but the idea of being more than two hundred miles away from Nick was not to be borne. Not, of course, that she cared a fig for him now, but he was her husband and she knew her duty.

'Yes, I am sure,' she said at last. 'I will live at Monkhurst and be your eyes and ears there.'

His chair scraped back. He stepped around the table and pulled her up into his arms. She put her hands against his chest, holding him off, but all the while her heart was beating a rapid, heavy tattoo against her ribs, leaving her breathless. He looked down at her, his mouth tantalizingly close.

'It could be dangerous,' he murmured.

'Being your *wife* is dangerous, Nick Wylder!'

With a laugh he bent to kiss her and it took all her willpower to turn her head away.

'No,' she gasped, closing her eyes as his lips feathered kisses down the line of her neck, causing her traitorous body to shiver with delight.

'You cannot deny you want me,' he murmured. His warm breath on her skin made her tremble, weakening her resolve.

'No, but I—do not—trust—you.'

The butterfly kisses stopped. He raised his head. 'Ah.'

'I'm sorry,' she whispered.

'You have nothing to be sorry for, sweetheart, it is my fault.' He cupped her chin and tilted her face up towards him. 'And I am to blame, too, for these dark circles under your eyes.' He ran his thumb gently across her cheekbone. 'What a villain I am to embroil you in this.'

Angrily she knocked his hand away. 'Yes, you are, and I shall *never* forgive you.'

'Never is a long time, sweetheart.' He grinned at her. 'I must try to make you change your mind.'

She hunched one shoulder and turned away from him. 'It will not work. I am wise to your charming ways now, Captain Wylder.'

He laughed softly. 'We shall see. But for now, we must feed you.'

'I do not think I could eat anything.'

He pushed her gently back on to her chair. 'Oh, I think you can.' He pulled a little piece of flesh from the chicken carcase with his fingers and held it out to her. 'Try this. The most succulent pieces are near the bone.'

Patiently he coaxed and cajoled her, offering her tasty slivers of cheese and the most succulent pieces of meat until she put up her hands, protesting that she was full. Only then did he look to his own needs. While he dined, Eve leaned back in her chair and sipped her wine.

'Nick? Why did you come to the Mermaid?'

'I was meeting a sea-captain, one with more information on the black-sailed lugger.'

'Did you see him? And did he help you?'

'Yes, and yes. He knows the lugger; she's called the *Merle* and sails out of Boulogne.'

'Is that not where you said Chelston has his warehouse?'

'It is. All I need now is evidence of where the smouch is being made and we can make our move.' He looked up at her. 'A few weeks more, my love, and all this will be over.'

Eve did not reply, but she watched him while he finished his meal. Light from the candles and the fire cast a warm golden glow over his face, enhancing the lean cheeks and strong jaw line, glinting off his raven-dark hair when he moved his head. A stab of longing shot through her and she clamped her teeth into her bottom lip to prevent a sigh. She must be careful or her wayward body would betray her. At last he pushed his plate away and gave a sigh of satisfaction.

'Our host knows how to please his guests, excellent food washed down by the finest French wines.' He refilled their glasses.

'And has the duty been paid on the wine?'

He grinned at her. 'I doubt it, but I am not going to ask. Now, one more thing to finish our meal.' He picked up an orange.

'No, really, I have had sufficient—'

'We will share it, then, but you will have some; it will do you good.' His lean fingers deftly removed the peel and broke the orange into segments. He leaned forwards, holding a piece out for her. 'Eat it,' he said. 'No, don't touch it; you will get juice on your hands.'

Obediently she leaned forwards and allowed him to put the segment in her mouth. She nodded, smiling slightly. 'It is good.'

He held out another piece and this time his fingers touched her lips; she yearned to take them in her mouth, to lick the sharp-sweet juice from his skin. It took all her willpower to pull away. Nick's eyes were on her face, reading her thoughts, piercing her very soul. In turmoil, Eve tried desperately to think of something to say. Anything, to break the dangerous mood that had settled around them.

'We should build a hot-house at Monkhurst. Fruit would do very well there. The gardens are sadly neglected but I have set Nathaniel and Sam to clearing the ground—'

'Eve.'

'We will need to employ a gardener, but Silas may know someone…'

Nick's chair scraped back. 'My love, you may

employ as many gardeners as you wish, but we will not talk of it now.' He pulled her to her feet and wrapped his arms around her. She kept her head down and braced herself. Her instinct was to give in, to lean against him and yield to his embrace, but she would not. She could not, for she knew only too well the heartbreak he would cause her. He cupped her chin with his hand and forced her to look up at him. When she saw his eyes darken with desire, felt his aroused body pressing hard against hers, she panicked.

'Of course as my husband you are entitled to take your pleasure of me, but I pray you will take it speedily. I am quite worn out with travelling.'

His brows snapped together. 'What is this? Do you think I am a monster, that I would force myself upon you?'

His hold slackened and she stepped back, turning away from him while she gathered her defences, dredged up every feeling of anger and resentment to protect herself from the attraction she felt for him.

'You are no monster, sir, but you must understand that I have suffered a severe shock. I set out this morning thinking myself a widow, only to discover that I have been deceived.'

'And I have explained to you why it was necessary!'

Eve spun around. 'Oh, so that is sufficient to make everything well again! You think that you only have to smile and say you are sorry and you will be forgiven.'

'No, of course not—'

She began to catalogue his offences, counting them off on her fingers. 'First, you married me because you suspected my family of being involved in smuggling. The day after our wedding you disappear, then you send your man to tell me you are d-drowned. I have told you, I shall *never* forgive you!' She put her hands over her face, fighting back the tears that were choking her. She longed to feel Nick's arms around her, to hear him utter some words of comfort, but there was only silence and it seemed to stretch on forever.

'You are quite right,' he said at last. 'I have behaved abominably towards you.'

She looked up. He was putting on his coat.

'Where are you going?'

'I must leave. I have no wish to force my attentions upon you, nor my company, if you find me so repulsive. Forgive me, Evelina.'

'Go, then!'

No, don't leave me! The words echoed in her head but Eve could not voice them. Nick buttoned up the old frock-coat.

'Richard will escort you back to Monkhurst tomorrow. If you are happy to remain there it will be a comfort to me to have you so close, but it could be dangerous. You need only say the word at any time and Richard shall take you to my brother.'

'Monkhurst is my home now. I shall stay there. What do you want me to do?'

'Watch and wait. But you must be careful, and tell Martha she must watch her tongue, because no one else at Monkhurst knows I am alive. Send a message with Richard if you want to contact me.'

'I will.'

Eve's heart leapt as he took a step towards her, but he stopped just out of arm's reach and gave her a wry, apologetic smile.

'Do not turn me into a monster while I am away from you, sweetheart. I shall give you no cause to distrust me ever again, I swear, but I need time to prove it to you.'

'Wait!' She gazed at him. Phrases such as 'do not go' and 'stay with me' rattled in her head, but instead she heard herself say, 'Should I not go on to Hastings? Granby will have told you it was my intention to visit the spot where you...died. It might look suspicious if I do not continue.'

'As you wish.' He smiled at her and the sight of that wickedly attractive dimple made the breath catch in her throat. 'Aye, go to Hastings. Let the world know that someone mourns my passing!'

Nick kissed his fingers to her, turned on his heel and disappeared through the door in the panelling. Eve watched the door close behind him, felt the stillness of the room envelope her again. Then, as if released from a trap, she dashed across the room and ran her fingers over the wood, trying to find a handle or lever to open the door. There was nothing. She pressed her ear to the panel. Straining, she thought she heard his boots on the wooden stairs and the dull thud of the outer door closing behind him.

He was gone.

There was a scratching on the servants' door and she went across to unlock it. Martha peeped in.

'Shall I clear away now, mistress? It's growing late and I don't want to be traipsing through these passages once they have snuffed out the candles.' She looked over Eve's shoulder. 'Where's the master?'

'He's gone.' Eve took a long breath, but she

could not stop the tears spilling over. Martha put her arms about her and guided her to the bed.

'There, there, Miss Eve. You come and sit here and tell Martha all about it.'

'Th-there's nothing to tell,' sobbed Eve. 'I—we…had a disagreement and…he l-left.'

Eve subsided into tears and Martha clucked over her like a mother hen.

'Good heavens, Miss Eve, never say he forced himself upon you!'

'No,' cried Eve in a fresh flood of tears. 'No, of course he did not, I told him to g-go and…and he d-did! Stupid, stupid man!'

Chapter Ten

The journey to Hastings was accomplished with ease, the Winchelsea road having been repaired and opened again for coaches to pass through. There was no reception party waiting for her when she reached the town and the road leading down the hill to the little harbour was rutted and ill-used. As Richard Granby opened the carriage door for her to alight she glanced at him.

'There is nothing here except fishing smacks. Tell me, Mr Granby, where are these business acquaintances that my husband was visiting?'

The valet's impassive countenance did not alter. 'I cannot say, madam.'

She pulled her veil down over her face. 'Well, help me out, Granby. We must continue with this charade, although there is no one here to witness it.'

'Oh I think you are wrong there, madam,' muttered Granby, giving her his hand. He nodded towards a group of fishermen who were mending their nets in the shelter of an upturned boat. Eve had noticed them looking at the carriage and as she stepped down one of the men came across to her, tugging at his forelock with his gnarled fingers.

'Beggin' yer pardon, mistress, we sees yer coming down the road and thinks—well, seein' yer widder's weeds—we wonders if you be the cap'n's widder? Cap'n Wyldfire?'

Eve looked towards Granby and, as if aware of her eyes through the thick veil, he nodded slightly. She turned back to the fisherman. 'Yes, I am,' she said softly. 'Did you—did you know my husband?'

A wide, black-toothed grin split his weather-beaten face.

'Aye, mistress, we all knew Cap'n Wyldfire. Proper sailor, he was, from the King's navy, no less, and very generous 'e was, too, allus ready to stand buff in the Stag of an evenin'. He told us he'd come down 'ere to take out the villains what is givin' us a bad name, sellin' us their smouch that was no more real tea than that there seaweed.' The grin disappeared and he shook his head. 'It were a sad day when he drowned, mistress, an' no mistake. We was all of us sorry to see the end o' such a brave one.'

Eve's heart skipped a beat. 'Were you with him, then? You saw my husband the night he—he—'

'Lor' bless you mistress, 'twas my boat, the *Sally-Ann*, he used that night. Wanted to get close to a brig that was sailing out o' Hastings, see?'

'And what happened?'

'Oh, we got close, right enough, the cap'n and some of us had already boarded the brig, being friendly-like, and pretending we was interested in taking some o' their cargo, but the Revenue cutter came up too soon. There was only a donkey's breath o' mist and as soon as they spotted her they set up the cry, knowin' as how they'd been tricked. Set upon us, they did. The cap'n was quick to sound the retreat, got us all safely back on board the *Sally-Ann*, but one o' they villains, he levels his pops at the cap'n and shoots him afore he can escape. Killed-dead he was. Went over the side without a murmur.'

'And did you not try to find him, to recover the body?'

'O'course we did, but there was no sign of him and we had to make sail, for the sea was carryin' us towards Nore rocks. It were dulling-up by that time and with the brig bristling with guns we decided to make for the shore. The Revenue cutter did give chase, but not long enough.' The fisherman showed his contempt for their efforts by turning his head to spit. 'They may've scared 'em off for now, but they'll be back, especially now they knows the cap'n ain't here to gainsay 'em.' The fisherman shook his head, and said in a reminiscent tone, 'Aye, a great one, was Cap'n Wyldfire; allus on the gammock he was, looking for excitement or any sort o' bobbery. We've been watching the beaches every day since then, missus, hopin' his body would be washed up so we could give 'im a proper Christian burial up at All Saints. And there's still time. We'll keep a lookout, don't 'ee worry.'

'Thank you.' Eve opened her purse and took out a handful of coins. 'Here,' she said, pressing them into the man's hand. 'When you and your crew go to the Stag tonight, I pray you drink a toast to my husband's memory.'

Again she was treated to the black grin.

'Well now, missus, that's very generous of 'ee, very generous. The sort o' thing the cap'n would approve, if you don't mind me sayin' so.' He tugged his forelock once again and turned to the little group behind him. 'Stan' up, lads, stan' up and pay yer respects to Wyldfire's widow!'

He tugged his forelock yet again as Eve turned back to the carriage.

'Back to Monkhurst, madam?' asked Granby, holding open the door.

'Yes, if you please. But we will stop at the church before we leave Hastings, I think.'

All Saints Church stood on the eastern edge of the town, high above the harbour and surrounded by its graveyard. As Eve climbed down from the carriage a shiver ran through her to think that this was where Nick might have been buried. The wind blew in from the coast, tugging at her bonnet and pressing the black veil to her face. She folded it back and breathed in the fresh sea air.

'What is beyond those houses?' she asked Granby, pointing to the cluster of buildings and the little lane beyond the church.

'Fields, madam, and the cliff.'

'Does it overlook the rocks the sailor mentioned?'

'The Rocks of Nore? Yes, madam.'

'Then let us go there.'

She strode off across the graveyard and through the little gate at the far side. She found herself in a lane that ran between rows of small, rundown houses. Raggedly dressed women and barefoot children stared at her with dull, unfriendly eyes as she hurried by and Eve was relieved that Granby was following close behind her. When they emerged from the lane on to the open grassland, there was no shelter from the elements and Eve was suddenly brought to a halt by the strong onshore wind. It buffeted her remorselessly, whipping at her pelisse and skirts and she put up one hand to hold her bonnet. Granby stepped up beside her.

'Allow me, madam.'

She took his arm and together they battled towards the cliff edge, until they could see the restless, grey-brown water breaking into creamy foam against the rocks beneath them.

'If last night had not happened,' Eve remarked, 'if we had not stopped at the Mermaid, I suppose you would have spun me a yarn about my husband's friends having left Hastings by this time.'

'I would have been obliged to think of something, Mrs Wylder.'

'Then you are an unmitigated scoundrel,' she told him. 'Now move away and allow me a moment alone to contemplate my fate.'

'Pray do not go to close to the edge, madam!'

Eve waved him away. She stood for a moment looking out at the choppy grey waters while the wind tugged at her skirts. She thought how much her life had changed. No longer was she Grandpapa's darling, living sheltered and secure at Makerham. She was a married woman now and there was no going back. Nick had married her for Monkhurst, but what else did he want from her? Was hers to be a marriage of convenience, was she to be installed in one of his houses and left there to run the estate while he was off adventuring? She squared her shoulders, narrowing her eyes a little against the wind. She had no idea what the future might hold, but as for the present…well, she had a part to play. She was a widow. Eve conjured up a picture of Nick as she had last seen him, wearing his old frock-coat with all the swagger and panache of a buccaneer. She was Captain Wyldfire's widow.

'What on earth am I to do now?' Evelina stood in the panelled drawing room and looked about her. She had returned to Monkhurst excited at the thought of playing her part in Nick's adventure, but now, as the comfortable stillness of her old home settled around her, she found it hard to believe that anything exciting could happen here. She turned to look at Granby, who had followed her into the room.

'I have no doubt your master thinks me safely out of the way here, while he pursues his dangerous games.'

'He is concerned for your welfare, madam. It was his wish that you should go north, to his own family, where he could be sure you were protected.'

'And do you blame me, Granby, do you think I am wrong not to take his advice?'

'I would not presume to criticise your actions, mistress.'

'Damn your eyes, you criticise me with every look!' she exclaimed, shocking herself with her unladylike language. With a sigh she sank down into a chair and dropped her head in her hands.

'Madam, I—' Granby broke off. She heard him take a few paces about the room before he began again, his voice devoid of all emotion. 'Captain Wylder ordered me to remain with you and I know he thought you would be safer at Wylderbeck Hall. Naturally, I do my best at all times to carry out his orders, but I admit that in this instance I was not— unhappy—to remain in Kent.'

She lifted her head. 'Thank you Mr Granby,' she said softly. 'We neither of us want to be too far away from him, do we?'

'No, madam.'

Nick's words came back to her. *It will be a comfort to me to have you so close.* It was a tiny crumb of consolation and it put new heart in her. Eve jumped to her feet.

'Well, there is no reason why we should not make ourselves useful here while we are waiting for this business to come to an end! We can at least make Monkhurst a home again.' She untied her bonnet and cast it aside. 'I may have to play the grieving widow, but there is no reason why I cannot be active in my own house!'

Over the following week Evelina found some outlet for her pent-up energies in making the old house comfortable. She accepted Richard Granby's offer to act as her general factotum until Nick returned and agreed that Aggie should bring in more girls from the village to help her with the cleaning. In an effort to prevent Silas and his sons from returning to smuggling she set them to work repairing windows and clearing even more of the garden. Eve herself donned an old dimity gown and joined Martha in the attics. They were packed with broken furniture, most of it only fit for firewood, but some of the better pieces she sent downstairs to be used in the house. It was hard work, but it helped to fill her days and at night she was so tired she would fall asleep as soon as she climbed into bed.

Once the attics had been cleaned, Eve turned her attention to the trunks that were stacked there. They were full of linen and fine fabrics, carefully packed away by some previous owner and Eve made a note of their contents for future use. There was one trunk, however, that caused her to cry out in delight when Martha dragged it forwards for inspection.

'I remember this one!' she exclaimed, running her hands over the battered top. 'It was kept in Mama's bedroom.'

'Nay Miss Eve,' exclaimed Martha. 'You can't recall so long ago, surelye.'

'Well, she is right,' agreed Aggie, who had come upstairs to help them sort through the trunks. 'This case was kept beneath the window in the mistresss's bedroom.'

'Yes!' cried Eve excitedly. 'It had cushions on the top, like a window-seat. Look, it has Mama's initials on the lid: H. W.—Helena Wingham.'

Aggie reached out one gnarled hand and traced the letters. She gave a loud sigh.

'I remember Miss Helena's father giving her this trunk when she was a girl and she always had it in her bedroom here, even after she was married and she couldn't come here quite so often. When your parents died Sir Benjamin moved all their personal effects to Makerham and closed up the house. If he left this behind, it cannot hold anything of value.'

'We must open it and see,' said Eve. 'It is locked. Try your keys, Aggie; one of them may fit.'

But after a fruitless quarter of an hour they were forced to admit that none of the housekeeper's keys would open the trunk.

'We could break the lock,' offered Martha.

'No-o, there were a few old keys in Mama's writing desk,' said Eve. 'I saw them when I was hunting for a seal to put on my letter to my Cousin. I did not tell you Martha, I received a note from him yesterday, such a wheedling letter, apologising for frightening me away from Makerham and asking if he could visit me here at Monkhurst.'

Martha snorted. 'I hope you told him it was not to be thought of.'

'I did indeed. I made it very clear that I will not have him in my sight.'

'You did very right, Miss Eve. Mr Granby will give him short shrift if he comes anywhere near this house, you may be sure o' that, miss. I told 'im how Bernard was makin' up to you, and you having just learned that the master was drowned.'

Eve shot her handmaid a warning glance.

'Yes, well, if my cousin should decide to visit Monkhurst I shall rely upon Granby and Silas to turn him away. And talking of those two, do you think you could run and find them now, Martha, and ask them to bring this trunk down to my room? Then we can try the keys I have found.'

The trunk was duly carried downstairs. Martha and the housekeeper accompanied it, Aggie declaring that the mistress should not be wasting her time with such trifles.

'It will be filled with old rubbish, you mark my words,' she said, shaking her head while Eve hunted through the drawers of the little writing cabinet.

'Perhaps, but I should like to be sure. I know I saw them here somewhere…ah, here they are.' She pulled a small bunch of keys from the back of a drawer and held them aloft, smiling triumphantly. 'Now we shall see!' She selected the likeliest key and fitted it into the lock while Aggie clucked her disapproval. At first the key did not move, but Eve gripped it tightly and tried again. This time it turned with a soft grating noise.

'You've done it Miss Eve!' Martha stared openmouthed as Evelina lifted the lid.

'There,' said Aggie, peering into the trunk. 'What did I tell you? 'Tis full of old clothes. Let it be, madam.'

Eve ignored her and rummaged through the contents. 'I do not understand.' She frowned. 'I know this to be my mother's trunk.' She pulled out an old brown jacket. 'But this is a boy's coat. It is far too small to belong to my father.'

'Now, Miss Eve, leave off, do,' exclaimed Aggie as Eve pulled out more clothes.

'Shirts, stockings, buckskins…and a pair of boots.'

'The stable-lad's cast offs, mayhap,' offered Martha.

Eve picked up one of the boots and held it against her own dainty foot. Excitement bubbled within her. 'Do you know what I think?' she said softly. 'I think these clothes belonged to Mama.'

Martha laughed. 'Now where are your wits gone a-begging, mistress? They's lad's togs.'

'I do not think so.' Eve fixed her eyes on the old housekeeper, who shifted uneasily. 'Well, Aggie?'

'Now, mistress, how should I know aught about these things?'

'Because you have lived at Monkhurst all your life. You were here when Mama visited the house as a child and you would have seen her grow up here. I can tell from your face that you know something.' She jumped up and caught at the old woman's hands. 'Do tell us, Aggie.'

'No, miss, 'tis nothing. It's all in the past. Let it be,' she implored, an anguished look upon her face.

'No, I insist.' Eve gave her hands a little shake. 'Tell me, Aggie. When did Mama wear these clothes?'

'They could be dressing up clothes,' suggested Martha, her eyes wide.

Eve shook her head and kept her own gaze fixed upon the housekeeper. 'No, I do not believe that. Well, Aggie?'

The old woman looked at her, read the determination in her face and capitulated. 'The mistress would sometimes go out in these clothes.' She paused, looking uncomfortable, but Eve's gaze did not waver and she added, in a whisper. 'At night. She would go out with the boys, the free traders.'

Eve clapped her hands. 'I knew it,' she breathed. 'She was a smuggler.'

'No!' declared Aggie, shocked. 'Your mama would be mighty offended to hear you speak so. There has always been trade twixt here and the Continent. Silas and the other lads from the village would bring in a few ankers of brandy every now and then. Only small, mind you—we had no truck with the big cutters bringin' in tea and brandy for the towns, we've only ever brought in enough for local use. Everyone knew about it and turned to the wall if the pack-ponies were coming through the village. Miss Helena discovered it on one of her visits here with the family. She could twist Silas round her little finger. Apple of 'is eye, she was, so when she wanted to go out with 'em, he couldn't stop her, short o' telling old Mr Wingham, and that 'e would never do. After all, it was only the local lads plying their trade, not one o' them nasty, vicious gangs that would cut yer throat as soon as look at you.'

'And did she stop going out with them once she was married?'

'Of course. She gave it all up when she became Mrs Shawcross.'

Eve gazed up at the portrait of her mother.

Looking into the demure smiling face, she thought now she could detect a gleam in those dark eyes that she had not noticed before. She laughed suddenly. 'Perhaps I am not such a poor match for Captain Wyldfire after all!'

'I beg your pardon miss?' said Martha.

Eve shook her head, smiling mischievously. She began to pack the clothes back into the trunk. 'It is nearly dinner time and this is such dusty work, I think I will have a bath, Aggie. We will continue sorting through the trunks tomorrow.'

However, the following morning, Evelina had barely risen from the breakfast table when Granby came in to tell her that she had a visitor.

'Lady Chelston has called, madam. I have shown her into the morning room.'

Eve stared at him. 'Lady Chelston! What in heaven's name can she want with me?'

'To offer her condolences, perhaps?' he suggested quietly.

She swallowed. 'And you think I must see her?' His steady look gave Eve her answer. 'Oh, heavens!' She bit her lip. 'I suppose I must do so, but I will not see her wearing this old gown! Do you go back to her, Mr Granby, and tell her I shall be with her presently—and if she objects and will not wait while I change, then so much the better.'

But when Eve entered the morning room some twenty minutes later she found her guest sitting at her ease, flicking through one of the periodicals that Eve had left on a small side table. Eve came in quietly, smoothing her hands over the heavy black bombazine skirts of her mourning gown. She wore no ornament save the plain gold wedding band upon her finger, and her hair was covered by a black lace cap. She looked, she hoped, very much the grieving widow.

'Lady Chelston. I am so sorry to keep you waiting.' She gave a little curtsy before raising her eyes to observe her guest.

Catherine Chelston was a tall, spare woman. Her once handsome face was heavily lined and at odds with the improbably black curls that peeped from under her large hat. Her Pomona-green travelling dress rustled as she hurried towards Eve, holding out her hands and saying impetuously, 'Oh my poor child, so beautiful, so like your dear mama.'

Eve blinked. 'You—you knew my mother?'

'Yes, yes. That was many years ago now, of course, we lost touch once we were married.

When I heard you had taken up residence at Monkhurst, I was determined to pay a morning visit and make myself known to you. And to offer you my condolences. So tragic, my dear, to lose your grandfather *and* your husband in so short a time. I thought to find you prostrate.'

'We bear it as best we can, ma'am.' Eve gently withdrew her hands and gestured to her guest to sit down. 'News travels fast here, I see.'

Lady Chelston laughed softly. 'It is the way in these country areas, and neighbours must offer each other such solace as they are able.'

'Oh, ma'am? Are we, then, neighbours?'

Again that soft, assured laugh. 'Chelston Hall is not much more than a dozen miles from here, and in an area where there are so very few *good* families, I do not like to be backward in my attentions.'

Eve inclined her head. She did not know how to respond, but was spared the necessity of a reply for Lady Chelston continued with barely a pause for breath.

'By the bye, my dear; who is that delightful young man who showed me in here? Not your butler, I vow.'

'No, that is Mr Granby. He was my husband's valet and has agreed to stay on with me,' explained

Eve, deciding that it would be best to stick as closely to the truth as she could. 'I have not yet set up my household here, and Granby is very useful. He fulfils the role of a major-domo very well.'

'He is certainly very personable,' murmured Lady Chelston, her eyes half-closed. 'When you have finished with him, my dear, you must send him to me and I shall find him a place in my household. I like to be surrounded by attractive young men. Oh, have I shocked you? I am sorry, Mrs Wylder, I allowed my tongue to run away with me, but you are so like your sainted mama that I quite forgot myself.'

'Did—did you know my mother well, ma'am?'

'Oh, yes, we were the greatest friends. Helena and I went off to school together, you know. We were both sadly wild, always falling into scrapes. It is difficult to know who was the leader! I was quite surprised when Helena married Shawcross— he was such a very quiet gentleman, not at all what I thought she would—' She broke off suddenly and smiled. 'But I am running on to no purpose and you will be wishing me at Jericho.'

'Not at all, ma'am,' murmured Eve politely.

'Now, my poor Mrs Wylder, you are here, all on your own, no family, no friends—'

'I have many loyal people around me.' Eve was quick to correct her, but Lady Chelston merely waved her hand dismissively.

'Servants. That is not at all the same thing. Life can be very lonely here on the Marsh. I know you will wish to live quietly, but it will do you no good to become a hermit. I know what you must do, you must come to Chelston Hall and stay with me! There is room and to spare, and you will very welcome.'

'That is very kind, Lady Chelston, but—'

'Better still,' cried my lady, ignoring her interruption, 'you must join my house party! I have friends coming to stay in a se'ennight and it would be just the thing for you to have some company. I am holding a masquerade, too, which is very exciting. I have already ordered a costume for myself and for Chelston. He is to be Hades and I am Persephone. It will be such fun…oh, do say you will come!'

'Really, madam, I cannot. My mourning is too recent—'

'Nonsense. Mourning in the country is a very different matter from the public show you would be obliged to put on in town, where everyone would know you and your circumstances. Here you are not known, and no one will be offended if you go about a little. I have never held with widows shutting themselves away, that only leads to deep melancholy. And you are not to think that I would be wishing for you to be merry all day long; Chelston Hall is a large house and you will be able to take yourself off and be quiet now and then, if you wish, but I shall be there to look out for you, to make sure you do not succumb to your dismal thoughts. Of course, you will not *dance* at the ball, but think how well you will look at the masquerade, dressed all in black and with a black satin mask to hide your identity! You will look so elegantly mysterious that all the ladies will be jealous and the gentlemen will be wild to discover who you are!'

Eve recoiled, shocked. 'Madam, I could not! It would be most improper.'

'La, but who is to know?' replied Lady Chelston, smiling. 'It is just such a spree as your mama would have liked.'

'Not if she was newly widowed!'

Lady Chelston's smile slipped a little, as if she realised she had gone too far. She sighed. 'Perhaps you are right,' she said, rising. 'I can see that you are not convinced, my dear, but believe me, a little lively company, a little stimulating conversation—

it can work wonders in assuaging your grief. But your countenance tells me you are determined to refuse me today. Well, I shall send you an invitation nevertheless; perhaps when you have thought it over you may change your mind.' She reached out for Eve's hands and took them, smiling down at her. 'You are far too young and pretty to bury yourself away, my dear. Send me word at Chelston Hall if there is anything I can do for you.'

'Thank you, my lady, but I am at a loss to know why you should be so eager to befriend me.'

Lady Chelston's blue-grey eyes widened. 'So frank—how refreshing,' she murmured. 'Let us say it is for your mother's sake. Now, I must go.' She squeezed Eve's fingers. 'To stay longer would be beyond the bounds of the propriety you set such story by. Goodbye to you, Mrs Wylder, and think upon my invitation!'

Eve could think of nothing else and when her disturbing visitor had left the premises she walked slowly to the kitchen, where she found Aggie shelling peas for their dinner. Richard Granby was piling logs into a large square basket beside the great fireplace.

'It is not for you to do that,' she told him, frowning.

'You have only one manservant in the house

besides myself and he has been on duty in the hall, waiting for your visitor to leave.' He grinned. 'I thought it best to play least in sight and let Matthew show her out; the lady seemed disposed to question me.'

'Lady Chelston did indeed ask about you. I told her you were my husband's valet and that you had stayed on to manage my house for me.' She chuckled. 'She was very taken with you and told me to send you to her when I have no further need of you.'

'I hope you will do no such thing, madam!'

'No, of course not, but I could not make her out. Aggie, Lady Chelston says she knew my mother. They were neighbours, and they went to school together. Do you remember her?'

Aggie shook her head, a crease furrowing her brow. 'I disremember any close schoolfriends of your mama's, madam, except—yes, there *was* one: Catherine Reade, merchant's daughter, about a year younger than Miss Helena she was. Spoiled little thing, nothing would do for her but she should follow Miss Helena to school in Tenterden. Yes, we thought it a good joke at the time, for Mr Reade was no more than your grandfather Wingham's tenant at the time, though 'e did buy the house at

Abbotsfield from your grandfather later. But what little Cathy wanted she must have. Made a good marriage, though; caught a lord with property across the border. We never saw her after that.'

'In Sussex? That could be Chelston Hall.' Eve sat down at the table and cupped her chin in her hands. 'If Catherine really had been such good friends with Mama, I would have thought you would know of it, Aggie, even if I couldn't remember her.'

'I am certain sure she never called upon your sainted mama after her marriage, at least not here at Monkhurst. I wonder why she should be calling upon you now?' mused the housekeeper.

Eve saw the warning look in Granby's eyes and shrugged. 'I think she was curious to see Helena Wingham's daughter.' She hesitated. 'She invited me to stay with her.' Aggie dropped the pea pod she was shelling and stared. Eve nodded. 'She thinks I will be lonely here on my own.'

'Well there is no denying, Miss Eve, that there's precious little company here for you. You should perhaps consider hiring a companion to live with you.'

Eve dared not look at Granby. 'I shall consider it, Aggie, but not yet. I am quite content here on my own for the present time. And there is plenty to do. Mr Granby, if you will meet me in the attics in quarter of an hour, I will go and change and then you can help Martha and me to empty the last few trunks.'

The busy afternoon passed quickly enough, but Catherine Chelston's visit still played on Eve's mind. It was not until dinnertime that she found the opportunity to talk it over with Granby. It had become the habit for the valet to wait upon her at dinner, overriding her objections by saying that he had done the same for his master on numerous occasions. She was glad of his company; it was a link with Nick and it was a comfort to be able to talk to him about his master. The September sun was shining in through the dining-room windows, making candles unnecessary as he cleared away the remains of her meal and placed a small bowl of sweetmeats upon the table before her.

'Aggie has surpassed herself,' said Eve, reaching for her wineglass. 'The lamb was delicious. Have you tried it, Mr Granby?'

'No, madam. I shall take my meal later. Mrs Brattee will leave a plate on the hob for me before she goes back to the Gate House.'

'Tell me what you make of Lady Chelston's visit.'

'I am not sure. I think she was sent here by her husband, but for what purpose I do not know.'

'We must tell Captain Wylder of this,' she decided.

'That is what I was thinking, madam.'

'Can you get a note to him, Mr Granby? He said you would know how to contact him.'

'Yes madam, I—'

'Good.' She rose. 'I shall write to him directly.'

'That will not be necessary, Mrs Wylder.'

'No, you are right, it would be best if we did not commit anything to paper.'

'That is not what I meant, madam.' Something in the valet's tone made her look at him intently. A glimmer of a smile was just discernible on his usually impassive face. 'You will be able to tell him so yourself, Mrs Wylder. The master is coming here tonight.'

Since their last meeting at the Mermaid Inn, Eve had spent many hours wondering just how she was going to deal with Nick Wylder. He was her husband, it was impossible for her to cut him out of her life, no matter how badly he had treated her. He had vowed to win her trust and she wanted to give him that chance, but that did not mean she was going to fall into his arms as soon as he smiled at her. No, she would be polite, she would help him catch his smugglers, but he should not have her love until he had earned it!

As the clock in the hall chimed eleven, Eve picked up her candle and left the drawing room to make her way through the dark, silent passages to the kitchen. Granby was sitting at the big table in the centre of the room, playing patience by the golden light from a single oil lamp. He glanced up as she entered.

'It is all right, madam, we are alone. Aggie has returned to the Gate House.'

'And I have told Matthew he may go on to bed,' she replied. 'He is not here yet?'

'No,' said Granby, rising. 'Have patience, madam, the captain will come. Pray, return to the drawing room; I will bring you word as soon as he arrives.'

Eve shook her head slightly and set her candlestick down upon the table.

'I will wait for him here. I cannot settle to anything. There is a chill in this house tonight, at least here the fire has been burning all day—'

She broke off as the valet threw up his head, listening. Soon Eve could hear it, too, the soft thud of a footfall followed by a quiet knocking on wood. Granby crossed the room and dragged aside the log basket. Seconds later the floorboards beside the fireplace began to rise.

'Welcome, sir!' Granby pulled back the trapdoor and Nick Wylder's head and shoulders rose from the black aperture. He grinned at Eve.

'Permission to come aboard, madam!'

She was so surprised by his unorthodox entry that her plans to remain cool and aloof were forgotten. 'You have used the riverside passage,' she exclaimed. 'But it is locked!'

Nick stepped up into the room. 'I know.' He patted his pocket. 'Dick left the key within reach for me.'

'You had no difficulty navigating the channel?' asked Granby.

'No, the waterway is clear from Jury's Cut as far as the boathouse.'

Nick drew up a stool and sat down, wincing slightly.

Eve said quickly, 'Your wound is still paining you.'

'It has not healed yet.' He gave her a wry smile. 'I do not rest enough.'

'When was the bandage last changed?' His

shrug told Eve all she needed to know. She went to the door. 'Stay there while I fetch some clean linen. I will re-dress it for you.'

'But I came here to talk to you!'

'You can do that while I bind you up.'

Chapter Eleven

When Eve returned to the kitchen, Granby had built up the fire and lighted more candles so that the room glowed with a rich golden light. A pitcher of ale stood on the table and three tankards had been filled to the brim.

'Richard has poured one for you,' said Nick, waving to the mugs. 'It is small-beer, but he will fetch you a glass of wine if you prefer.'

'No, I will drink ale with you.' She began to tear the old sheet she had brought with her into strips. 'You must take off your jacket and shirt, if you please.'

She did not look up as Granby helped Nick to take off his coat, but as he stripped off his shirt she found her eyes straying to Nick's broad shoulders. She watched the way the muscles rippled under the skin as he pulled the shirt over his head, the sinuous contours accentuated by the candlelight.

Swallowing hard, she forced herself to concentrate and shifted her gaze to the tight bandaging around his ribs. There was a dark stain low on his left side.

'Good God, sir,' exclaimed Granby, frowning. 'Has it been changed at all since I last saw you?'

Nick perched himself on the table and held up his arms as Eve began to remove the bandage.

'Of course,' he said. 'Rebecca did it for me about a week ago. She is landlady at the Ship, ma'am, in case you were wondering.'

'Is that where you are staying, at an inn?'

'Yes, outside Hastings. The risk of being recognised is too great to stay in the town, but I am well hidden at the Ship. It was Rebecca who looked after me when I was first brought ashore.'

Something of Eve's thoughts must have shown in her face for Nick laughed. 'You need not be jealous, sweetheart; she is married, and old enough to be my mother.'

'I am not at all jealous,' she retorted.

He reached out for her. 'No?' he murmured, pulling her closer.

She put her hands against his chest and pushed hard. 'Of course not!' she said crossly. She went over to the pump in the corner and worked the handle vigorously. The water slopped into the bowl. She drew more than she needed, but she wanted the heated flush in her cheeks to die down before she went back to Nick. She heard Granby's angry mutter.

'I should have stayed with you, Captain.'

'It would have made no difference. Besides, Dick, I needed you here to look after my wife.'

Eve refused to allow herself any comfort in Nick's words; he was merely looking after his interests, scoundrel that he was! However, when she turned her attention to the wound in his side, all other thoughts were driven out by the sight of the red, angry gash.

'You told me it was a little flesh wound.' Her hands trembled slightly as she washed away the dried blood and gently cleaned around the injury. 'This is very deep. You are fortunate it did not touch any vital organs.'

'I've had worse than this,' he reassured her cheerfully.

'But I have always been there to look after you!' put in the valet quickly.

'Oh.' Eve paused. 'Then perhaps, Mr Granby, you would like to carry on here—'

'No he would not!' exclaimed Nick. 'Richard's ministrations have always been of the rough-and-ready sort. I much prefer your gentle touch.'

Eve scowled, revolted by her pleasure at his words. She picked up a small ointment jar.

'What's that?' asked Nick suspiciously.

'Comfrey paste, to help the skin to heal.'

'It is healing well enough alone,' he muttered, looking sceptically at her.

She held the jar in front of her. 'I made it myself,' she coaxed.

At length he sighed and raised his arm. 'Very well, apply your witch's potion!'

She dipped her fingers into the jar and began to smooth the ointment over the wound. Standing so close to Nick was playing havoc with her insides, making it difficult to concentrate. She was aware of his chest rising and falling just inches from her face, the faded scars on his skin reminding her of the adventurous life he had led.

She did not realise she had stopped applying the comfrey paste and was staring at a neat round scar on his shoulder until she heard him say, 'I told you it was not the first hole I've had in me.'

'I think you court danger,' she said in a low voice.

'No, but it seems to find me.'

She looked up to see that devil-may-care smile curving his lips. He held her eyes, inviting her to share in his excitement and, oh, she wanted to! She wanted to throw her lot in with him and declare the world well lost, but it frightened her.

Eve dragged her eyes back to the red, ugly wound in his side. Just looking at it made her shudder for what might have happened. She was about to suggest that Mr Granby should apply the final bandage when she heard the valet cough and excuse himself. When the door closed behind him, the silence that settled over the kitchen was heavy with tension.

She took up a strip of clean linen and turned to face Nick. Obligingly he raised his arms for her but he was still sitting on the table, and Eve had to move forwards, to step in between his legs and put her arms about him to pass the bandage around his back. Her face came very close to his chest, so close she only needed to lean a little more and her cheek would press against him. His skin smelled of the outdoors, of salt and sea air, overlaid with hints of spice and soap. She breathed deeply; he was so strong, so reassuringly solid. Safe. Nick jumped.

'Oh—did I hurt you?' She looked up quickly.

'No, sweetheart. I had forgotten how good it was to have you near to me.'

The dark glow in his eyes sent her heart skidding round in her chest. She knew an overwhelming desire to stretch up and kiss the dimple that appeared at the side of his mouth when he smiled down at her. With an effort she wrenched her eyes away, reminding herself what a troublesome individual he was.

'I am only doing this because I do not want your death laid at my door!'

'Yes, of course.'

She bit back a smile at his meek tone and continued to pass the bandage around him. When she had finished, her hands lingered on his skin, reluctant to move away. Nick reached up and covered her fingers, trapping them. He slid off the table and stood before her, his body tense and aroused. A thrill of anticipation trembled through her, quickly followed by a terrible, aching pain as she remembered his betrayal. She had mourned him, grieved for him and he was not dead.

'You need your shirt.'

'Eve.'

With a tiny shake of her head she pulled her hand away from him and stepped back, blinking rapidly. 'I have no time for dalliance, sir.'

'Dalliance! I merely desire a moment's tenderness from my wife.'

Eve stared down at her hands, clasped tightly before her. The room was silent save for the merry crackle of the fire that seemed to mock her unhappiness. She said in a low tone, 'I do not trust you. Not yet. It is still too painful for me—'

'Then I will wait,' he replied quietly. 'Until you are ready.'

The constriction in Eve's throat threatened to choke her as the tears welled up. There was a heavy tread from the passage, a rattling of the door handle and Granby entered the kitchen. Nick quickly turned, putting himself between Eve and the door. Retreating to the shadows, she pulled out her handkerchief and wiped her eyes.

'I have brought in more ale,' said Granby. 'I thought you might care for another cup?'

'Thank you, yes, but I cannot stay too long, the tide will be turning soon.'

He guided Eve to a chair, then sat down beside her. Granby refilled his tankard.

'So, Captain, what news have you?'

'Very little, I am afraid. I have been to Boulogne and can find no sign that they are making this false tea there. It brings me back to my original suspicions that the stuff is made here, in this country, but where? My searches around Chelston Hall have drawn a blank. I cannot find out that Chelston is carrying out any large-scale production of the smouch on his estates.'

'Surely it would be very dangerous for him to do so,' murmured Eve.

'It would, of course, but the production needs to be somewhere secluded, and he has acres of woodland. Unfortunately, after the fiasco at the Rocks of Nore there has been very little activity; the Revenue men's sources have no new leads for us to follow. It is like the Marsh, the villages are isolated and people do not talk readily to strangers.'

'So what happens now?' asked Granby.

'We continue to watch and wait. Chelston cannot hold off indefinitely, he will need to move the goods soon.'

Despite Nick's cheerful words Eve felt the chill of despondency curling around them

'Well, we have had some excitement,' she said, trying to be cheerful. 'I had a morning visit today, from Lady Chelston.'

'The devil you did!' exclaimed Nick.

'Yes. She knew my mother. She said they had lost touch when they both married. I cannot imagine that Mama liked her—I did not take to her at all.'

'And what did she want?' asked Nick eagerly. 'Did she ask to look around the house, or was she looking for you to invite her to stay?'

'Quite the contrary, she wanted me to join her house party next week. At Chelston Hall. Of course I declined. It would be most improper, especially as she is holding a masquerade.'

'Is she, by Gad?'

'Yes. Although she tells me I need not attend.' A reluctant smile dragged at the corners of her mouth. 'She sees herself as Persephone, with Chelston as Hades.'

Nick laughed. 'How appropriate, Hades being known as both the unseen one and the rich one! That fits very well with my idea of the man.'

'But not so appropriate for his lady.' chuckled Eve, 'Persephone was an innocent, and I cannot think that term applies to Lady Chelston!'

'True, but I like the idea of a masquerade, it could be very useful to us.'

'Now what are you planning?' she asked, suspicious of Nick's wicked grin.

'Well it would be an advantage to have someone inside Chelston Hall. We might learn something.'

Eve backed away, shaking her head. 'Oh, no!'

Nick gave her a pained look. 'I would not expect you to search the house, sweetheart, merely to open a door or a window to let me in.'

'Certainly not! It is impossible for me to go. I am a widow.' Nick raised an eyebrow at her. 'Well,' she temporised, 'I am still mourning my grandfather.'

'Of course you are,' he agreed, reaching out to clasp her hand. 'You could not be expected to attend the ball, or even to join the company after dinner. Your widow's status would make it perfectly acceptable for you to keep to your room a good deal, but think how useful you could be, inside Chelston Hall.'

'I thought you wanted me to live retired,' she argued. 'It would be most improper for me to go out in public.'

'This is a private party at a country house where no one knows you. Your situation would allow you to keep your distance from the other guests.' He squeezed her hand and gave her the full force of his charming smile. 'I promise you will come to no harm.'

She felt herself weakening and rallied a final, desperate argument. 'You cannot know that. Lord Chelston may be planning to coerce me into giving up Monkhurst, or even to have me murdered in my bed.'

'Chelston is outwardly very respectable. I would not send you if I thought you would be in any real danger. I do not believe he would show his hand quite so plainly. You will take Martha with you, of course.'

'And where will you be?' asked Eve suspiciously. She was not reassured by the wicked gleam in his eyes.

'Oh I shall be close at hand, never fear.' He squeezed her fingers. 'Say you will do this for me, sweetheart. Write to the lady and tell her you have changed your mind.'

'I shall do no such thing! I can think of nothing more likely to rouse her suspicions.'

'I thought you *wanted* to help me.' His reproachful gaze made her falter.

'Lady Chelston did say she would send me an invitation, even though I told her I should not come. If she does so, then I will accept.'

He lifted her hand and pressed it to his lips. 'Thank you. I knew I could rely upon you.'

'Should I go too, sir?' asked Granby. 'If there is any danger—'

'No, I do not think Mrs Wylder will be in any

serious danger while she is at Chelston Hall, Richard. I would rather you stayed here, in case they try to break into the house.'

'You still think there is something here that they want?' exclaimed Eve, snatching her hand away. 'And you are happy that I should continue to live here, when I may be in mortal danger? Oooh...' She almost stamped her foot in vexation. 'You are despicable!'

Chapter Twelve

Eve wanted to believe that Lady Chelston's visit had been no more than a neighbourly gesture and that, having done her Christian duty, the lady would forget all about it. She was therefore disappointed and somewhat surprised when an invitation to visit Chelston Hall arrived a few days later. Having given her word to Nick, Eve sent back a civil acceptance, but it was not to be expected that her decision to visit Chelston Hall would be welcomed by her household. Aggie tut-tutted at the idea of her mistress going away so soon after her arrival at Monkhurst.

'There is so much yet to do here, mistress,' she complained. 'We have but emptied the attics!'

'I shall not be gone more than a se'ennight,' said Eve. 'And you do not need me in residence to have the house swept out from top to bottom. In fact,' she added, 'I would as lief *not* be here.'

They were sitting in the kitchen, where Eve had been going through the week's menus with her housekeeper. She looked up from her lists as the outer door opened and Sam strode in with an armful of logs.

'Morning, mistress,' he greeted Eve cheerfully as he dropped the logs into the basket. 'There now, Mother, dry logs from the store. Nat and I should finish clearing the shrubbery today and then I'll chop some more firewood for 'ee.'

As he straightened and turned to go, Eve noticed his left eye was blackened and there was a livid bruise spreading over his cheek.

'Heavens,' she exclaimed. 'What has happened to you?'

Sam grinned and put his fingers to his face. 'Oh, we had a set to a few nights ago with some lads down at Jury's Cut. There was a bit of argle-bargle going on: they wanted to stop us using the inlet. Jumped us, they did, when we was lying up there.'

Aggie shook her head as she stirred the contents of the black kettle hanging over the fire. 'There's been a fair few fights recently,' she said. 'I do hope we aren't going back to the bad days. Some says it's the Hawkhurst gang come back.'

Eve frowned at Sam. 'Silas promised me that if

I could find you work you would all give up the smug…free-trading.'

'And so we will, mistress, surelye, but there's some obligations that has to be dealt with first.'

'It is a matter of honour,' put in Aggie, anxious that Eve should understand. 'Some o' the villagers has already paid you see, but once the final orders are settled then the boys will not be going out again. And glad of it I shall be; I shan't rest easy in my bed until they've completed their final run.'

Sam looked pained. 'Now then, Mother how can you say that when Father has been free-trading all his life?'

'Ah, but it weren't so dangerous in the past, it's been a gentlemanly business since the worst o' the gangs was taken out…'

Eve went out, leaving them to argue, and ran upstairs to inform her maid of the forthcoming visit. Martha was even more disapproving than the housekeeper, and much more vocal.

'Well I don't like it, Miss Eve and so I tell you! To be putting yourself in the hands of that villain, not to mention the disrespect to your sainted grandfather.'

'There will be no disrespect,' returned Eve with quiet dignity. 'I shall wear full mourning, and I have made it clear in my letter to Lady Chelston that I will not participate in any of her entertainments.'

Martha sniffed 'Nevertheless, to be staying in the house of the captain's enemy is a risk, miss, you cannot deny it.'

'You seem to know a great deal about this, Martha; I suppose you have been talking with Richard Granby.'

Her maid blushed rosily. 'Mr Granby and I do have an understanding, madam.'

'Ahh. So that's it; you do not wish to leave him and come with me to Chelston Hall.'

'Miss Eve! How could you think that I would ever see you go off without me to look after you! And you to be thinking that Rich—Mr Granby would countenance such a thing! Now cease your teasing, do, and leave me to get on with the packing, since you are determined to go!'

Chelston Hall was a sturdily-built Palladian villa which had been extended at some recent date with two new wings and an imposing pediment over its entrance. It stood atop a slight hill, affording its occupants unrivalled views over the surrounding countryside and even, on a good day, a glimpse of the sea. The wind whipped around Eve as she stepped from her carriage. Through her black veil she observed the tall, wooden-faced lackey who welcomed her to the house and took her into the huge marble hall. A grand staircase led up to a gallery that ran around the upper floor, supported on gleaming marbled pillars. A second footman escorted her to her room. Sounds of laughter drifted down to her from the main reception rooms leading off the gallery, but she was in no hurry to see her fellow guests and requested that Lady Chelston be informed that she would rest until the dinner hour.

Her allotted bedchamber was in the east wing, overlooking a wide terrace and formal flower gardens. Ivy leaves surrounded the window and spilled over the stone windowsill, the growth so abundant it threatened to invade the room. A quick glance assured Eve that the stout door to her room had a serviceable lock and key and there was a small adjoining dressing room that also contained a narrow bed for her maid. She set Martha to the task of unpacking her trunk, deciding that her gowns would be better hung on pegs in the dressing room rather than folded in the large linen press, which already contained a colourful assortment of folded satins and velvets. Eve then lay down upon her bed until it was time to join the other guests for dinner. Despite her outward calm she was excited at the thought of what was to come: she had a part to play, but although she was a little nervous, she did not think that any harm could come to her in a house full of guests. Eve wondered how soon Nick would contact her. She had sent Richard Granby to him with the news that she was going to Chelston Hall, but Nick's reply had been disappointingly brief; he would seek her out.

'What?' she had exclaimed upon hearing this. 'Did he give no indication of when I might expect to see him?'

'The captain prefers to leave matters to take their course, Mrs Wylder,' Granby replied woodenly. 'He finds that the most satisfactory way to work.'

'Well, I find it most unsatisfactory,' retorted Eve. 'I am to put myself into danger with no idea what I am expected to do.'

She thought she saw a faint curving of the valet's lips, but it was gone in an instant. He said quietly, 'Captain Wyldfire runs with the wind, ma'am. That is his way. But you need not be anxious. He will always come about.'

'Well, let us hope that this time is no exception!'

* * *

'Mrs Wylder, how glad I am that you could join us!'

Catherine Chelston hurried forward in a rustle of satin skirts to greet Eve as she came into the drawing room. Lady Chelston gestured to the lavishly dressed gentleman following more slowly in her wake. 'Madam, may I present to you my husband?'

Eve observed the man bowing before her. Lord Chelston was of slight build, not above average height, but there was a sense of ruthless strength beneath the satin and lace, and when he fixed his eyes upon her they held such a cold, calculating look that Eve had to suppress a shiver. His thin face was very pale with a high forehead and she guessed that beneath his powdered wig his own hair would be thin and receding. He took her hand in a limp, almost damp clasp.

'My dear Mrs Wylder, it is very good of you to honour us with your presence, especially when you have suffered not one, but two losses so recently—'

'I told my lord that you were reluctant to take up my invitation,' broke in Lady Chelston.

'I am still not sure if I should be here,' murmured

Eve, withdrawing her hand and resisting the impulse to wipe her fingers on her gown.

'Your scruples do you credit,' returned Lord Chelston. 'And be assured, no one will intrude upon your grief, but on these occasions it is sometimes better to be amongst friends.'

Eve inclined her head. 'Did you know my husband, sir?'

'I regret I did not have that pleasure, but you are not to be thinking that you are totally alone here in your grief, for your cousin is also staying with us.' He stepped aside and Eve saw Bernard smiling at her from across the room. She looked away without acknowledging his bow. Catherine laughed gently.

'Poor man, he told us he had allowed his passions to run away with him and declared himself far too early. But you need not worry, my dear Mrs Wylder; I have his word that he will be on his best behaviour here.'

'You will forgive me, madam, if I reserve judgement on that,' returned Eve.

'Of course.' Lady Chelston reached out and touched her arm briefly. 'But I beg you will allow him to take you into dinner tonight. We would not wish to give the gossipmongers cause to think there was any dissention in your family, now would we?'

'Very well, ma'am, to oblige you. However, please let me say, as I made plain in my letter, I cannot join in all your entertainments, and I certainly cannot attend your masquerade.'

'No, no that is quite understood,' agreed her hostess. 'I hope you will be able to join us for the dinner beforehand, but after that you may keep to your room and you can send down for such refreshments as you require.' Lady Chelston patted her hands. 'We want you to feel at home here, my dear; I hope we can be of some comfort to you at this time. Mayhap your visit here will help you to forget your grief, at least for a short time.'

Eve inclined her head. 'I think we can be sure it will do that, Lady Chelston.'

'We have been here for three days, and still no word from him!'

Eve stared into the mirror as Martha brushed out her hair.

'Hush madam. The captain will come to you when he is ready.'

'And in the meantime I feel such a fraud,' sighed Eve, keeping her voice low. 'Everyone is so very considerate to me as the poor, grieving widow. My host and hostess have not said or done anything out of place and even Bernard is keeping his distance!'

'As well he might,' growled Martha. 'Now sit still Miss Eve, do, while I put up your hair again. You cannot go down to my lady's grand dinner looking a fright.'

Eve slumped a little. 'I wish I did not have to go. Lady Chelston knows I will not attend the ball, but she has planned her dinner table to include me. I shall feel so out of place in my widow's weeds.'

'The black show off your fine complexion,' returned Martha in a bracing tone. 'Every lady will envy you and the gentlemen will all admire you excessively.'

Eve pulled a face in the mirror. The thought shot through her mind that there was only man she wanted to admire her, and he would not be present. She watched as Martha fixed the black lace cap over her curls, then she stood up and shook out her gown. She had chosen to wear a black overdress of cobweb-fine lace over her silk skirts, the deep mourning relieved only by a single string of pearls around her neck. 'I thought it an unnecessary extravagance when I bought this gown, but now I am glad I have it. The feel of the silk gives me more confidence. Well…' she gave her skirts a final twitch '…wish me luck.' An irrepressible gleam of humour tugged at her mouth. 'I may well find that my grief is too great and I shall be obliged to rush away from the dinner table.'

She set off along the maze of corridors, keeping her gaze modestly lowered and taking no notice of the statue-like footman who were on duty at regular intervals along her route. Within hours of their arrival at Chelston Hall, Martha had passed on to her the servants' gossip that the mistress of the house had a predilection for handsome young footmen and Eve noted that every one of the liveried menservants in the house was over six feet tall. Observing Lady Chelston's lingering glances at these lackeys, Eve suspected that some of them at least provided her with more intimate services than was usually required of a footman. She was approaching the main gallery when one of these liveried statues spoke to her.

'Good evening, sweetheart.' The sound of the familiar voice was so unexpected that Eve's knees threatened to buckle and she put out a hand to the wall to support her. Raising her eyes, she gazed in astonishment at the tall figure in the white-powdered wig and blue coat with its gold facings. The deep blue eyes and wicked grin were unmistakable.

'Nick! What in heaven's name are you doing?' she hissed.

With a quick glance to make sure the corridor was deserted, he gripped her wrist and pulled her through the nearest door into a small, empty bedroom. 'I told you I should come.'

'But not like this! You look…strange.'

He grinned. 'And you look breathtaking. I have missed you.' His eyes darkened with desire and she looked away quickly, finding it difficult to catch her own breath.

'This is madness! You will be recognised.'

'*You* did not know me,' he pointed out.

'That is different.'

'No, it is not. People only see what they expect to see. Besides, who is there here that knows me?'

'My cousin Bernard, for one!'

Nick shrugged. 'He will not notice me. I had thought to look through Chelston's papers while I am here.'

'As far as I can tell, there are two places where he might keep important documents. There is a desk in the library, but that room has been opened up for his guests tonight. However, his office is below here, on the opposite side of the hall to the kitchens and servants' rooms. The passage leads only to the office and the back stairs for the east wing, so it should be very quiet this evening.'

'Well done, Eve. You have been busy.'

'I have had little to do but acquaint myself with the house.'

'I commend your foresight.' He cast an appraising glance over her. 'Are you going down to dinner in that? The gentlemen will have eyes for no one else.'

She flushed. 'That was not my intention.'

'No, but you do not appreciate just how beautiful you are.'

She tried to ignore this, but was aware of the flush creeping into her cheeks and the fluttering excitement in her stomach. 'How did you get in?'

'It is common knowledge in this area that the Chelstons take on more staff when they are entertaining. Once I learned that Lady Chelston likes to pick the servants herself, it was not difficult to be chosen.' The wicked laughter was in his eyes again. 'After all, I have all the attributes she looks for in her footmen.'

'You would be well served if she was to select you for her favours tonight!'

'It is the lady who would be well-served,' he murmured.

Eve gasped at his audacity. Nick merely laughed and swept her into his arms.

'No, no, I am jesting, sweetheart. There is only room for one woman in my life now, and you know it.'

His words and the feel of his arms about her sent Eve's senses spiralling out of control. She had no time to gather her scattered wits and turn her head before he was kissing her, his mouth rough and demanding against her own. Her fingers clutched at his coat as she responded, urgent desire heating her blood.

'Must you go in to dinner now?' he muttered, covering her face and throat with warm, tender kisses.

'We will be discovered,' she whispered as reason threatened to leave her.

He groaned. 'You are right. You will be missed.' He gripped her shoulders and possessed her mouth for one last, lingering kiss. 'There. Go now before I forget that I am a servant and ravish you.'

She did not smile as she stepped away from him. 'Will we speak again?'

'I shall find you later, trust me.' He opened the door and cautiously looked out. 'It is clear. Off you go now.'

Still bemused with the shock of the encounter, Eve made her way to the drawing room. She was one of the last to arrive and her entrance went almost unnoticed in the noisy confusion. The room was packed with guests who laughed and chattered and exclaimed over each other's masquerade costumes. Lady Chelston came up, looking magnificent in green and gold.

'Persephone in Spring, my dear,' she said, when Eve uttered a compliment. 'Chelston had these yellow diamonds made up into the shape of a primrose cluster for my corsage—are they not exquisite?'

She hurried away and Eve watched her flit around the room, too distracted to spare more than a few words to anyone. A small group of house-guests welcomed Eve in a kindly manner, then continued their discussion with no more than an occasional glance or word in her direction. This suited her perfectly, unlike the protracted dinner, which proved to be a sore trial.

She was seated next to her cousin and she nearly fainted when Nick filed in with the other footmen to serve the first course. She kept her eyes resolutely lowered, praying that she would do nothing to give him away. Conversation ebbed and flowed; Eve had no idea what she said or what was said to her. The elegant and colourful dishes prepared for the delectation of Lord Chelston's guests tasted of nothing in her mouth. Eve filled her plate and ate mechanically and all the time she was aware of the footmen gliding silently around the room, refilling glasses, clearing dishes and setting down fresh ones.

'Cousin, let me help you to a little of the baked pike,' said Bernard presently. 'It is quite delicious.'

'No, I thank you.'

'You are still angry with me,' he said in a low voice. 'I should not have declared myself so soon. It was the violence of my regard for you that made me so precipitate.'

Eve froze. Nick was directly before them, serving the gentleman seated on the opposite side of the table. Anxious that Bernard should not look up, she gave him a much warmer smile that she had intended, desperate to keep his attention. 'So you told me in your letter, Cousin.'

'Your reply did not lead me to hope you had forgiven me.'

'*Your* letter implied you thought your suit might still succeed,' she countered.

'And will it not?'

Nick had moved out of sight and Eve relaxed slightly. 'No,' she said. 'Never.'

'Never is a long time, Cousin.'

The complacent smile on Bernard's face made her long to slap him. She restrained herself, regretting her earlier friendliness. She said with false sweetness, 'Then you will have plenty of time to recover from your disappointment.'

Very deliberately she turned her shoulder and began to converse with the gentleman on her right. *There*, she thought. *I have told him; I will not speak to him again, and Nick must look out for himself!*

The meal progressed with no oaths, no clatter of dropped dishes to draw attention to a clumsy servant. A glance at each end of the table showed Eve that Lord Chelston and his wife were both at ease and too engrossed in their guests to look at the footmen. When at last her hostess gave the signal for the ladies to withdraw, Eve knew a moment's panic. What if something happened to Nick later, when she was not there? Reason told her there was nothing she could do to help, but she would have preferred to remain near him. As the ladies slowly processed out of the room she risked one swift glance along the line of liveried servants. She saw Nick almost immediately, but although he met her eyes for a brief moment, he gave no sign of recognition. A wild bubble of laughter welled up within her; he might be daring, but he was not so reckless that he would risk a look being intercepted. It gave her some comfort, but it was still a struggle to maintain her composure, knowing he was courting danger.

After a brief word to her hostess Eve slipped away to her room. As she passed along the gallery she could hear the orchestra tuning up below. The notes reverberated around the empty hall, but Eve knew that once the vast space was filled with people the hollow echo would be replaced by a much more melodious sound. It would be very busy, she thought, all the footmen would be required to attend to the guests and Nick would not be able to slip away unnoticed.

She paced around her bedchamber, her body buzzing with nervous energy. It was absurd for her to sit idly doing nothing. The idea nagged at her so much that after an hour she could bear the uncertainty no longer and she went back to the gallery. There were no servants now in the dimly lit upper corridors and she guessed that they had all been pressed into service downstairs. Eve peeped over the balustrade. The hall was packed with a noisy, colourful throng. Many of the guests were in elaborate costumes with silk masks over their eyes, but dotted between them were mysterious figures enveloped in swirling silk dominos. The liveried footmen moved through the crowd offering fresh glasses of wine. She walked round the gallery until she could see the entrance to the saloon that opened off the hall. The double doors had been thrown wide and more servants were busy setting out supper on long tables.

'Mrs Wylder, does the noise disturb you?'

She jumped and turned to find Lord Chelston beside her. 'N-no, sir.' She tried a wan smile. 'I merely wished to see how the ball was progressing.'

He held out his arm. 'Let me take you down—'

'No, no, my lord, I thank you.' She shrank away. 'My black gown does not lend itself to such gaiety, and it might make some of your guests uncomfortable. Forgive me, I have seen enough and will retire now.'

'Then allow me to escort you back to your chamber.' He pulled her hand on to his arm and walked beside her through the dimly lit corridor. 'To find you watching the dancers makes me wonder if you are perhaps lonely, ma'am.'

'L-lonely, my lord? No, I assure you—'

'Shawcross informs me that Makerham was your home for many years. It must surely be a wrench for you to leave it, to leave all your friends and move to Monkhurst, which I am well aware is very isolated. You are young, would you not prefer to be living in Tunbridge, or Bath, where you would find a little more society?'

'I am very content at Monkhurst, my lord.'

He stopped, his sharp eyes searching her face. 'Are you sure?' he said gently. 'Are you not putting a brave face upon your plight? If it is money, madam, then perhaps I can help you. I could buy Monkhurst. I know this country, Mrs Wylder; Monkhurst is not like to suit everyone. I would be happy to take it off your hands for a generous sum—and we need not wait for the legalities to be complete. I could make you an advance to allow you to move immediately to somewhere more suited to your nature.'

She put up a hand. 'Please, my lord, say no more. I assure you Monkhurst suits me very well. Perhaps, perhaps in a year or so, when my grief has lessened…' She allowed the sentence to remain unfinished and lowered her eyes before his cold, piercing gaze. After a moment he bowed.

'As you wish, madam. I shall take you to your room now. But do not be afraid to send your maid to me, if there is anything you require. Anything at all.'

'You are very good, sir.'

He escorted her to her door and when she entered she found Martha anxiously waiting for her.

'Oh, Miss Eve, thank heaven you are back safe! I was that worried.'

'And rightly so.' Eve pressed her ear to the door, listening. 'Lord Chelston discovered me on the landing. It is plainly not safe for me to wander the house like this.' Excitement fluttered in her chest. She crossed to the linen press and opened the doors.

'Whatever are you about, madam?' Martha demanded. 'We never put any of your things in there.'

'I know it,' Eve said, hunting through the cupboards. 'But I saw something when we arrived... ah, here it is.' She emerged from the cupboard, a triumphant smile upon her lips, and held up a cherry-red domino.

'Lawks, miss, you are never going to join the dancing?'

'No, but I saw several red dominos amongst the revellers, so no one will recognise me if I wear this tonight!'

Creeping out of the room again a short time later and enveloped in cherry-red silk, Eve made her way along the empty corridor and slipped down the backstairs. As she reached the ground floor there was shrieking and loud laughter, and she flattened herself against one of the panelled walls as a lady dressed as Gloriana rushed past, dragging a puffing and be-whiskered Falstaff behind her. They paid no heed to Eve, shrouded in her domino, and once they had disappeared she moved on. Reaching the study, she tried the handle. The door opened easily, but the room was in darkness. Calmly she picked up a candlestick, stepped along the corridor and held the candle to the lighted ones burning in the wall sconces. With some small, detached part of her brain she marvelled that her hand was so steady, but she was aware that a show of nerves now could be her undoing. She slipped into the study and closed the door carefully behind her. Lifting her candlestick higher, she looked around the room.

Eve was suddenly at a loss. She had no idea what she was looking for. Glass-fronted cupboards lined two walls, while shelves flanked the chimney piece and the window, where a large map-chest stood, its top level with the sill. A heavy mahogany desk occupied most of the floor space with a selection of stamps, inkwells and pens arranged neatly on the top, but it was clear of papers, as was every other surface in the room. She moved to the fireplace and inspected the mantel-shelf, but there were no invitations propped against the snuff-jars nor opened letters tucked behind the ormolu clock. Eve scolded herself for naïvety in thinking Lord Chelston would leave evidence of his wrongdoing lying around for anyone to find. The sudden scrape of the door handle made her jump and she almost dropped the candlestick. She swung around, her heart leaping into her mouth, but it settled into a rapid tattoo against her ribs as Nick stepped into the room.

'I saw the light under the door,' he said quietly. 'Chelston is dancing, so I knew that it must be you here. What have you discovered?'

'Nothing yet.' Eve put the candlestick down upon the desk. 'I was about to try the drawers.'

'A very good notion.' He crossed the room in a few quick strides and slid open the top drawer. Eve watched him lift out a pile of papers and carefully flick through them.

'But is it likely that he would keep anything here that could incriminate him?' she asked.

'No, but there may well be some clue for us.'

'What sort of clue?'

'I have no idea, but I shall know when I find it.'

Eve stepped back. The glow from the single candle was barely enough to light the area where Nick was searching so she did not attempt to help. Instead she wandered over to the window. A half-moon was rising, bathing the gardens in a silver-blue light and casting a soft gleam on the top of the map-chest. Idly she pulled open the first drawer. The moonlight illuminated a large and detailed map, but there was insufficient light to read the names. She lifted the document out of the case and held it closer to the window, but it was no use. She thought it might be a map of the Chelston estate, but the writing was too faint to read in the poor light. Eve was about to put it back when the next map in the drawer caught her eye. The outline of the coast was picked out with a bold, dark line and even in the pale moonlight she recognised it immediately.

'Nick,' she whispered, 'here is a plan of Monkhurst.'

She pulled out the map and laid it on the top of the chest as Nick crossed the room. He held up the candle and its feeble glow was just enough to show the bright colours of the map and the carefully marked place names.

'Look.' She pointed to the map. 'The River Rother, Jury's Cut and the inlet leading up to the boathouse. It is all picked out in a darker ink.'

Nick peered closer. 'Yes, but it is not primarily a map of Monkhurst. It is the neighbouring estate that is at the centre of this map.' He moved the candle slightly and peered closely at the writing. 'Abbotsfield.'

'Nick,' breathed Eve, her voice trembling with excitement. 'Aggie told me that Lady Chelston's father bought Abbotsfield from my grandfather Wingham. It might have been part of her marriage settlement.'

'In which case Chelston might be using it. This shows Abbotsfield to have a substantial portion of woodland. Perhaps we have been looking in the wrong place for Chelston's manufactory,' said Nick slowly. 'Perhaps it is not in Sussex, but in Kent!'

Eve gripped his arm. 'Earlier this evening Lord Chelston offered to buy Monkhurst from me. He offered to fund me to leave the house immediately.'

'So there might well be a connection,' said Nick. The little clock on the mantelshelf chimed repeatedly. 'Midnight,' he muttered. Carefully he placed the maps back in the drawer. 'I must get back. And you should return to your room, now. The un-masking will take place soon and it would not do for you to be found out.' He moved to the desk, checking that nothing was out of place, then he put down the candlestick and turned to take Eve by the shoulders. 'I am sorry I must let you go again so soon. I—' He froze, listening.

Eve heard footsteps and a stifled giggle outside the door. As the handle rattled she hurled herself at Nick, throwing her arms around his neck.

'Oh, we are too late—someone is here before us. A thousand apologies, madam, for intruding upon your…assignation.' Eve recognised the voice as that of the man sitting on her right during dinner. She kept her face buried against Nick's chest, thanking Providence that she was still covered from head to toe by her domino. The door clicked shut and Nick exhaled with a long, low whistle. He hugged her, giving a low laugh that rumbled against her cheek.

'Quick thinking, sweetheart.'

She leaned against him, suddenly weak. 'This is too much excitement for me,' she murmured. 'I fear I shall faint.'

His arms tightened. 'Not you, my love. You are made of sterner stuff.' He put his hand under her chin and tilted her face up. 'Admit it,' he said, his eyes glinting, 'you are enjoying this adventure.'

The familiar tug of attraction liquefied her insides. She was exhilarated, reckless. 'When I am with you…' she began.

'Yes?'

Eve closed her lips tightly. It would be madness to confide in him. 'You bewilder me,' she ended lamely.

Nick held her eyes for a moment longer, then kissed her brow. 'I wish I had time to ask what you mean by that, love, but you must go back to your room now.' He snuffed the candle and took her hand as he led the way out of the study.

The sounds of revelry coming from the hall were even louder than before. Shrieks and wild laughter echoed between the panelled walls of the dark corridor and several empty glasses had been abandoned on a narrow shelf. They approached the back stairs; grunts and sighs were coming from the darkness beyond and Eve tried not to think what might be going on there.

Nick's hand pressed in the small of her back. 'Go,' he whispered. 'Quickly.'

She turned for one last, fleeting look at him then picked up her skirts and fled.

Nick watched her run up the stairs and disappear into the darkness without one backward glance. He had seen the spark of desire in her eyes when he held her, but he had also noticed her withdrawal, her lack of trust. She was not ready to give herself to him, not yet. But she would, for he had glimpsed in her a passionate spirit to match his own and he was determined to capture it.

As he turned away from the stairs he heard heavy footsteps and voices and the butler appeared around the corner, talking to one of the regular footmen. They stopped at the sight of him.

'Now, my lad,' barked the butler, 'what do you think you are doing here?'

Nick scooped up some of the empty glasses. 'Collectin' these.'

As another dance ended and the music in the hall died away, the heavy grunts and gasps from behind the staircase could be clearly heard. Nick grinned and jerked his head in the direction of the noise. It drew an answering grin from the footman, but the butler merely scowled.

'Your place is in the saloon attending the guests, not skulking here in the passage! Get back there now. You can collect up the glasses when everyone has gone.'

Nick dipped his head. 'Aye, sir.' He slouched away, grinning to himself as he heard the butler complaining to his companion.

'Heaven help us, the mistress takes on these extra hands for what they have in their breeches rather than in their heads…'

Nick made his way downstairs to the kitchen where he found Lord Chelston's bad-tempered French cook shouting at his minions. He slipped past them and into the servants' hall where a tired-looking scullery maid was clearing the remains of the servants' dinner from the table.

'Here, let me help with that.' He began to stack up the plates. 'Do you always eat so well?'

She giggled. 'No, silly, 'tis only when there's guests that there's so much left over for us.'

'So have you worked here long?'

'Aye, since I was a nipper.'

'Then you've seen lots of balls like this one.'

The maid paused and rubbed her nose. 'None so many. But I do believe they is always having balls and parties at the house in Lunnon.'

'Oh? Is that their only other house, then?'

'Lawks, no! The master has his huntin' lodge somewhere up north, and there's another house in Devon.'

'What about Kent?' asked Nick. 'I thought I heard one of the stable lads mention property in Kent. Abbots-something.'

'You means Abbotsfield. 'Tidn't a house, though. That burned down years ago.'

Nick carried the plates through to the scullery and the maid gave him a quick, appraising glance.

'But you isn't supposed to be 'elping me, you should be upstairs, serving supper.'

'I should, I know, but I reckons there's enough of 'em up there for now. I'll go up in a minute, when we've finished clearin' the tables.'

'Well, mind you don't get the mess from the plates on yer coat,' she warned him. 'They'll knock a charge off your money for cleaning if you do.'

He grinned. 'Well then, they'll have to pay me first!'

Eve hurried up the stairs and through the empty corridors to her bedchamber. She launched herself through the door and quickly locked it after her, leaning against the heavy wooden panels, breathing heavily. A single candle burned on the mantelshelf and Martha was sitting on a stool, gazing dejectedly into the empty fireplace. When she saw her mistress she jumped up.

'Ooh, Miss Eve, thank heavens! Where have you been, and why on earth are you smiling in that way?'

'I am smiling, Martha, because I think I am having an adventure!'

Eve quickly scrabbled out of her clothes and into her nightgown. The cherry-red domino was neatly folded and returned to the linen press and Martha took away her gown to hang it with the others in the dressing room. By the time she returned, Eve was sitting at the dressing table, unpinning her hair. She resisted her maid's attempts to take the brush from her. 'Get you to bed, Martha. You must be very tired.'

'Not so tired that I cannot see you safely tucked up, Miss Eve.'

'I am quite capable of blowing out my own candle, I assure you! Off you go now; as soon as I have finished brushing my hair I shall retire, I promise you.'

However, it was long before Eve slept that night. She could not say that she was disturbed by the masquerade because very little noise reached her bedchamber, save Martha's gentle snores coming from the dressing room, but the events of the evening had left her brain racing with conjecture and there was the underlying fear that Nick had been discovered. She tossed and turned in her lonely bed, wondering where he was, what he planned to do next. It did not matter that she told herself this was a fruitless exercise, it kept her awake until the grey light of dawn crept into her room.

It was with some trepidation that she went down to breakfast the next morning but the few guests who were not sleeping off the excesses of the night before greeted her quite normally, and there was no sign that she was about to be denounced as a fraud or a spy. She asked about the ball and was told it had been an outstanding success with the last carriages rolling away soon after dawn. No one mentioned intruders posing as footmen, and the servants in attendance in the breakfast room looked as sleepy and indifferent as ever, so she could only hope that Nick's disguise had gone undetected.

It was not to be expected that the party would be very animated after such an exhausting entertainment and the day passed quietly, with Eve making sure she remained in the company of the ladies at all times. She was relieved that neither Bernard nor Lord Chelston made any attempt to single her out, but her cousin's very civil attentions during dinner tried her patience and, pleading fatigue, she fled to her room before the gentlemen joined the ladies in the drawing room.

Eve was indeed very tired after her sleepless night and she lost no time in donning her night-gown and dismissing Martha. Within minutes she was asleep, only to wake with a start some time later. The room was very dark, for her maid had closed the curtains to shut out the bright moonlight which might disturb her mistress. Eve lay still, straining every nerve to listen. She had locked the door herself, but wondered if it had been the sound of someone trying the handle that had woken her. Then she heard it again, a gentle but insistent tap-tapping on glass. For a moment she hesitated, won-dering if she should call Martha, but she decided against it. Eve slipped out of bed and padded across to the window. With her heart hammering hard against her ribs she threw back the heavy curtains.

There was no one there.

The nearly full moon sailed in a cloudless sky, bathing the gardens in its serene light. Eve threw up the sash and cool night air flooded into the room. She rested her hands upon the sill, puzzled. There was no wind, nothing to cause a loose tendril from the ivy to tap at her window.

She gasped as a hand shot out and grabbed her wrist.

'Stand back, sweetheart, and let me come in.'

Chapter Thirteen

The ivy rustled and creaked as Nick hoisted himself across and in through the open window. He was wearing soft boots, black breeches and a dark linen shirt, clothes chosen deliberately so that nothing would stand out against the ivy-covered walls. He grinned at Eve, who was staring at him, open-mouthed. His heart contracted as he looked at her. She was so appealing, standing there with her hair in a dark cloud about her shoulders. 'Well, will you not welcome me?'

She ignored his open arms. 'How did you know this was my room?'

'I saw Martha at this window when I was here yesterday. By the bye, where is Martha?'

Eve indicated the dressing room. 'She sleeps very heavily, but pray keep your voice down. Have you been here all day?'

'No, we were paid off this morning. Which reminds me, how much do we pay our servants, Evelina?'

She blinked at him. 'I—um—I do not know…'

'Well, whatever it is we must increase it. I was given a paltry sum for working here last night, and I've never worked so hard in my life. I'd rather be a raw recruit on board a man o' war than to do that again.'

Eve tried to stifle a giggle and failed. She pressed her teeth into her full bottom lip, but could not suppress an unruly dimple. Nick was enchanted. He resolved to make her laugh a great deal more in future.

'You have led too pampered a life, sir!' she told him severely.

'I am beginning to think so, too.'

'Well, never mind that. Why are you here? What have you learned?'

'In one day? Not much. Catherine inherited Abbotsfield when her father died. It would appear all the old retainers were turned off when the house burned down about five years ago and no one knows much about the place since then. I have sent someone to search the woods and report back to me.' He moved away from the window, taking care that his feet made no noise on the bare boards. 'I wanted to tell you that I have sent a couple of men to Monkhurst. They will act as your servants, but they are Revenue men and are there to protect you. I still think Chelston's schemes involve Monkhurst in some way, and I want to be sure you are safe.'

'Thank you, but you could have sent me word of that. There was no need for you to put yourself at risk by coming here.'

'But I wanted to see you. No—' he held up his hand. 'Don't move.'

'Why not? What is wrong?'

'Your nightgown.'

'What about it? It is a very fine nightgown.'

'I know, sweetheart. With the moonlight behind you I can see every line of your body.' And a very shapely body it was, long legs tapering down from the swell of her hips and above that the narrow waist that seemed to beg for his hands to span it. He remembered how she had stood before the window on their wedding night. It had been his undoing. With a gasp she stepped quickly out of the moonlight and Nick laughed softly.

'You are no gentleman!' she hissed.

He reached out and pulled her to him. The feel of her body against his brought an instant reaction.

'If I were not a gentleman I would carry you to that bed and ravish you!'

He must not rush her, but he could not resist pressing just one kiss on her neck, where the lacy edge of her nightgown had slipped off her shoulder.

'That would be the action of a true scoundrel!'

Reluctantly he raised his head. 'I know,' he agreed mournfully. 'And I have vowed I shall not impose myself upon you.'

She put her hands against his chest and his heart thudded, as if trying to reach her. She tilted her face up, her lips parting to form a very inviting O of surprise. His arms tightened and the next moment he was kissing her, slowly, sensuously. For a brief, exultant moment she responded, then he felt her struggle and push against him.

'No,' she hissed, turning her head away. 'I will *not* give in to you, Nick Wylder!'

She tried to pull away from him but he caught her wrist, saying impatiently, 'By God, woman you are *my wife*!'

Her head went up. Even in the moonlight he could see the haughty flash of her eyes. 'You forfeited any rights you had when you deceived me,' she said, her voice vibrating with fury.

His head snapped back as if she had struck

him. Nick looked at the tightly-coiled bundle of pride and passion standing before him and for the first time in his adult life he was afraid of doing the wrong thing. Pure, animal instinct told him to take her, to kiss her into submission. He knew he could do it, he had sensed the passion within her, had tasted it in her kiss moments before. But something held him back, warned him that passion might win her body, but it would not win her trust.

Eve trembled. In her head she was determined to fight him, but every nerve of her body strained with desire. If he ignored her protests and dragged her into his arms, she knew her defences would crumble almost immediately for her heart was crying out for him to hold her, to make love to her. She kept her head up and met his gaze defiantly. 'I think you should go now.' She marvelled at how steady her voice was when inside she was burning up.

'Yes,' he said, releasing her wrist. 'I think I should.' Nick saw the flicker of surprise in her eyes and smiled, knowing he had made the right choice. 'I do not consider that I have any— *rights*—over you, sweetheart. Neither do I want you to give in to me. You are my wife, my partner.

We will meet as equals, you and I. Or not at all.'
He flicked a careless finger across her cheek and
slipped back out of the window.

Eve stood looking at the space where he had
been. She told herself she was relieved, but there
was also a vague sense of disappointment that he
had given way so easily. Perversely she was not
at all sure it was what she wanted. She ran to the
window and leaned out. Nick was little more
than a dark shadow amongst the bushes. His
words echoed in her head: *my wife, my partner.*
We will meet as equals, you and I. Equals. Could
he really mean that?

As she peered down he stepped out into the
moonlight and raised his hand to blow her a kiss.

Two days later Eve was back at Monkhurst.
Lord and Lady Chelston had been reluctant to let
her go, but she had stood firm, declaring that she
must attend to her estate. Richard Granby was
clearly relieved to see her safely returned and lost
no time in presenting to her Davies and Warren,
the two men Nick had sent to protect her. They
bowed to her and declared themselves happy
enough to help Granby around the house.

'We thought it best to keep it quiet that we are

with the Revenue,' grinned Davies. 'The people hereabouts are none too fond of us.'

Eve nodded. 'Then we shall just say that I asked Mr Granby to bring in extra staff. There should be no surprise at that; there is a deal to be done.'

However, Eve was surprised at Silas's reaction to the news.

'If you thinks I'm too old, missus, then just say so,' he told her when they met in the gardens later that day. Eve tried to be patient.

'You are not too old at all, Silas. But we can use the extra help, and it is always useful to have a few more men around the house.'

'What's wrong with Sam and Nat? They'll protect you, if that's your worry.'

'They are very useful, and have made a big difference already to the gardens, but they have families of their own to look after in the village, and cannot be at Monkhurst day and night. Pray do not be offended, Silas.'

'Well I don't see how you needs anyone else,' he grumbled. 'Especially when they're not Kentish men.'

'Perhaps you are right, but Granby did what he thought best. And they will be very useful in turning out the last few rooms for me.'

* * *

Eve was determined to continue with her plans for making Monkhurst into a comfortable home, but after the excitement of her visit to Chelston Hall, life at the old house seemed sadly flat. There was no news from Nick, but that did not surprise her; he was born for adventure, not the day-to-day domesticity that comprised her own life. Her depression deepened; she was far too ordinary to satisfy the dashing Captain Wyldfire for very long. She blinked back a tear. True, she was his wife and he would come to her occasionally, when he needed to rest, or perhaps—the thought turned her insides to water—when he wanted her body, but then he would be off again, seeking excitement. Well, thought Eve, if that was how it must be then she would not complain. To have such a man, even for a short time, was as much as she could hope for. She would not pine.

To keep herself from moping, Eve threw herself into the role of housewife, but this served only to highlight how humdrum her life was compared with the unimaginable dangers Nick was facing. The only drama at Monkhurst was provided by Silas, who fell off a ladder in the barn and cracked open his head.

'He should never have been on that ladder in the first place,' declared Aggie, bustling around the kitchen. 'Sam told 'im he would do it, only he was that determined to prove that he was every bit as good as these new lads you brought in, that he would go up.'

'Oh dear, poor Silas. Is it very bad?'

'Well, he can't see straight for the present, besides bein' sick as a dog, so he won't be able to—' Aggie closed her lips and shook her head before saying with a sigh, 'But don't you be worrying, Miss Eve, we shall manage.'

'Perhaps you would like to go back to Silas now,' suggested Eve. 'Martha and I will do very well with a cold dinner.'

'You will do no such thing, mistress. Why I never heard of such a thing! Silas has young Nat to look in on him during the day and I shall cook your dinner as I always do, so let's not hear any more about it!'

Eve hurriedly begged pardon and left her affronted housekeeper to her work.

She thought no more about it until Martha came in tutting because Aggie had left her basket by the back door. It was after dinner and Eve was in the drawing room, sitting by the window and making the most of the remaining daylight to work on her embroidery.

'Full of pies it is, too, Miss Eve,' said the maid, carrying a lighted taper to each of the candles. 'I hope Silas wasn't expectin' them for his supper.'

'Poor Aggie was looking very harassed today,' remarked Eve. 'She was in a hurry to get away, too.' She put aside her embroidery and looked out of the window at the golden sunset. 'Do you know, it is such a lovely evening that I would like to take a walk, so I will carry Aggie's basket to the Gate House. It will save her walking back for it.'

'Well, you can't go out alone in the dark. I'll fetch Davies to go with you.'

'There really is no need…' Eve began, but Martha's look silenced her. Meekly, she collected her shawl and set off towards the Gate House with Davies for company. It irked her to have someone dogging her every footstep, but she realised the necessity of it and smiled at the man. After all, it was not his fault that he had been ordered to protect her. Most likely he would prefer to be off chasing smugglers rather than walking behind her.

There was a lamp burning in the window, but when she knocked on the door it was a long time before there was any response, and then it was only Aggie's rather nervous 'Who's there?' from within.

'It is only me,' Eve called cheerfully. 'I have brought your basket. You left it in the kitchen.' The door opened a crack. 'Well, Aggie, will you not invite me in?'

Aggie peered out into the gloom.

'Aye, mistress, but your man must wait outside.'

'What is the matter, Aggie? Are you in your nightgown with your hair in rags?' Eve chuckled as she slipped in through the door but her smile was replaced by a look of surprise when she saw Aggie wearing one of Silas's smocks and a pair of baggy trousers. 'What on earth—?'

'There's a run tonight, and as Silas can't go I shall have to,' explained Aggie, looking anxious. She ran a hand over one leg of the trousers. 'These sailor's slops fits me better nor most of Silas's clothes.'

'Surely this cannot be necessary.'

Aggie's mouth pursed. 'Do you think I'd be going if it wasn't? There's not enough boys to go out tonight as it is, and without Silas they'll be short of hands. I'm waiting now for Nat to call for me.'

'You must not go,' said Eve, setting down her basket.

'That's just what I bin tellin' her,' said Silas, appearing at the door. 'I'll be fine as soon as I gets me sea-legs.'

He swayed as he spoke. Aggie and Eve both rushed to take his arms and help him to his chair.

'You ain't goin' nowhere,' Aggie told him crossly. 'You'd be a danger to yourself and to the boys.'

'She's right, I'm afraid, Silas,' said Eve.

Silas hunched in his chair, scowling. Eve took the older woman's shoulders and looked into her face. 'Why is it so important to go out tonight, Aggie?'

'It's the last run. You will remember, miss, that Silas promised they would do no more once the orders was filled, but John the waggoner and his son are gone off to Ashurst and we daren't wait for their return, because the moon's on the wane. It has to be tonight.'

'But there must be other men in the village.'

Aggie shook her head. 'Since Sam and Nat had the run-in with that other gang, the village lads is afeard to go out. So with Silas laid up they're too short-handed.'

'Well, you cannot go,' said Eve decidedly. She

stood for a moment, tapping her foot. 'What time do you expect Nathaniel here?'

'Soon as it's properly dark.'

'Then I have half an hour. I can be back by then.'

Silas looked up. 'What d'you mean, mistress?'

'Miss Eve, what are you going to do?' demanded Aggie suspiciously.

Eve turned, her eyes shining with mischief. 'Why, go in your place, of course!'

Eve hurried back to the house, dismissed her escort and ran lightly up the stairs to her bed-chamber, calling for Martha as she went. By the time the maid arrived Eve had pulled a selection of clothes from the trunk at the bottom of the bed. 'Quickly, Martha; help me out of this gown.'

'Whatever are you about now, mistress?'

'You must not ask me,' replied Eve. She was unable to keep the excitement from her voice, nor could she resist confiding in her maid, 'I am going out.'

'You never are, madam!'

'Yes, I am.' Eve stepped out of her skirts and reached for the soft leather breeches. 'But you are not to tell anyone.'

'Heavens to mercy! You cannot be going out in those!'

'I am. I only hope Mama's clothes fit me…they do, thank goodness!'

'Miss Eve—' Martha put her hands to her mouth. 'You're never goin' out with the traders?' She collapsed on to the bed. 'Oh, gracious heart-alive!'

'Hush, Martha. Now where is the shirt—? Oh, and my hair, I cannot possibly wear it like this. Quick, now, remove the pins and I'll tie it back…there, what do you think?'

'I think it is a dreadful idea, Miss Eve, and I cannot let you go!'

'If you try to stop me, I shall turn you off,' retorted Eve, giving Martha such a fierce look that the maid went pale.

'You wouldn't,' she whispered.

'Of course not, as long as you do as I bid you.'

'But what would the master say!'

'The master is not here,' replied Eve. 'And if he was, it is just the sort of thing he would do.'

Eve clapped the battered tricorn hat upon her head and stared at herself in the mirror. In the flickering candlelight a stranger stared back at her. The tricorn shaded her eyes, leaving only the mouth and chin visible, and if Eve considered these far too dainty for a man, she thought that at least she could not be recognised. The breeches were close-fitting, but thankfully she could still move in them, and the shirt billowed out from her shoulders, adequately disguising her form. 'It will have to do,' she said, dragging on the dark woollen jacket.

'You need a muffler around your neck,' said Martha. 'You must make sure every bit of that shirt is covered and your face, too; your pale skin will show up bright as day under this moon.'

'Martha, how do you know about such things?'

'You can't live in these parts without knowing something of the trade,' retorted the maid. 'But oh, Miss Eve, I wish you would not go.'

'I have to, Martha. They are my people out there and they need me.' She drew herself up as she said these words, a *frisson* of pride threading through her excitement. She kissed her maid. 'Now, you had best come down and lock the door after me. And remember, tell no one I am gone!'

Eve slipped out of the kitchen door and stopped for a moment, listening until she heard Martha slide the bolts back into position, then she ran silently through the garden and across the park to the Gate House. The moon that had been so full during her visit to Chelston Hall was no more than a sliver, giving barely enough light for her to find her way and she guessed that anyone watching would see little more than a shadow flitting between the trees. She arrived, breathless, at the Gate House and scratched at the door.

'Miss Eve, I cannot like this,' muttered Aggie as she let her into the house. She led the way through to the little kitchen, where Nathanial was waiting, twisting his cap in his hands. His mouth gaped when the saw her in her coat and breeches. Eve merely nodded at him.

'Good evening, Nat, I see you are wearing a smock, too—must I wear one?'

'The boys all do, mistress,' said Aggie. 'It's common garb here on the Marsh. That way the ridin' officers can't tell one from t'other.'

'Then I should put it on, I suppose. Help me, Aggie. There.' She grinned at them. 'Well, will I do?'

'Nay, mistress.' Nathanial cast an anguished look towards his mother.

Eve's grin disappeared. 'For heavens' sake, Nathanial! Would you rather it was your mother out on the marshes with you? I can handle the ponies as well as Silas—' she paused, then added with a touch of irrepressible humour, 'and run a great deal faster, if necessary.'

'I'd rather it was neither of you,' mumbled Nat.

'Now that is very uncharitable.'

'Well you mun promise to do just as I say,' he retorted, gaining a little courage.

'Of course I will.' He did not look very reassured by her assertion and she put her hand on his arm, saying gently, 'I have no wish to ruin your last run, Nathanial, but Aggie says you need an extra pair of hands, and I am offering you mine.'

Nathanial frowned at her for a long moment, then he seemed to make up his mind. He straightened. 'Well then,' he said, 'Let us be off.'

They walked for a mile or so along the shadowy lane until they reached a crossroads, where Nathanial gave a low whistle. At first, Eve could hear no sound on the still air, but after a few moments there was the faint clop of hoofbeats. Black shapes appeared, a line of ponies led by a stocky figure, his face a pale disc in the moonlight.

'Gabriel.' Nathanial's murmured greeting received only a grunt in reply, but there must have been some whispered question about her presence for she heard Nathanial say, 'Oh, he's my cousin's boy, from Tenterden-way.'

The man called Gabriel peered in her direction,

Eve lowered her head so that the brim of her hat shadowed her face.

He grunted again.

'And Robert and Adam?' muttered Nathaniel.

Gabriel jerked his head. 'Bob's 'ere. Adam's comin' in on the galley with Sam. That's all the help we could muster this night.' Gabriel beckoned to them to follow him.

For the next few hours Eve found herself in a dark, alien world where familiar objects such as houses or trees loomed black and menacing around them. All her senses were heightened, every nerve alert to pick up the merest hint of danger. She strained her eyes to see through the near-darkness, and once she grabbed at Nathanial's arm. 'Look!' she hissed, pointing. 'A light over there!'

The pack stopped and for a moment there was a tense silence. Then she heard Nat's low rumbling laugh. 'It's nought but a shiney bug. You've seen they before, surelye.'

Eve was aware of the grins of the other men and she hastily begged pardon, hunched her shoulders and walked on, berating herself for allowing her nerves to get the better of her.

* * *

'Come up, Admiral.'

Nick touched his heels to the horse's glossy sides and the animal responded immediately. Soon they were moving through the lanes at a steady canter. There was no time to lose, but to press Admiral to go too fast across the dark, unfamiliar territory was to risk a fall at best, and a broken neck at worst, neither of which would help his cause. He had learned only an hour ago that Captain George had received word of a run tonight at Jury's Cut. Privately, Nick had no doubt that it would be Silas and the boys, but although he argued strongly that these could not be Chelston's men, the Revenue officer knew his duty. He could not ignore the report and had despatched a party of riding officers to apprehend the smugglers. Nick was powerless to stop them. His only hope was to reach Silas in time and warn him.

The pale moonlight illuminated a stretch of flat, clear ground and he pushed Admiral on to a gallop. He could have found someone to carry the message for him, someone who knew the area better than he, but at the back of his mind was the thought that once he had discharged his errand he might call at Monkhurst. He laughed out loud, causing Admiral to throw up his head, nervously breaking his stride. 'Fool, it will be gone midnight by the time you get there,' he muttered to himself. No matter. He would wait until dawn, creep into her room and be there when she awoke.

He thought of Eve as he had last seen her at Chelston Hall, warm and drowsy with sleep, her hair tumbled over her shoulders. Damnation, just the thought of it made him hot for her! He eased himself in the saddle. Better not even to think of Eve until he had delivered his message.

He pushed on, cantering past Monkhurst village and through the leafy lanes until the Gate House was in view. He judged it was gone midnight and Silas might already have set off. Suddenly he was aware of a movement to his left. He pulled Admiral to a halt in the shadow of the trees and peered into the darkness.

'Richard!' His call brought the figure to a stop. Nick walked his horse forward. 'Richard? What are you doing here?'

'It's Mrs Wylder, sir.' Granby ran towards him. For once he had lost his imperturbable calm. Fear chilled Nick's bones. He said tersely,

'Well, man?'

'She's gone off with Nat and Sam to Jury's Cut!'

Chapter Fourteen

Eve had no idea how long they walked in the near-darkness. Their progress was silent save for the gentle clip-clop of the ponies and the creak of leather harness. Eve wanted to ask Nathanial where they were going, but she was afraid to speak and break the hush that lay over them like a palpable blanket, so she merely walked, striding out in her mother's old leather boots. It was a still night and only the lightest of breezes stirred the leaves. The steady walking gave her far too much time to think of Nick, and the darkness in her mind was even thicker and more engrossing that the night. She knew now that she loved him, but although she knew he wanted her she thought that his passion for her was cooling. What else could explain the way he had accepted her rebuttal at Chelston Hall? Twice now she had refused him and twice he had walked away. She was very much afraid that he no longer found her attractive. In fact, she thought miserably, he must be regretting ever having married her.

And did she regret Nick coming into her life and dragging her out of her cosy little world? *If I had not met him, I would not have disguised myself and searched Lord Chelston's office. Nor would I now be walking through the near-darkness to collect a cargo of contraband.* Even as the words formed in her head, Eve realised with a little jolt of surprise that she would have been very sorry to miss the visit to Chelston Hall and, in a strange way, she was even enjoying being out on the Marsh in the middle of the night.

Eventually they left the houses and farms behind and the lane was no longer shadowed by high hedges. Instead deep ditches lined the causeway and the land stretched away on either side, a vast, flat expanse of marshland where the faint, salty breeze whispered through the rushes.

Eve could smell the sea and make out the line of sand dunes that rose up to meet the midnight-blue sky in the distance. A few yards away a narrow channel of water wound like a pewter ribbon through the Marsh towards the inlet known as Jury's Cut. Eve could feel the tension in her companions now: this was where Nathanial and Sam had been attacked and she looked about her nervously, her body tense and ready for flight.

Suddenly Nathanial stopped. The ponies came to a stand, blowing gently. Eve heard a short, low whistle and a quiet splash of oars. A long, low boat nosed its way between the rushes. Several figures leaped out and pulled the hull up on to more solid ground.

The men worked quickly and silently to unload the boat. Nathanial pulled Eve into line and she found herself part of a human chain, passing goods hand to hand from ship to shore. Her arms began to ache and soon she was uncomfortably warm in her smock and heavy coat, but she dare not remove them, nor unwind the concealing muffler from the lower part of her face. She realised now why they needed more men. There was some distance between the boat and the causeway where the ponies waited patiently to be loaded. When goods were passed she had to reach out to take each packet and stretch to pass it on to her neighbour. The bundles wrapped in oilcloth were weighty enough, but the half-ankers, the small barrels holding the brandy, were so heavy she had to take a step each time to complete the operation.

At last the final barrel had been strapped to a pony and the last packet of lace tucked away in a pannier. Eve eased her aching back and watched as half the men pushed the galley off the mud and began to row away, the oars dipping almost silently into the grey waters. A touch on her arm told her that they were ready to move off and she clambered back to the causeway where the ponies were already beginning the trek back inland. She tugged at Nathanial's sleeve. 'The last pony carries no pack,' she whispered.

Nat grinned, his teeth gleaming briefly in the pale light. 'We always keep one saddled and ready. In case.'

'In case of what?'

'Just in case.'

He put his hand to his lips and strode ahead. Eve followed on, puzzled and determined to demand an explanation as soon as they were safe.

The crescent moon hung low in the sky by the time the first farm came into sight, a black outline in the distance. Eve realised how tense she had become and made a conscious effort to relax her shoulders. Soon they would reach the comparative shelter of the tree-lined lanes again. She was about to say as much to Nathanial when there was a warning growl from the head of the line.

'Riding officers. Run!'

The ponies began to trot, their packs creaking ominously.

'Where are they?' muttered Eve, peering into the darkness.

Nathanial raised his hand and pointed. 'Between the barns over there.'

Eve only had time for one swift look. The blackness between the tall square outlines of buildings was shifting and moving. Riders, and they were coming swiftly towards them. When they realised their quarry had spotted them, the riders abandoned their stealthy progress and shouted, their cries carrying on the night air.

'Stop, in the name of the King!'

Nathaniel pushed Eve before him. 'Run.'

The little ponies moved with surprising speed and Eve followed, her heart pounding. The road snaked between deep drains and on one corner stood a small copse of stunted trees, which screened their flight from the pursuing riders. A sudden slackening of the ponies' pace made Eve look up. At the head of the line, Sam was leading the ponies off the road and into the ditch. She gasped, expecting the animals to plunge into deep water, but they merely dipped a few inches before disappearing into the shadows on the far side of the drain.

'Where are they going?' she asked Nathanial as one by one the ponies were swallowed up in the darkness.

'Sunken causeway,' he replied. 'Once the fence and reeds are in place no one can see us.' She heard him chuckle. 'We've been doing this, man and boy, for so long that we're experts at fooling the Revenue.'

As they trotted to the edge of the drain, Nathaniel untied the final pony and held him back while the others splashed across the ditch and into the darkness.

'Come along, Miss Eve,' called Sam with no attempt to hide her identity. 'The water's only ankle-deep.'

She hesitated. 'What about Nathaniel?'

'I'm going to draw them off.'

'But isn't that dangerous in the dark?' she asked.

'No, these ponies know their way,' said Nat. 'Better'n the Revenue men anyway.'

'Miss Eve, come *on*!' Sam was already pulling the reed-covered panels into place.

'Then let me go.'

'No, by heaven!' exclaimed Nat, revolted.

Eve put her hand out and took the reins. 'You must,' she insisted. 'I'm lighter than you and can make better time. And do not worry, I will find my way home.'

Nathanial gasped as she pushed past him and scrambled into the saddle. He reached up as if to pull her from the pony, then stopped, unable to bring himself to lay hands upon a lady.

'No, Miss Eve, 'tain't proper! What would the master say?'

'What would Aggie say if you were caught?' she countered. 'You and Sam have your families to think of. They need you.' *There is no one to miss me.* She pushed aside the unspoken thought and said briskly, 'Quick, now, they will be here any minute.'

'Mistress, please!'

'Go. We shall all be caught if you do not go now!'

Nathanial hesitated for another moment, until Sam's urgent hiss reminded him of the danger. He splashed through the water and helped Sam to put the final panels into place. Then there was silence.

The water in the drain grew calm again, mirroring the starry sky. Eve looked at the high wall of reeds; there was no sign of an opening. She stood up in the stirrups, but could see nothing more than the reed tops, rippling and whispering in the breeze. The pony stamped impatiently, but she held him still, curbing her own impatience to be moving as she looked back for her first sight of the Revenue men. She did not have long to wait. A rumble like distant thunder grew steadily louder, and as the first rider appeared round the bend she dug her heels into the pony's flanks and set off at a gallop. Shouts from her pursuers told her she had been seen. The race was on.

The track was a grey ribbon in front of her, occasionally disappearing into darkness where trees threw their black shadows across the path. Her capacious smock billowed around her as the little pony flew over the ground. Eve marvelled at his sure-footed flight, but drew on the reins, steadying the headlong pace; she must not lose her pursuers too soon. Ahead lay the outline of a jumble of buildings; a village or farm, Eve could not tell, but she knew that as they moved inland there would be more buildings and more roads where she might slip out of sight and escape. Through the gloom she could see that the road turned sharply to the left beside a large wall. Eve risked a glance over her shoulder. She still had a good lead, but it could not last; the pursuing horses were covering the ground much quicker than her little pony.

She leaned into the corner, pulling her mount round, but as she straightened up and settled into the saddle again she was aware of a black shape breaking away from the shadows behind her. Alarmed, she dropped her hands and leaned forwards over the pony's neck, allowing him his head. The lane was flanked by tall trees and they were galloping in and out of the shadows. The wind was in her face, tugging at the wide brim of her hat. She dare not lift a hand from the reins and moments later it flew off behind her. Eve pressed on at a gallop, praying there were no obstacles or deep holes in the path. They were flying through the darkness, but she could hear the drumming of other hoofbeats. Someone was close on her tail. Eve dug in her heels, her heart hammering against her ribs. The little pony pressed on courageously, but the thunder behind her was growing louder. The next moment a wild-eyed horse was alongside her, foam flecking its mouth. Panic jolted through her and for one heart-stopping moment she imagined the devil was at her side. A black shape loomed, Eve screamed as the rider leaned over, grabbed her around the waist and lifted her bodily from the saddle.

'Release the reins, sweetheart.'

The shock of hearing Nick's voice almost sent her into a swoon. The reins fell from her nerveless fingers as he pulled her up in front of him. The riderless pony galloped away and Nick slowed his horse, swerving off the road into the deep shadow of a high wall.

'Quiet now.'

His warning was unnecessary. Eve could not have spoken even had she wished to. She watched the pony racing along the road and minutes later a dozen riders thundered past in hot and deadly pursuit.

They remained in the shadows, still and silent until the riders had disappeared into the darkness. The thunder died away and was replaced by the quiet whisper of the salt winds through the trees.

'With any luck they'll be following that little fellow until the morning.' Eve heard the words, felt Nick's breath warm on her cheek. She wanted to pinch herself, to make sure this was not a dream. He spoke again. 'Where are the others?'

'Safe, I hope. They took the hidden causeway.'

'Ah. Then they will be able to evade the Revenue men. Time to get you back to Monkhurst, I think.'

Eve clutched at him as the horse began to

move forwards. His arms tightened around her, holding her fast.

'How did you know?' she murmured, breathing in the familiar smell of his closeness, soap and spices and a male muskiness that made her close her eyes and inhale again.

'The officers received word that there was a drop tonight. I rode over to warn Silas, but I was too late. Thankfully so were the Revenue men. Hush now; let me see if I can find my way back to Monkhurst. I would be much more at home on the water than on these winding lanes.'

Eve settled herself more comfortably against him and wrapped her arms around his body, being careful to keep her grip well above the wound in his side. Admiral moved over the ground in a long, loping stride and she tried to relax, to sway with the movement of horse and rider. Her whole body was still buzzing with the excitement of the chase, the blood was singing in her veins. Was this how her mother had felt when she had gone out with the free-traders? Was this how Nick felt when he was engaged in some dangerous adventure? She hugged the question to her as they rode through the darkness, the rough wool of Nick's coat against her cheek, his arms enclosing her, holding her safe.

Nick settled Admiral into an easy canter and stared ahead into the near-darkness. The sliver of moon was low in the sky and the tall trees cast inky shadows on the road. He was very conscious of Eve's slim form leaning against him; wisps of her hair had escaped their ribbon and tickled his chin. He turned his head briefly to rest his cheek upon her tangled locks, relieved to have her safe within his arms. He had been surprised when Richard had told him that Eve had taken Silas's place with the boys. At first he had been far too intent upon racing after her to dwell on the danger, but gradually fear had crept into his mind, fear unlike anything he had experienced before. He knew the Revenue officers, they were good men, but ill disciplined and God knew they had no cause to love the free-traders. If they had captured Eve, there was no telling what they might have done to her when their blood was up. Now, with her soft body resting against his, he had nothing to do but to think of what might have happened if he had not seen her racing towards him, if he had not been in time to rescue her. The heady relief of finding her safe diminished and was replaced by an ice-cold chill as his imagination ran wild.

* * *

Admiral clattered into the stable block at Monkhurst. A sleepy groom fumbled with a lantern, but Nick did not wait. He lowered Eve to the ground, then jumped down and thrust the reins at the bewildered boy. 'Don't unsaddle him,' he barked. 'I will be leaving again shortly.' He took Eve's arm in a painfully tight grip and marched her towards the house. Granby opened a side door as they approached.

'I was looking out for you,' he said quietly. 'I'm glad to see you back safely, Miss Eve. If you would like to go to the morning room, Martha has built up a fire in there for you.'

Nick gave her no time to reply; he almost dragged her along the dark passageway and into the little room off the great hall, where they found the maid waiting for them, her hands twisting nervously in her apron.

'Oh Miss Eve, thank heaven—' Martha broke off, eyes widening in surprise. 'Captain Wylder! I didn't think you knew of this.'

'I didn't.'

'Yes, and why was Granby waiting for us?' asked Eve, shaking off Nick's hand. 'Did you tell him, Martha?'

The maid bowed her head. 'I did, miss. I'm sorry, I know you said not to tell anyone, but I was that worried!'

Nick stood by the door, holding it open. 'Leave us, please.'

The maid's face was alive with curiosity, but Nick merely stared at her and without a word she bobbed a curtsy and scurried away.

'Poor Martha is agog,' remarked Eve, tugging off her gloves. 'She will not rest until I have told her everything.' She looked up at him, her face alight with laughter. The rage that had been growing inside Nick during their moonlight ride now boiled over.

'Of all the crack-brained starts! Whatever possessed you to be so foolish?'

She blinked. 'I beg your pardon?'

'Did you think it a good jest, to play at smuggling? Do you not realise how deadly serious it is?'

'Of course I realise it! That is why I wanted to help them. Silas had promised me this would be the last run they would do, but they could not let their people down.'

'Did you not stop to think about the risks you were taking? That you would be putting them all in jeopardy with your inexperience?'

She smiled. 'What experience does it need to follow a pack-pony, and to shift half-ankers from the boats?' She rubbed her arms. 'I think I did quite well.'

Her calm response only enraged him further.

'I credited you with more sense than to risk your reputation, your life even, going out with the Brattee boys.'

'They were short-handed. Silas must have told you—'

'Aye, he told me, but do you really think your presence made that much difference?'

'Yes, I do! The chain was stretched enough as it was, and you know that the risks are greatest during the unloading! It has to be done quickly.' She stared at him. 'You are really angry with me.'

'Of course I am angry!' He advanced upon her and before she knew what he was about he had wrenched the linen smock up over her head and dragged it off. 'The others might be able to put this on and pass for simple farm workers, but not you! Think what would have happened if you had been caught.' He bundled the offending cloth into a ball and hurled it into the corner of the room. 'How dare you do such a thing!'

Eve frowned. A shadow of uncertainty clouded

her eyes. 'These are my people. I must help them where I can.'

His hands slammed on the table, making her jump. 'Do you think it would help them if you were to be clapped in gaol? Damned idiotic idea. And with Revenue officers in the house, too! How the hell do you think it would have looked if they had discovered what you were up to? Damnation, you are my wife!'

'I am your *widow*!' She drew herself up, her lip curling. 'You made me thus, and I have no wish to be anything else to you—ever!'

Eve dashed away a tear. This was no time to show weakness, especially to Nick. She had ridden back to Monkhurst in a mood of elation, relieved that the others had escaped, pleased with her own part in it. Nick's fury was like a bucket of ice-cold water, but her nerves were still tingling with excitement and anger swept through her; she would not be cowed by his irrational rage. He took a step towards her and she moved away, making sure the solid oak table was between them.

'And what makes it so different for you?' she flung at him. 'You have been engaged on far more dangerous enterprises.'

'That is different. I risk being injured, killed perhaps, but you, if they caught you—'

She slammed her own hands down on the table. 'Do you think my anxiety is any less, when I am left here to imagine what might be happening to you? Not that I care any more,' she added quickly. 'I have no wish to be deceived by you again. In fact, I shall be much happier without you.'

'Evelina—'

'I do not think you can have anything more to say to me.' She folded her arms and glared at him. 'Make sure Granby locks the door behind you.'

Nick was like a statue, looking at her from under his black brows. She forced herself to meet his eyes, hoping hers were showing nothing more than scorn and disdain. The silence was unnerving. Anger held her body rigid. She would not yield. Finally, after what seemed like an hour, but she knew could be only a few moments, Nick turned on his heel and strode out, slamming the door behind him.

All the anger and excitement in Eve drained away. Trembling, she sank down into a chair and dropped her head in her hands. She knew he did not love her, but she had been foolish enough to hope that he might like her better now she had shown him she had some spirit. He did not. It was not at all what he wanted and now she had lost him completely.

Nick had stormed out of the house, managing only a curt word for Richard as he strode past him. He had collected Admiral and was a mile away from Monkhurst before he even realised it.

I am your widow. I have no wish to be anything else to you.

Eve's words had hit Nick like a physical blow, winding him. She did not trust him, did not realise that his anger was born out of anxiety. He had never been afraid for himself, but the idea that the fragile little woman he had married might be in danger had almost driven him out of his wits.

You should have told her that. You should tell her you love her.

This blinding revelation jolted through him. He jerked on the reins and obediently Admiral halted. *Did* he love her? He had always enjoyed his en-counters with women, but he had never loved any of them. He had thought that love, when it came, would be a warm, comfortable feeling. What he felt for Eve was far from comfortable. It was a mixture of joy, desperate desire and anxiety. He was afraid for her, afraid she might be in danger, that she might be unhappy.

And for himself there was the dark, terrifying prospect of life without her.

He turned his horse. He would go back, explain it all, suggest that they should start afresh. A few yards on he stopped again. The first fingers of dawn were pushing into the sky. Eve would be asleep. She would not thank him for waking her when she had already been up for most of the night. Besides, he could offer her nothing until the business with Chelston was resolved. Better to wait. When all this was over he could woo her properly. He turned once more.

'Easy, Admiral,' he muttered as the horse snorted in disapproval. 'You think your master is an old fool, don't you?' He sighed. 'Well, mayhap you are right.'

Chapter Fifteen

Eve dragged herself through her morning duties. Her body ached from the unaccustomed activity of the night and there was a bleak heaviness within her as though some spark of hope had finally been quenched. It would pass, of course, but for the moment she felt desperately lonely. She knew a sudden, searing moment of agony as she thought of her grandfather. How she missed him and the quiet, peaceful life they had shared. How she wished he had never invited Nick Wylder to Makerham!

The thought of Nick brought her back to the events of the previous night. Nick's fury at her going out with Nat and Sam had hurt her deeply, all the more so because she had thought he would share her exhilaration. The heady excitement she had felt during the chase was intoxicating. She had wanted to explain that to Nick, to let him know that she understood now why he thrived on danger. But instead of catching her up in his arms and making love to her he had berated her, turning her adventure into a foolhardy scrape, causing nothing but trouble. The thought made her eyes sting and she blinked away her tears. She would not cry. It had all ended well; there had been word from Sam that everyone was safe and that was all that mattered.

'Pardon me, madam, there is a note for you.'

Granby approached, holding out a letter. Eve took it, but had to blink several times before the words stopped swimming before her eyes.

'It is from Catherine Chelston,' she said. 'She says that she is even now on her way here, determined to carry me off to Appledore to see the new muslins that have just arrived at Mrs Jameson's.' She refolded the note. 'I will not see her.'

'There will be some plan afoot,' murmured Granby. 'It would be interesting to know what it might be.'

'Interesting for you and your master, perhaps,' snapped Eve.

'I beg your pardon, madam.'

She rubbed her brow. 'No, it is I who must

apologise, Richard. I am very tired, and have no heart for these games.'

'But, madam, the captain would—'

'No!' she exclaimed. 'After the rating I received last night I want nothing further to do with any of this. You may see Lady Chelston if you wish; after all someone must ride out to meet her, to tell her I will not go!'

She turned on her heel and swept away, leaving Granby to stare after her.

The day dragged by and after a solitary dinner Eve retired to her room, telling herself that everything would seem brighter after a good night's sleep. Eve guessed that Granby had told Martha of her outburst, for the maid was determinedly cheerful and bustled about the chamber lighting the candles and talking all the while, as though afraid of silence. Eve allowed herself to be undressed and coaxed into her silk wrap, then she sat quietly upon the stool in front of her mirror while Martha brushed out her hair with long steady strokes. The rhythm was soothing and some of the tension went out of her shoulders. Martha met her eyes in the mirror and smiled.

'There, Miss Eve, is that better? It's no wonder you are so tired, being out of doors until dawn! It's all Aggie can talk of, you goin' out on a run, just like your sainted mother. Well, that and the fact that the captain is alive. I must say I'm relieved that I don't have to watch my words with her any more. She and Silas are that pleased you'd think he was one of their own. Of course the captain told 'em not to spread it abroad, but he did say they could tell Nat and Sam, since they can all hold their tongues—'

'And I wish that you would do just that, Martha!' Eve dropped her head in her hands. Everyone wanted to talk of the captain, when all she wanted to do was to forget all about him. Before she could apologise for her incivility, Martha was patting her shoulder.

'Ah, my poor lamb! There I am, talking nineteen to the dozen, and I've no doubt at all that your head is aching. Well, my dearie, what you need is something to soothe you off to sleep. What say you to a cup of warm milk?'

'Thank you Martha, I would like that. If it's not too much trouble.'

'No, madam. The kitchen fire will still be warm enough to heat up a pan, I'm sure. You just slip into bed and I'll be back upstairs directly.'

She bustled away, but Eve remained on the

stool, staring disconsolately at her reflection. She should plait her hair, she thought. It would prevent tangles in the morning, but it seemed too much effort. Perhaps she would ask Martha to do it when she returned.

She heard a light step on the landing, the click of the latch as the door opened and closed again. She expected to hear Martha's breezy chatter, but there was nothing, only a continuing silence. Eve turned. Nick was standing just inside the room, his greatcoat hanging open and swinging slightly, as if he had been moving quickly only moments before. He regarded her intently, his eyes shadowed.

'I was frightened for you,' he said abruptly. 'Last night. Men can turn into animals in the heat of battle. That's why I was angry. I know what can happen if they find a woman. And riding officers are not all gentlemen.'

'But they did not catch me.'

'No. But it did not stop me thinking about it. My blood ran cold to think of what might have happened to you.'

She rose. A tiny spark of light glimmered. She knew him well enough to realise this was the nearest he would come to an apology.

'I did not think of the danger when I went out. I only wanted to help.'

'I know. You were very brave.'

The glimmer strengthened, but she damped it down, kept it under control. 'You said I was foolish.'

'Did I? Eve—' He took a step towards her and she put up her hand, savouring the feeling of power.

'*Damned idiotic* were your exact words.'

A smile lifted the corners of his mouth, 'That could equally apply to me. I should tell you now that I am very proud of you, Mrs Wylder.'

'Y-you are?'

'Oh, yes. Not many women would willingly put themselves in such danger.'

He was coming closer. Another few steps and he would be within arm's reach. The tug of attraction was very strong, but she fought it.

'M-Martha is coming back with a cup of milk for me.'

'No, she is not. I have sent her to bed.'

Eve gasped. Her hand fell to her side. 'Oh! Of all the arrogant, high-handed—'

He pulled her into his arms and stopped her mouth with a kiss. The shock of it sent a tremor right down to her toes. Eve gripped his coat as his tongue raided her mouth. She was so relieved to have him with her that she responded eagerly, kissing him back with a ferocity that left them both breathless. Eventually, when Nick raised his head, Eve rested her cheek against his chest, listening to the heavy thud of his heart, revelling in the feel of his arms around her.

'You were magnificent last night,' he murmured, pressing a kiss on the top of her head. 'You were riding like the very devil; I doubt they would have caught you.'

She pushed her arms around him under the greatcoat and hugged as hard as she could. 'I wanted to make you proud of me.'

'I *am* proud of you, my love.'

She almost purred with pleasure at that. 'Really?' she murmured into his chest and felt him growl in response. She raised her head to find him gazing down at her. She responded to the look of dark desire in his eyes by tilting her head up, inviting his kiss.

As his head swooped down he swung her up into his arms and walked across to the bed. Even before he put her down her fingers were reaching for the buttons of his shirt. She wanted to run her hands over his bare skin, to feel again the pleasure she knew he could give her.

When he lowered her on to the bed and released her, Eve scrabbled to her knees. She knew a moment's panic as she thought he might be leaving her, but instead he shrugged himself out of his coats and pulled off his neckcloth. Impatiently she reached out for him, pulling him to her. As he climbed on to the bed she kissed him, throwing her arms around his neck, her lips parting beneath the onslaught of his deep, urgent kisses. Desire raged through Eve, she found herself plucking at his shirt, desperate to touch his skin, to run her fingers over the smooth, hard curves of his body. There was more to discuss, many more questions to be answered, but for now she need to know he was really here, that it was not some sweet dream from which she would wake up, lost and unsatisfied. His fingers tangled with the ribbons at her neck and all the while he continued to kiss her mouth, his roving tongue wreaking havoc with her senses. He lifted his head and gently ran his hands over her shoulders, pushing away the nightgown. It slid down, unre-sisting, to pool around her on the bed. Eve reached out for his shirt and tugged at it.

'This is unfair,' she whispered. 'I must see you, too.' Eve grappled with the buttons of his breeches but her hands stilled as Nick pulled off his shirt in one sweeping movement and she saw the bandage just below his ribs.

'Merely a precaution now,' he said, following her gaze. As if to prove his words he unwrapped the dressing to reveal the thin, jagged line. 'There. It is almost healed.'

Gently she reached out and placed her fingers near the wound. The skin was pale and cool to the touch. No sign of inflammation. 'Does it hurt?'

'Not much.' He grinned at her and that wicked dimple peeped. 'It will not impair my performance, I promise you.'

While he slipped off the bed and quickly removed his boots, breeches and stockings, Eve pulled away her nightgown and tossed it aside, but all the time she kept her eyes on Nick, enjoying the way the candlelight played on the muscled contours of his back, enhancing the curving sweep of his spine. It was as if she was seeing him for the first time; she marvelled at the broad width of his shoulders, the way his body tapered to the narrow waist and taut, finely carved buttocks. As he turned back to her the sight of his aroused body drew a faint gasp from Eve.

Nick tumbled her back onto the bed, laughing. 'I told you I had missed you.'

She pulled him down to her, driving her hands through his hair, cradling his head while he trailed kisses along her collar-bone. Her body arched as his hands cupped her breasts, thumbs gently caressing her. She breathed in the faint, spicy fragrance that clung to him. It was so familiar she had even dreamed of it. She threw back her head as his mouth trailed across her breast and closed over one hard peak. His tongue circled slowly, causing such sweet agony that a soft moan escaped her. She felt so alive, every inch of her skin was crying out for his touch and it positively burned beneath his fingers when they travelled over the flat plain of her stomach. The aching desire intensified as his hand moved downwards. Muscles deep within her pelvis seemed to be pulling her apart. Her thighs opened in anticipation, her body tilted, eager for his fingers to slide into her. Even so the shock of his touch jolted through her and she cried out as a surge of excitement flooded her body. Still his tongue continued to caress her breast, creating waves of almost unbearable pleasure while his fingers continued their rhythmic stroking. She writhed beneath him, crying his name, no longer able to control her body.

In one smooth movement he rolled on to her. His

fingers slid away and she felt him inside her, hard and smooth. Gasping, she reached up to his face, pulling him close so that she could plunder his mouth, wanting to repay something of the pleasure he was giving her. He tasted of salt and wine. Her senses were reeling with the feel of his body upon hers, their limbs tangling together in the semi-darkness. She felt rather than heard his groan as his self-control slipped away. She matched her movements to his, revelling in the joyous release as they both approached the final, shuddering climax. Eve clung to him, crying out as a wave of passion crested and broke. Consciousness splintered and Nick's rigid body was above, around and within her, possessing her totally.

With a sigh Nick collapsed, panting, beside her on the bed. Gently he drew her into his arms. 'I think,' he murmured into her hair, 'that you have missed me, too.'

She snuggled closer and gave a sleepy sigh. 'I did not realise how much.'

He gave a soft laugh. 'Then we are equal in that.'

Eve awoke to find herself alone in the bed. The early morning sun peeped through the window and she raised her head to look around the room.

Not again! Memory stabbed at her.

Nick was already dressed, bending before her mirror to tie his neckcloth. She remembered their wedding night at Makerham, waking to find Nick dressed and about to leave her. An icy chill settled over her heart. Would it always be like this?

She sat up, pulling the sheet up in front of her. 'You are going?'

'I must.' In two strides he was at the bedside, cupping her face and kissing her. 'We had word yesterday that Chelston will be moving a large consignment soon—perhaps tonight. I have to get back. The Revenue cutter is patrolling the mouth of the Rother; nothing can slip by.' He kissed her again. 'Another couple of days should see this wrapped up. Then I promise you my roving days are done.'

'Do you really mean that?'

'I do.'

She released the sheet to put her arms around his neck for one final kiss. Her body arched upwards as his hands cupped her breasts.

'Damnation, Evelina, you make it hard for a man to leave you!'

She gave a low laugh, using all her new-found powers to detain him. 'Do I?'

He put his hands on her shoulders and held her

away from him. 'Yes, but it must be done.' His eyes held a promise that made her tremble with anticipation. 'I shall return: be ready for me!'

One final, hard kiss and he left her.

Chapter Sixteen

As Eve made her way downstairs some hours later, Nick's words sang in her head. Her spirits soared when she recalled the way he had looked at her, his admission that his anger was not for what she had done, but for the danger she faced. It was true, it had been a reckless escapade and it was not something she should repeat, but she had known a wild pleasure in outwitting the riding officers. She chuckled to herself as she crossed the hall. Sam and his friends were very enterprising, the hidden causeway had been effective; no one would guess that there was any route other than the road.

Eve stopped. 'Of course!' she exclaimed. 'I wonder—' She looked up to find Granby had come into the hall and was watching her.

'Madam?'

She looked at him, hardly able to contain her excitement. 'Mr Granby, I want you to come with me, now, to the boathouse passage.'

'The passage? But why, mistress?'

'I cannot say,' she replied, her eyes twinkling with mischief. 'It may be nothing, but…come along. And bring a lantern!'

She was too excited to waste time changing her gown, but made Granby precede her down the stepladder and look away while she pulled her skirts about her and negotiated the narrow steps. Aggie, holding open the trapdoor, tutted her disapproval and uttered dire warnings about headstrong females.

'I have seen those novels you keep by your bedside, Miss Eve. They do you no good, filling your head with outlandish ideas and making you think you can act like the heroine in a romance!'

Eve paused long enough to laugh up at her. 'Tush, Aggie, if I really thought of myself as a heroine I should not tell anyone where I was going and put myself in great danger. As it is, I am being very sensible and taking Mr Granby with me. Now shut the door after us, if you please.'

By the time Eve had descended to the floor of the passage the trapdoor had closed above them and they were in darkness save for the pale gleam of the lantern. She shivered in the cold, damp air and was inclined to wish she had brought a shawl.

'So, madam, what are we looking for?' asked Granby.

'I am not quite sure. Let us go on to the boat-house—and keep the lantern shining forward. I can hear things scrabbling around in the dark, and I have no wish to see what it might be.'

Granby laughed. 'There might be the odd rat, Miss Eve, but they won't bother you. After all, we must look like monsters to them.'

'Your reasoning may be sound, Mr Granby,' said Eve with studied calm, 'but I really do not wish to think about it! Let us get on.'

She grabbed his arm as he strode along the passage, telling herself that the noises she heard were no more than the drip of water from the roof of the passage, or the soft moan of the wind blowing in from the grating at the end of the winding tunnel. She found herself breathing a little easier once they reached the final bend and the locked grating stood before them. Beyond it, the wooden panels that made up the back wall of the boathouse were sadly rotted and sunlight reflecting off the gently moving water of the drain glinted between the weathered boards. Instinctively Eve moved towards the light.

'Shall I unlock the grating, madam?'

'No.' Eve stopped, considering. 'The passage winds so I have lost my bearings. Tell me, Mr Granby, if we stand with our backs to the opening, on which side of this passage would be Abbotsfield?'

Granby did not hesitate. 'That side,' he said, pointing. 'To the north.'

Eve looked at the way the passage curved slightly northwards. 'Excellent,' she said. 'Then that is where we must look.'

'Look for what?'

'A concealed entrance. When I was out with Sam the other night he said that the families in these parts had been hiding their tracks from the Excise men for generations.'

'That is true, madam, but I don't see—'

She took the lantern from him and began to inspect the walls very carefully. 'We know Silas has always been involved in free-trading: the very presence of this tunnel suggests that Monkhurst was used for smuggling at one time, but my family also owned Abbotsfield, which is no more than half a mile north of here. What if there is a tunnel from Abbotsfield to here? Sam and his people use a sunken causeway; it is hidden from the road by fencing covered in reeds so that the riding officers went straight past it, following the road. If the King's men ever searched the boathouse they might well discover this tunnel and would follow it to Monkhurst, but would they look for another opening? The bend in the passage makes this wall particularly dark…aha!' Eve held the lantern higher. 'There is a gap here!'

Granby stepped up, running his hands over the wall. 'This looks like part of the wall but—it's a door.'

'There's no lock,' said Eve, moving the lantern to and fro.

'No, but—there's a latch!'

The click echoed around the passage, Eve tensed, expecting the shriek of metal against metal as the door swung open, but it moved smoothly and in near silence.

'The hinges have been oiled very recently,' murmured Granby.

Eve's heart hammered painfully against her ribs. 'Careful!' she gasped. 'What if there is some-one—?' Her words trailed away as the door swung wide and the lantern's glow illuminated the space beyond. The light did not reach very far, but it showed them a cavernous tunnel stretching back into the darkness. Piled high against its walls were dozens of wooden chests.

Granby gave a low whistle. 'You were right, Miss Eve.' He took the lantern from her and stepped through the doorway. He bent closer to one of the chests 'Tea,' he said. 'Or rather, not tea. Smouch.'

Eve swallowed. 'Nick said the Revenue men are watching the river,' she said slowly. 'They are watching the wrong place. These casks will be taken out through Jury's Cut.'

'Then they'll miss it, mistress.'

She turned and gripped his arm. 'Mr Granby, you must go immediately to tell Nick. There may still be time for him to act.'

They ran back along the passage.

'Quickly,' she said when they had once more reached the kitchen. 'Take the fastest horse and do not stop for anyone.'

'But what of you, madam? Captain Wylder ordered me to stay with you.'

'I shall be safe enough, I have Davies and Warren to look out for me. Now go!'

Eve went off to change her gown. She was sure she would not be able to settle to anything until she heard from Nick, but she could not be idle. After partaking of a very late breakfast she sorted out a pile of sheets for mending and was carrying them downstairs when she saw a figure crossing the hall.

'Bernard!' He stopped and looked up, raising his hat to her. 'How did you get in here?'

'I walked in from the kitchen garden, Cousin. Are you not pleased to see me?'

Eve hoped her face did not show her dismay. She was a little surprised to see him in topboots and breeches, and despite the warmth of the day he carried a travelling cloak over one arm. She said shortly, 'I am very busy, Bernard. Pray tell me what it is that you want.'

He followed her into the morning room, where she placed the sheets next to her sewing basket.

'I thought you might like to take a little walk with me. Let me put it differently,' he said as she opened her mouth to reply. 'You *will* take a little walk with me.' He lifted the travelling cloak slightly to reveal a small silver-mounted pistol in his hand. 'Do not think I will not use this,' he continued. 'From this distance I could not fail to kill you.'

Eve stood very still, her eyes upon the small black mouth of the pistol that was pointed at her stomach. 'What are you about, Bernard?'

'I will explain presently. For now you will

precede me out on to the terrace, if you please, and from there to the park.'

'And if I refuse?'

'I will choke you or shoot you.'

Eve stared at his face. There was a grim determination in his eyes that made her think he would really do it. He gestured towards the door. 'Shall we go? And pray do not think to call to your servants,' he murmured as she went out before him. 'If I think you are giving them any signal at all, I shall shoot you.'

She stepped out of the house and upon Bernard's instruction walked ahead of him towards the archway that led into the park. It was a balmy day, yet Eve found herself shivering, aware of the pistol's muzzle only inches from her back. She could only hope for some distraction so that she could get away, but for the moment there was no one in sight, no one who knew of her plight.

'Where are we going?' she asked, trying to keep her voice calm.

'Walk straight on towards the row of beeches over there. My carriage is parked just beyond the wall.'

'You are kidnapping me.' It was a statement, and Eve was surprised that she could sound so matter of fact about it.

Bernard laughed. 'Yes, I suppose I am. It would have been simpler if you had agreed to accompany Lady Chelston yesterday, but there it is. She was most put out that you would not see her, but we thought it might arouse suspicions if she came bang up to the house and demanded you go out with her.'

'We? Who might that be, Bernard?'

'Why, Lord Chelston and myself, of course. I—'

A sudden shout behind them made him stop. He grabbed Eve's arm and pressed the pistol hard against her ribs.

'It—it is my maid,' she said, looking back. 'I will need to speak to her, to reassure her.'

'Then be very careful, Cousin. Remember the pistol at your back. I have its twin in my pocket and I can use it just as well with either hand. Do not give me cause to shoot your maid as well as you.'

Keeping close, he turned Eve to face Martha, who was running up to them.

'Madam, I saw you from the house—'

'Yes, Martha. I am going for a walk with my cousin.' The maid hesitated, frowning, and Eve found herself praying that she would say nothing out of place.

'You may return to the house,' said Eve quietly. 'I do not need you.'

Martha shifted uncomfortably from one foot to the other. 'Madam, it—it is going to rain; would you not be more comfortable indoors?'

'That is why we are taking our walk now,' said Eve smoothly. 'Although it means I shall not be able to ride out on Persephone this afternoon. When Mr Granby returns, Martha, pray tell him I shall not require Persephone.'

Eve smiled brightly while all the time she was in terror that her maid would look puzzled and ask her what she meant.

'Would you like me to come with you, mistress?'

The hard muzzle prodded warningly in Eve's back. She managed a laugh, although it sounded brittle to her strained nerves.

'Goodness me, no. You would be much better employed mending the sheets I have left in the morning room. You know I was going to tackle them myself, until my cousin here beguiled me with the idea of a walk. Of you go now. I shall not be long.'

'She is suspicious,' muttered Bernard, watching the maid make her way back to the house.

'Of course she is,' retorted Eve. 'She knows I dislike you. However, it is not her place to question my behaviour. She will sit over her sewing until dinner.'

'By which time you will be far away.'

Another few minutes brought them to the edge of the trees. Bernard pushed her on to a narrow path and soon she saw a gap in the palings and a carriage beyond. Eve tensed. If she was going to run, it would be better to do it now. Once in the carriage she could be miles away before she had another chance to escape. Her hands had closed on her skirts, ready to lift them and take to her heels, when she felt a stunning blow to the back of her head. The force sent her down on to her knees, the daylight was replaced by blackness and she lost consciousness.

Chapter Seventeen

'Four o'clock.' Nick consulted his watch as he guided Admiral through the gates and into the park at Monkhurst. 'We have made good time, Richard, though not quite as speedy as your ride to me this morning!'

'I thought it necessary to get the information to you with all speed, sir.'

'And you were right. You arrived in time for me to discuss the new plans with Captain George, rather than send fresh instructions after him.'

'I only hope we've got it right, Captain,' murmured Granby.

'Well it all makes sense, Richard. And it explains Chelston's interest in Monkhurst.'

Nick urged his horse to the trot. His heart was singing, not only with anticipation of the forthcoming action, but with the thought of seeing Eve again.

As they clattered into the stable yard he was surprised to find it already bustling with people. Warren and Davies were leading horses out of the stables while Silas Brattee and his sons turned as Nick trotted up. Eve's maid pushed them aside to run forward. Richard was off his horse in a flash to meet her.

'Martha? What is it?'

'Oh, Dick, I'm so glad you've come.' Martha caught at his hands, then turned a tear-stained face towards Nick. His brows snapped together.

'What's happened?' he barked.

Silas strode forwards. 'It's the mistress, Cap'n. She's gone. We was just getting up a party to go and find her.'

'Gone? Where?' he demanded.

'We don't know, sir,' cried the maid. 'She went out walking with that cousin of hers and never came back.'

'Shawcross was here?' said Granby. He turned towards Nick, a frown in his eyes.

'Aye,' muttered Martha, wiping her eyes with her apron. 'Davies let him in.'

'That I did, Cap'n.' Davies stepped up, an anxious frown on his round face. 'I'm that sorry, sir, but when he came walking in by the side door and said he was Mrs Wylder's cousin—'

'You weren't to know,' said Nick. 'He's abducted her, that's certain.' He turned again to Martha. 'What time was this, when did you last see her?'

'It was about noon, Captain. When Davies told me Mr Shawcross was here I wasn't happy about it and went to find her, not wanting her to be alone with him. I saw them walking away from the house, so I ran after them, but Miss Eve sent me away, saying to tell Mr Granby that she wouldn't be needin' her horse this afternoon.'

Richard frowned. 'Horse? We had made no arrangement.'

Martha shrugged. 'I'd said it looked like rain— trying to get them to come back to the house, but she just laughed at me and said in that case she wouldn't be needing Pers—Persephone.'

Nick turned to stare at Granby, who shook his head. 'She doesn't own a horse by that name.'

'No,' said Nick slowly, 'but she used it for Lady Chelston recently.' He grinned. 'Clever girl, she's telling us where Shawcross is taking her!'

The unpleasant tang of smelling salts stung at Eve's nose and instinctively she twisted her head away. As consciousness returned she was aware that she was lying on a narrow couch. She did not open her eyes, but she could feel the slippery satin beneath her hand. A woman's voice sounded very close.

'She's coming round.'

There was something familiar in the low, husky tones, but her head ached and she could not quite remember where she had heard it before. Then she heard a voice that she knew only too well.

'She has been unconscious for hours; I did not think I had hit her quite so hard.'

Bernard's tone was querulous, defensive. Eve kept her eyes closed, as though by doing so she could avoid the truth of her situation. Her memory was returning. Bernard had carried her off. The soft, gravelly voice belonged to Catherine Chelston, and suggested they were at Chelston Hall. Eve knew she must find out for herself. Cautiously she opened her eyes a little. The room seemed very bright and she closed them again with a moan.

'It is very hot in here. Throw up the sash, then pour some wine for her!' Lady Chelston began to chafe one of her hands. 'Come along, madam, you have lain there long enough. We need you awake.'

With a shudder of distaste, Eve pulled her hand free and tried opening her eyes again. She found Catherine leaning over her, and beyond the painted face and powdered hair she could see a white rococo-patterned ceiling. She had seen that design before, it was Lady Chelston's drawing room.

Eve struggled to sit up. Bernard was standing before her, his eyes narrowed.

'What am I doing here?' she asked frostily.

'I apologise for the rough treatment, Cousin, but it was entirely necessary.'

'Was it necessary to hit me over the head?' she demanded, taking a glass of wine from him.

'Oh, yes,' he replied with a cold, self-satisfied look. 'I knew you were considering flight, and I had no wish to drive through the village with you struggling like a wildcat.'

'So what do you want with me?' She glared at them. Anxiety gnawed at her. Did they know Nick was alive? Did they know of his plans to intercept the consignment? Bernard's next words gave her some reassurance.

'It is very simple: Monkhurst.'

She took a sip of the wine, hoping it would revive her. 'And how do you propose to get it?'

Bernard's sly smile made her skin crawl with apprehension. 'You will marry me. I have to admit the idea holds some appeal for me. I have always had a fondness for you, Cousin.'

Eve turned away from him. She glanced at the clock on the mantelpiece; Five o'clock. Martha would know by now that something was wrong, but could she get word to Nick? And would she pass on her parting message? It was a very slim hope, but it was all Eve had. She must not lose her courage now. She must play for time.

'I feel very ill, is there somewhere I could wash my face, and perhaps brush my hair?'

Catherine Chelston regarded her for a moment. 'Very well, come with me.' She escorted Eve upstairs to one of the guest rooms, but any hopes Evelina might have had of overpowering her were dashed when Lady Chelston called to her dresser to accompany them.

Eve took as long as she dared tidying her hair and splashing her face with cold water. When she returned to the drawing room she felt considerably more alert, although no nearer finding a means of escape.

'Ah, my blushing bride. I trust you are feeling a little better, Cousin?'

Bernard stopped pacing the floor and tried to take her hand. She snatched her fingers away.

'You cannot force me into marriage. Everyone knows I detest you.'

'Do they?' Catherine pushed her down on to a chair. 'Your presence at my house party did not go unnoticed, Mrs Wylder, nor the fact that Bernard was so very attentive. What more natural than a lonely widow finding solace with her cousin and unable to wait to satisfy her passion? So you slip away quietly to be married by special licence—'

'Which I have obtained,' added Bernard, patting his pocket. 'I cannot wait to make you mine, Cousin.'

Eve tried not to think of it. 'But Mr Didcot advised caution; I might not yet be a widow.'

Bernard gave a snort of rude laughter. 'Didcot's an old fool. Wylder's dead. There's no one to contest our marriage. I'll have you wedded and bedded by dawn.'

A shudder ran through her. 'Why is Monkhurst so important to you?' she asked.

'There are certain—goods—at Abbotsfield that need to be shipped abroad,' said Lady Chelston. 'Revenue men are watching the Rother, so we want to move them out on the Monkhurst Drain.

We have already taken steps to make sure that no one else uses the inlet at night.'

'So you have been attacking my people in Jury's Cut.'

'Your people—how feudal that sounds,' Bernard scoffed. 'Yes, we sent our men to frighten off the locals. And we made sure the Revenue was aware that there was going to be a drop the other night. Normally they would not concern themselves with such a small affair, but they are very active here at the moment; they think it will lead them to a large smuggling gang.'

'Led by Lord Chelston and yourself, perhaps?' retorted Eve.

Lord Chelston's cold voice came from the doorway. 'Very acute, madam, but it is dangerous for you to ask so many questions.'

Catherine turned to him. 'You are back, my dear! You have the parson?'

'He is in the chapel.' He nodded towards Eve. 'How much does she know?'

Bernard shifted uneasily. 'Very little, my lord. Mere conjecture—'

Lady Chelston lifted her fan. 'Still enough to make her a threat,' she said.

'She will be safe enough once we are married,' said Bernard. 'I promise you.'

'You promised me Monkhurst if I would make you a partner in this business,' snapped Lord Chelston. 'I want you and your new wife back at Monkhurst as soon as maybe. If her servants set up a hue and cry, there will be the devil to pay.'

'If he takes me back to Monkhurst, what is to stop me telling everyone the truth?' demanded Eve.

Lord Chelston's cold grey eyes settled on her. 'Do not underestimate your cousin, Mrs Wylder. If you give him too much trouble, he will have to kill you just as he killed your husband.'

Eve did not have to pretend to look shocked at these words. Although she knew the truth, she was horrified to hear Lord Chelston speak of murder so coolly.

'Wylder was working with the Revenue,' said Bernard. 'If I had not shot him, he would have ruined everything—'

'We have no time for this now,' Lord Chelston interrupted him. 'Bring her to the chapel.'

'Wait!' cried Eve as Bernard dragged her to her feet. 'What if I refuse? You cannot force me into this!'

Lord Chelston looked at his wife, who pulled a small bottle from her reticule. 'Laudanum,' she said. 'You will not be in a position to refuse.'

'No!' Eve protested as Lord Chelston stepped behind her and pinned her arms to her sides. Bernard took the bottle and removed the cork. Eve stared, horrified. If he forced her to swallow the laudanum she would be lost. She might even give away Nick's secret. She struggled desperately but Lord Chelston held her fast. Bernard stepped closer, a cruel curl to his lips.

'Now, now, my dear, why should you object so much to taking me for a husband?'

'Because she does not wish to commit bigamy.'

A stunned silence fell over the room. Eve's head snapped round towards the sound of Nick's voice. Relief flooded through her at the sight of him sitting in the open window, his legs astride the sill and a deadly-looking pistol in each hand. She knew a sudden and irrational desire to laugh; he looked completely at his ease and that familiar, gleaming smile made her heart leap.

Bernard dropped the laudanum bottle and its contents spilled out to make dark, spreading stain on the carpet.

'Wylder!' he spluttered. 'But it can't be. I sh-shot you. You are dead!'

'Obviously not,' drawled Lord Chelston. He gave Eve a little shake.

'Well, madam, did you know he was alive?'

'Not at first.'

Bernard turned to glare at Eve, his mouth working convulsively. 'No, I'll swear she did not. I was there when his man broke the news.'

She tried to shrug herself free, but Lord Chelston's grip only tightened painfully. He held her before him like a shield.

'Congratulations, Wylder,' he said coolly. 'You fooled us all.'

'Yes, I did, didn't I?' Nick grinned as he swung his leg over the sill and stepped into the room, Richard Granby and Sam following him. 'So much so that we know all about your plan to send out the next consignment of smouch through Jury's Cut. Captain George already has his orders to intercept the black-sailed lugger and haul in your people at Abbotsfield, to keep everything ship-shape. It is all up with you, Chelston.'

'Oh I think not. I still have one ace in my hand, Wylder.' He yanked Eve's arms behind her, holding them with one hand while his other reached into his pocket and pulled out a pistol. He pressed the cold muzzle against her head, just below the ear. Eve swallowed, trying not to tremble, and kept her eyes on Nick. His smile did not waver, but he was very still. Tension crackled around the room.

'Let her go, Chelston,' he ordered. 'There is no way you can escape now.'

'Perhaps not. But what have I got to lose if I shoot your wife first? I should like to think I made you suffer for your victory.'

Eve closed her eyes. It would not help Nick to see how terrified she was.

'Don't be a fool, man.'

Chelston laughed softly 'Oh I am no fool, Wylder. I have your measure. You will not risk the life of this pretty lady, now, will you? One wrong move by you or your friends and I shall pull the trigger.'

There was a brief, heart-stopping silence before Nick spoke again. 'We seem to have reached an impasse.'

'Whatever happens now, your wife will die,' said Chelston. 'Unless…'

The word hung in the air. Eve's nerves were at breaking point. She forced her tense muscles to relax, afraid that if she shuddered or trembled that deadly pistol might go off.

'Unless?' Nick prompted quietly.

'Call your men off, Wylder. Let the consignment go through.'

'That is out of my hands. Chelston. The Revenue is aware of your whole operation.'

'True, there is little I can do about Abbotsfield; if the government knows of its purpose then it is too late to save it. It matters not, since it would appear you have made it impossible for us to remain in England. However, this final consignment is valuable and I would rather not lose it. You can send word to your Captain George, Wylder; tell him you were mistaken and that the original orders stand: his ship should continue patrolling the Rother.'

Eve's eyes flew open. 'No,' she whispered, gazing at Nick. 'You cannot let him get away.'

'Would you rather he let you die?' sneered Chelston.

Eve ignored him. She kept her eyes upon Nick. *I'm sorry*. She mouthed the words, hoping he would understand her. Lady Chelston took a step forward.

'Everything depends upon how much our gallant Captain values his wife.'

Eve drew herself up. She said proudly, 'Not above duty to his country! I would not expect that.'

Nick stared at the little group in front of him and weighed up the odds. With Richard and Sam both armed he did not doubt that Shawcross, Chelston and his lady could all be overpowered, but neither did he doubt that the pistol pressed against Eve's head was loaded and that Chelston would use it if they made any attempt to rush him. His heart contracted painfully as he saw how bravely she stood her ground. He looked into her soft brown eyes. They were dark now, the dilated pupils the only sign that she was afraid. Bless her, did she really think he could put duty before her?

'Very well,' he said at last. 'I will call off the Revenue.'

Eve gave a little sob. 'No.' Her voice was little more than a whisper. 'You were sent here to prevent this,' she said. 'When they find out, you will be ruined.'

'Yes, that gives another pleasant twist to this episode,' Chelston jeered. 'The heroic Captain Wyldfire, a traitor to his country.'

Nick ignored this taunt. He signalled to Sam and Richard to lower their pistols. 'Release her,

Chelston, and you have my word that you will not be intercepted tonight.'

'No, no, Captain, you have *my* word that once the *Merle* has loaded her cargo and set sail again I will let your woman go free,' Lord Chelston replied. 'I do not fear your ships once the *Merle* is moving. I would back her to outrun anything you may have in your fleet. You and your men will leave here now. You will send word to the Revenue officers that their cutter is to remain at the mouth of the Rother and make sure that nothing happens to prevent this last consignment from reaching the *Merle*, or to prevent my own little party boarding my yacht at Hastings. Is that agreed?'

'And my wife?'

'Mrs Wylder shall be my guest aboard the *Maestro* and we shall watch the proceedings from there. And now, Captain Wylder, I would ask you to make your decision quickly. My arm is beginning to ache and this trigger is so very sensitive.'

'What assurance do I have that you will keep your word?'

'Why, none, my good Captain; but then, what assurance have I that you will keep yours?' He laughed softly. 'Mrs Wylder is my guarantee of safe passage out of the country. But time is getting on. You must leave now if your instructions are to reach your gallant Revenue captain in time. And remember, Captain Wylder; your wife is safe only as long as matters go smoothly, so you had best make sure I see the Revenue cutter in Rye Bay this evening. I shall look out for her when we sail past in the *Maestro*. From this moment Mrs Wylder will be accompanied at all times by Shawcross, Catherine or myself; we are all like to hang if we are caught, so we are none of us afraid to pull the trigger, am I not right?' He looked at his companions, who nodded, and Chelston fixed his cold eyes on Nick again. 'If I suspect you are trying to trick me, then she will be the first to die. Well?'

'Your consignment will not be intercepted. You have my word upon it.'

It took all Nick's self-control not to react to the flash of triumph he saw in Chelston's face. He had schooled his own to a look of indifference and forced himself to watch without emotion as Chelston pulled Eve closer to him and stroked her cheek with the pistol.

'Well, my dear, do you trust him?' That purring voice grated on Nick's raw nerves. 'After all, he fooled you before, did he not? He allowed you to think he was dead. What sort of trick is that to play on a loving wife?'

Nick saw the anger in Eve's eyes and the scornful curl of her lip. He gave her a rueful smile and said quietly, 'Well, sweetheart?'

Her chin went up. 'Yes,' she said clearly. 'Yes, I trust him. Implicitly!'

Despite their desperate situation a blaze of happiness lifted Nick's spirits. He met and held Chelston's challenging look. 'You harm her and I will make sure you do not live to see the dawn.'

Lord Chelston's thin lips curled. 'I am no uncivilised savage; keep to our bargain and she goes free. Shawcross, ring the bell, if you please. Our guests will leave by the main door, I think.'

Chapter Eighteen

'Captain?'

Nick heard Richard call his name, but he did not answer as he strode out of the house. He made his way quickly to the walled garden where they found Silas and Nathanial waiting with the horses. A tight knot of anxiety twisted inside him, worse than any fear he had ever felt for himself. Walking away from Eve was the most difficult thing he had done in his life. Her brave smile had wrenched at his heart; although he had a plan forming, there was no guarantee that it would work. She had put her trust in him and he was not at all sure he would succeed.

'Captain?' Richard spoke again. 'What are you going to do?'

'There's enough of us, Cap'n,' said Sam, anxious eyes fixed on his face. 'What if we were to storm the house—?'

Nick shook his head. 'You heard Chelston, Sam. If we try anything of that nature he will shoot Eve. I cannot risk it. Let's get out of here.' He mounted and cantered down the drive, Richard and the others behind him. He did not stop until they were well clear of Chelston, then he pulled up in a wooded glade at the side of the road and waited for them to come up to him.

'Well, sir?' Richard's usually impassive countenance was grim.

'I do not think Chelston will harm her, at least until the smouch has been transferred to the lugger,' said Nick. 'The first thing to do is to get word to Captain George.'

'I'll go, Cap'n!' declared Sam eagerly.

Nick shook his head. 'I've other work for you, Sam. Silas, how many oarsmen does that galley of yours hold?'

'Why, twenty, sir, but we can manage with half that number—'

Nick interrupted him. 'For what I have in mind you'll need a full complement. You said your brother has a similar vessel, over at Dimchurch.'

'Aye, sir, 'e has.'

'You'd be better setting off from there. Could you find me enough oarsmen? Could you find them for tonight?'

'Aye, Cap'n, reckon we can, if it will help rescue Miss Eve.' Silas stuck out his chin. 'She helped us on our last run, now it's our turn to repay the debt.'

Nick grinned. 'Very well then, Silas. You are always telling me that the Kentish oarsmen are the best in the world, now you are going to prove it to me!'

Chapter Nineteen

It took all Eve's willpower not to cry out to Nick as he walked out of the room. As soon as the door had closed behind him Lady Chelston pulled one of cords from the window and bound Eve's wrists. After that she became the still centre of a whirlwind of activity. She was obliged to sit passively and watch while all around her bags were packed, orders shouted and servants despatched. Her forced inactivity was deeply frustrating. And at all times Lady Chelston, her husband or Bernard hovered near her, a constant reminder that if anything should go wrong she would be the first to suffer.

Eve half-expected an attack on Chelston Hall by the dragoons or a party of riding officers and she was a little disappointed when an hour dragged by with nothing more exciting than Lady Chelston's maid dropping a scent bottle on the marble floor of the hall and filling the air with the pungent, sickly smell of overblown roses. Eve told herself that Nick was protecting her, that he would do nothing to risk her life, but it irked her to be so helpless. She remembered Mr Granby's words: *Captain Wyldfire runs with the wind, ma'am.* Well, he was running with a very ill wind now and she did not see how he could turn it to his advantage.

The drive to Hastings was slightly more interesting, but less comfortable, for she was bundled into the carriage with Lady Chelston and her maid, who cried into her apron and declared that she did not want to leave her family.

'Why can't I stay behind, m'lady, like 'is lordship's man?'

'Griffin is not staying behind, you foolish wench,' retorted Lady Chelston, 'He is staying to pack the rest of the trunks and will follow us as best he can.'

'But I don't like the water, ma'am; you know I gets sick!'

In reply Lady Chelston boxed her ears and told her to control herself, but the maid's sobs only increased.

Eve looked away in disgust. Outside the windows

she could see her cousin and Lord Chelston riding beside the carriage. She felt trapped and as the coach bounced and rocked over the uneven road she was obliged to reach up with her bound hands and cling on to the strap for the most uncomfortable journey of her life.

They boarded the *Maestro* at Hastings. With her hands tied Eve found it difficult to climb up on to the yacht, but she closed her lips stubbornly against any complaint. As Bernard helped her on to the deck she heard Lord Chelston addressing the first mate.

'Mr Briggs, where is your captain?'

The man snapped to attention. 'Sick, me lord,' he replied smartly. 'Flux. Running out of 'im somethin' dreadful…'

'Yes, yes, no need to give me all the details.' Lord Chelston waved him away. 'Well, get on with it, then man. You know what to do.'

Lady Chelston and her maid immediately retired to a cabin, complaining of sickness and Bernard bundled Eve to a quiet spot near the stern of the yacht while the bare-footed sailors moved quickly about their tasks as they prepared to put to sea. Everywhere she looked there was a profusion of ropes, wooden spars and huge canvas sails that to Eve's untutored eye made the *Maestro* look top-heavy. As the crew adjusted the sails to make the most of the light breeze, she heard the first-mate informing his master that with so little wind it would be fair nigh impossible to make good time. If that was true, then perhaps the *Merle*, too, would be late to the rendezvous; no one could blame Nick for that.

Eve waited until the first fevered activity of setting sail had died down, then she thrust her bound wrists towards Bernard.

'I would be obliged if you would untie me now. After all, I can hardly escape from here.' She looked out over the calm grey water that surrounded them. 'You know I cannot swim, Cousin. What harm can I do you here?' She directed a steady look across the deck at Lord Chelston, who nodded.

'Take off the rope, Shawcross, but watch her.' He turned to Eve. 'Any tricks, madam, and you will be trussed up and locked below. Do you understand?'

Eve met his eyes without flinching. 'Perfectly.'

Once her wrists were free, Eve made her way towards the bow of the ship where she hoped she would not be in the way of the crew. She rubbed her arms, hoping that the balmy night would stay warm since she had only the silk shawl Lady Chelston had given her to keep out any chill winds. The sun had set, the daylight a mere thin line of pale grey on the horizon. There was no moon and the only light came from the stars that were beginning to twinkle in the east, although above her head the mass of ropes, spars and huge sails blotted out the sky. She moved past the pin-rail, where a bewildering number of ropes were tied off, and dropped down by the railing so that she could peer out under the rigging at the empty sea before them. Despite the lack of wind the ship seemed to be travelling quickly through the water, the prow slicing effortlessly through the waves with a gentle rocking motion that she found quite soothing. The sea air was cool on her cheeks and she could taste the salt on her lips. It was invigorating; it reminded her of Nick. Bernard came up and sat down beside her. She hunched her shoulder and turned her back on him.

'Look, Cousin.' He pointed towards the dwindling coastline with the ancient town of Rye on its hill, standing guard like some medieval fortress. 'You see the sails over there? It is the *Argos*, cruising at the mouth of the Rother. Captain George will have a long wait.'

Eve did not answer. The Revenue ship looked so far away, she could expect no help from that quarter.

'The *Maestro* is a very fast cutter,' Bernard continued. 'She's clinker built with a lute stern so she's very light and fast. She's rigged fore-and-aft—'

'Bernard,' Eve interrupted him wearily. 'Do you have the slightest idea what any of that means?'

'It means, dear cousin, that we have the advantage of any government vessel. Chelston tells me the *Maestro* was built at the self-same shipyard as the lugger that is waiting for our longboats to row out to it with the casks full of smouch. It means,' he said with great deliberation, 'that even if your husband tries to give chase tonight he will not catch us.' Bernard gave a self-satisfied sigh. 'It is common practice, I believe, for the shipwrights to build boats for both the free-traders and the Revenue, but 'tis the free-traders who get the faster vessels.'

'With so little wind I do not see it makes any difference,' remarked Eve.

'Oh, it will pick up presently. For now we are in no hurry. The *Merle* is not expected at the rendezvous until midnight.' He settled himself more comfortably. 'Seems damnably dark to me. Barely enough light to see your hand in front of your face, but I'm told the crews prefer it that way.'

'How will the *Merle* know this is not an enemy ship?' she asked. She added hopefully, 'It might turn around and sail away.'

'There are pre-arranged signals. Chelston informs me that we shall be able to watch the consignment being transferred to the *Merle* and when it is all done we shall follow her to Boulogne.' He reached out and put a hand on her shoulder. 'I am looking forward to getting you ashore, my dear.'

Angrily she shrugged him off. 'Lord Chelston gave his word that if the consignment went ahead I should be freed.'

She caught the quick gleam of his teeth in the near-darkness.

'Yes, Cousin; but Lord Chelston did not say where. If we set you down in Boulogne with no money, no maid and no baggage, I think you might soon find yourself in difficulties. What do you think, Cousin?' He leaned closer until she could feel his hot breath on her face. 'A young lady, unattended, in a busy seaport—you would not last five minutes. Much better to put yourself under my protection, my dear. Besides, I think your husband owes me something for obliging me to undertake this precipitous flight, with not even my valet to attend me. At least I shall have you to warm my bed—'

She brought her hand up and caught him a stinging slap on the face. With a snarl Bernard jumped up, his black shape looming over her.

'Why, you—'

'Quiet, damn you!' Lord Chelston's voice cut like a whiplash across the deck. 'We have reached the rendezvous.'

With a muttered curse Bernard lounged away. Eve watched him go with some relief. She looked towards the shadowy figure of Lord Chelston, pacing to and fro across the deck.

'What happens now?' she asked him as he came near.

'Now we sit and wait to see if your husband is as good as his word.'

A heavy darkness fell, trapping them between the velvety sky with its myriad twinkling stars and the silky blackness of the sea. The only sound was the gentle lapping of the water against the hull or the occasional snap of a sail overhead. Eve hugged her shawl about her and wondered what she could do when they reached Boulogne. The idea of remaining under Bernard's protection was unthinkable. Nick would come for her, she was sure of that, but how soon? Perhaps she could find a priest to take her in while she sent word to him. She closed her eyes, summoning up that last glance he had given her before he had walked out of the drawing room at Chelston Hall. No words, but a look in his blue, blue eyes that had promised he would find her. It was a small hope, but it was all she had and she clung on to it desperately.

'There she is, m'lord.'

The first mate's quiet growl roused Eve. She strained her eyes until they watered. At first she could see nothing in the gloom, but at length she could just pick out a black shape in the distance. A light glimmered, the barest flash in the darkness. One of Lord Chelston's crew swung a lantern in response and a murmur of anticipation ran around the deck. Eve remained beside the rail, watching and waiting. Minutes passed. At last a faint movement caught her eye; she could see a line of small shapes on the water, inching towards the *Merle*. She knew they must be the long boats, laden with casks of bogus tea to be hauled aboard the lugger. Her pulse quickened; perhaps Nick and his officers had replaced the longboatmen and were even now aboard the *Merle*, overpowering the crew and capturing the ship for the crown. Perhaps…

A series of lights flickered from the black outline of the ship and Eve heard Lord Chelston give a grunt of satisfaction.

'Good. All is well; she's loaded. Any sign of enemy ships, Briggs?'

'No, sir.'

Eve's heart sank as she watched the tiny boats moving away from the *Merle*. At such a distance they looked like a string of jet beads on a bed of dark satin. Once the *Merle* set sail there was little chance that any Revenue cutter could prevent her from reaching Boulogne. Depression as black as the night settled over her. Once it was known that Nick had allowed the smugglers to escape, his good name would be lost. And she was to blame. Nick had sacrificed everything in a desperate bid to save her. Eve squared her shoulders. She must not be despondent; if the tales she had heard were to be believed, Captain Wyldfire had successfully recovered from worse situations than this. For now there was little she could do except to stay alert.

As Eve watched the black shapes of the longboats slip back towards the shore, a question occurred to her.

'What will happen to those men?'

Chelston shrugged. 'I have no idea.'

'But you could have warned them. If they return to Abbotsfield, they will be arrested.'

'That is not my concern; I have no further use for them.'

'How can you be so cold?' She shook her head, disbelieving. 'Have you no thought for the people you have abandoned?'

'No, none.' Lord Chelston put his telescope to his eye and slowly turned around, raking the seas. 'Well, well; the *Merle* is underway and not another vessel in sight. Wylder was as good as his word. He must really love you, my dear.'

'Oh I do, Chelston. Never doubt it.'

'*Nick!*'

Eve hurtled across the deck towards the tall, familiar figure that had appeared by the main mast. Nick reached out and drew her to him with one hand, while the pistol in the other never wavered from its target, which was Lord Chelston's heart. She noted that Richard Granby was beside him, his pistol aimed at Bernard, who had raised his hands. Even in the darkness she could see that he was shaking.

Nick leaned down to plant a kiss upon her head. 'Have they hurt you, sweetheart?'

She clung to him, pressing her cheek against his rough wool jacket. 'No, not at all. But I am so glad to see you.'

'Curse you, Wylder, where did you come from?' snarled Lord Chelston.

'I was 'tween decks with Richard. We didn't want to ruin the surprise by your spotting us too early.'

'Much good it may do you, when you are outnumbered by my crew. Take them!'

Eve gasped as Chelston dived to the deck, but Nick did not move. No shots were fired, and no one attempted to lay a hand upon Nick, who merely laughed.

'Get up, Chelston, you look very foolish lying down there. I think you will find they are not your crew any longer. I've hired them.'

'You have *what*?' It was too dark to see Chelston's face, but Eve could hear the astonishment in his voice.

'I have hired them. You kept 'em too long ashore, Chelston, and on half-pay too. A mistake, but although they were anxious to get to sea again not one jack tar wanted to turn pirate, which I convinced them they would be if they followed you. I admit it was the reward for your capture that finally persuaded them to come over to me. I've a mind to have the *Maestro*, too; after all, you will have no use for her now. Of course, your captain could not be bought, so we had to leave him behind, but I think once he learns you have been arrested he will consider his contract with you void.' He raised his voice. 'Mr Briggs, take them aft and secure them, if you please.'

'Aye, aye, Cap'n.'

Eve gripped his coat 'Nick, Lady Chelston—'

'Safely locked in her cabin, sweetheart. I do not think she is yet aware of what is happening; she dosed herself with laudanum as soon as they set sail.'

'And the maid?'

'Locked in with her. She's cast up her accounts, but still looks decidedly green. But what of you, my love, no sea-sickness?'

Eve shook her head. 'I have been on deck all the time.'

'That's my girl.' His arm tightened around her, pulling her against his chest. He dropped his pistol into the pocket of his coat before cupping Eve's chin in his hand and turning her face up towards him. 'Are you sure you are not hurt?'

'Yes, I am sure.'

'Were you frightened?'

She smiled up at him lovingly. 'No. I knew you'd come for me.'

He threw back his head and laughed. 'What? No fits, no vapours? You are a woman after my own heart, Evelina! No.' He looked down at her, suddenly serious, and said softly, 'No, you *are* my heart.'

It was too dark to see his face clearly, so she reached up her hand to touch his cheek. A muscle in his jaw quivered beneath her fingers, he pulled her even closer until she could feel his body hard against hers.

She drew his head down, turning her face up to him. The next instant his mouth was crushing hers, possessing her. She pressed herself against him, consumed by a fierce, urgent desire until Nick's hands moved to her shoulders and he held her off a little.

'Gently, sweetheart,' he said unsteadily. 'Much more of that and I'll have to take you here, on the deck. Think how that would shock poor Richard!'

She stared at him, dizzy, uncomprehending. All she knew was that she wanted him. She managed a shaky laugh. 'I said I was not frightened, but that's not true; I was afraid I would never see you again.'

He stroked her face gently. 'You'll never know how much it cost me to leave you at Chelston Hall.'

She covered his hand with her own and rubbed her cheek against his captive fingers. 'It is over now—'

She broke off at a sudden shout of alarm. Nick looked up and instantly pushed her away from him. As she hit the pin-rail Eve saw the dark figure of Lord Chelston crash into Nick, who fell to the deck with a grunt of pain. Chelston straightened. There was a flash as the starlight glinted on the blade in his hand. Eve seized a belaying pin from the rail and swung it as hard as she could. It caught Chelston's arm with a sickening, bone-breaking crack and the knife fell harmlessly to the deck.

There was an infinitesimal pause, a brief moment of stillness for Eve to catch her breath before she was surrounded by figures. One sailor gently prised the belaying pin from her fingers while two more laid hands on Lord Chelston, who yelped with pain. Richard Granby was helping Nick to his feet, Mr Briggs hovering beside him, anxious to make his apologies.

'I'm sorry about that, Cap'n. He was so quiet-like and I just took my eye off 'im for a moment—'

'Yes, well, don't take any more chances with this one,' replied Nick, putting a hand to his side.

'You're hurt,' said Eve, her voice not quite steady.

'No, no, merely winded,' he replied. 'He caught me on my wound, but no harm done, I hope. A capital hit, Evelina, well done, my love.' He reached out one hand for her and looked over her head to address the first mate. 'Briggs, take Lord Chelston away and bind him up securely this time—and be careful with his arm; I think 'tis broken. Now, Mr Granby, cram on all sail and let's see if Captain George has captured the *Merle*.'

'But how can he?' Eve frowned. 'The *Argos* is still in Rye Bay; I saw it myself, when we sailed from Hastings.'

'His ship may be at Rye, but Captain George and his men should be near Boulogne by now, as guests of Silas and his brother in the old galley!'

Chapter Twenty

There was no opportunity for Evelina to demand a full explanation. A freshening wind had sprung up and Nick was busy ordering his new crew to set course for Boulogne. The stars were already fading by the time they came upon the *Merle*, which was now flying a red customs ensign and pendant above its black sails. As the *Maestro* came alongside the lugger, Eve recognised several Monkhurst men on her deck and guessed they would be helping the customs officers to sail the lugger back to England. As the two ships prepared for the return journey Silas sprang nimbly over the rail on to the deck of the *Maestro*. When he saw Eve, he stopped and tugged his forelock.

'I'm glad to see thee well, mistress, and that's a fact. I tell thee straight I didn't think the cap'n's plan would work when he first suggested it—'

'Then damn your eyes for doubting me, Silas Brattee,' cried Nick, coming up. 'You'd best come below deck; we'll break out a bottle of rum and you can give me your report.'

Eve stepped forwards.

'I'm coming too.' She sensed the men's hesitation and added belligerently, 'I have been kidnapped, tied up and forced aboard this, this floating prison: I think I am entitled to know just what is going on!'

Silas looked stunned at this outburst, but Nick merely laughed.

'Very well,' he said holding out his hand to her, 'Come below, my dear, but you will find it very cramped!' He crossed to the companionway leading below deck. Eve hesitated at the dark, cavernous opening, wondering how she was going to negotiate the steep, ladder-like stairs and keep her dignity. 'Allow me,' said Nick, and before she could protest he threw her up over her shoulder and carried her to the lower deck where he set her down, grinning.

'Thank you,' she said through gritted teeth, 'You need not have done that. I managed the ladder in the boathouse tunnel and I could have managed this one.'

'I am sure you could,' he replied soothingly, 'but my way was much quicker—and far more enjoyable.'

Blushing furiously, she turned away as Silas climbed down the steps to join them. Nick lifted a lantern from its hook and led them to a small table. Moments later she was sitting beside him while he poured a red-brown liquid into three cups, saying as he did so, 'Well, Silas, tell me just how you enjoyed having a full complement of Revenue officers on board.'

The old sailor gave a slow smile. 'I think they considered our galley a bit beneath their dignity, Cap'n, but once we was underway they realised we could beat any sailing vessel on the sea last night, there being no wind, like.'

'So you rowed out in the galley to intercept the *Merle*?' asked Eve.

'Aye, mistress, that's right. The cap'n here daren't risk Lord Chelston spotting any ships *following* the lugger, so he sent a message to Captain George, asking him and his men to meet us at Monkhurst. From there we rode like the very devil across to Dimchurch, to me brother's place.' Silas tossed off his drink and gave a fat chuckle. 'You should've seen old Ephraim's face when we arrives with a parcel o' Revenue men! Thought we'd turned traitor, dang 'im, it took a fair few minutes to convince 'im to let us have the galley, but he come round in the end and we made good time after that. Sea was like a mill pond, she was.'

Silas paused and stared hard at his empty cup. His lips twitching, Nick finished his own drink and reached for the bottle. When he had filled Silas's mug and his own he looked at Eve, one eyebrow raised. She shook her head. She had taken a few small sips of rum and managed not to cough, although the thick, sweet liquor had made her eyes water. She realised she had eaten nothing since breakfast and wondered if it was wise to drink at all. She turned away from the mischievous glint in Nick's eyes and addressed Silas.

'But how did you find the *Merle*? After all, the sea is so…' she spread her hands and ended lamely '…big.'

'Lord love you, mistress, we just rowed for Boulogne like we always do—I mean…' he coughed, and looked a little sheepish. 'As we used to do in the old days. Then we just laid on the oars and waited for the *Merle* to come to us. Took some time, of course, with no wind for her sails. 'Twas dark and the galley so low in the water that the *Merle* didn't see us 'til it was too late. Cap'n George sends a volley o' shots across 'er decks and we boarded her with no trouble. French crew. No fight in 'em,' he ended almost sadly.

Eve took another cautious sip from her cup. The rum left a burning trail as she swallowed, but now there was a pleasant warmth spreading through her limbs. She leaned back and listened as Nick told Silas all that had happened aboard the *Maestro*. Their talk became steadily more animated, full of nautical terms as they passed from discussion of the night's activities to reminiscences of the adventures they had shared together in the King's navy. The little cabin rocked with their laughter.

'Aye, those were the days,' sighed Silas. 'I'll never forget '76, Cap'n—do you remember? Admiral Howe gave you command of your first ship.'

'How could I forget? We took Newport and Rhode Island, although we had to defend it from the French a couple of years later, before we could sail for home.'

'So we did—' nodded Silas as Nick refilled their mugs yet again. 'Rare times they was, so far from home and the enemy all around us. But we were all for 'ee, sir, every man jack of us wanted to sail with

Cap'n Wyldfire. We'd all go to hell and back for you, Cap'n, 'cos we knowed you'd be there with us.'

Eve closed her eyes and let their talk wash over her. A tiny cloud was shadowing her heart. This was Nick's world, this life of adventure and danger. It was not hers. She heard the chink of glass against a cup. Nick was serving out more rum; most likely he had forgotten she was there. The cloud darkened as Bernard's words came back to her. *You cannot tame a tiger, only cage him.*

'Aye, they was good old days, surelye,' Silas was saying, his tone contemplative.

'And do you miss it?' asked Nick.

'That I do, sir. Pottering about near the shore ain't the same as sailing halfway round the world. No, the sea's a harsh mistress, Cap'n, but she don't ever let you go.'

Eve felt the depression settling more heavily inside her. She let out a sigh. Immediately Nick turned to her.

'Tired, my love?' The warmth in his voice was unmistakable; that was a comfort, but Eve realised just how weary she was, and when Nick called Richard Granby to escort her away she went quietly, content to rest in what Richard explained was once Lord Chelston's cabin. She lay down upon the narrow bunk, and even the muffled sounds of Lady Chelston's hysterical shrieks from her makeshift prison did not prevent her from falling into a deep, dreamless sleep.

Eve awoke some hours later to find that they were at Rye. Making her way to the deck, she found Richard Granby overseeing the crew. He turned and bowed when he saw her.

'Good morning, ma'am. The captain sends his apologies; he was obliged to meet with Captain George, and they are taking the prisoners to the gaol in the tower. He expects to return soon and begs that you will wait for him at the Mermaid. If you will give me but two minutes to instruct Mr Briggs, I will escort you.'

At the inn she found that Nick had already reserved a bedchamber and the genial landlord informed her that the small coffee room was also at her disposal. Eve declined any refreshment and allowed her host to escort her upstairs. The room set aside for her was the same one she had used on her previous visit, but she had no time for memories, because no sooner had she stepped through the door than Martha rushed across the room and enveloped her in a fierce, tearful embrace.

'Oh, Miss Eve, I'm that glad to see you! I was so frightened when I had the message from the captain, and he begged most politely that I should come to Rye to wait for you here. As if anything would stop me coming to you, mistress!'

'Yes, yes, thank you Martha.' Eve gently disentangled herself from her maid, resisting the urge to burst into tears. 'I am very glad you are here, and I shall be even more glad if you will fetch up some hot water for me to wash.'

'Of course, madam, immediately. And you will see that I have brought you some clean clothes. The master sent for his things, too, but without Rich—I mean Mr Granby to pack for him, we can only hope that we've brought the right clothes.'

'But where is his trunk? Oh…' Her spirits flagged a little. 'He bespoke a separate room, I suppose.'

'Why yes, Miss Eve, which the landlord tells me is just such a thing as the greatest lords and ladies do.' Martha chuckled. 'Nothing but the best for our Captain Wylder! But you are looking very pulled, mistress, and no wonder, being out on that nasty rough water all night. But don't you worry, we will soon have you feeling as fresh as a daisy. Um…' Martha stepped back, twisting her hands in her apron. 'I'm supposing you *all* came back safe? I mean, is Mr Granby...?' She trailed off, a rosy glow spreading over her round cheeks. Despite her low spirits a smile tugged at the corners of Eve's mouth.

'Richard Granby escorted me here,' she replied. 'It is very likely that he is still here at the inn.' She added innocently, 'Perhaps you could find him, and tell him I have no further need for him today.'

The blush on Martha's cheeks deepened. 'Ooh, yes, mistress, I will!' She dropped a series of hurried curtsies as she backed towards the door, then she was gone and Eve was alone.

She sat down on the edge of the bed and let the silence of the room settle around her. It was as if she was still for the first time in many, many weeks, for the first time since Nick Wylder had ridden into her life. She had lived a quiet and un-exacting existence at Makerham; the most exciting thing in her life had been a short visit to Tunbridge Wells. But Nick's arrival in her sheltered world had changed all that. He was Captain Wyldfire indeed. She had been pitched headlong into the sort of adventure that should have left her swooning. Only she had not fainted away. Instead, she had relished the excitement. She regretted nothing. Except, perhaps, that she had fallen in love with an adventurer. And adventurers, like tigers, could not change their nature.

Eve wrapped her arms across her stomach. She could not tame her tiger, but neither would she confine him. To do so would surely kill any love he had for her. No, he must be free to go his own way, however much it hurt her.

Chapter Twenty-One

It was late morning before Eve received a message from Nick. She was sitting in the small coffee room when Martha came in with a note. Eve almost snatched it from her hands.

'Hmm,' she said, scanning it quickly. 'Typically high-handed. No apology, he merely says he will be here as soon as he can. *"I have ordered dinner to be served in your room."* Hah! I am tempted to countermand that.'

'Ooh, Miss Eve, I beg you won't! The captain don't want you eating with the common folk.'

'We could use this room. Well,' she said as Martha shifted uncomfortably from one foot to the other, 'why not?'

'Well, mistress, you see, Richard and me...' Martha almost squirmed before her.

'Ah, I understand,' said Eve, trying not to smile. 'You are planning a private dinner with Mr Granby. As your employer, I should perhaps ask him if his intentions towards you are honourable.'

'No, Miss Eve, pray don't do anything like that! 'Tis only a dinner, after all, and better for the both of us than listening to the coarse talk in the kitchens. I was so worried about him, you see…'

'Very well, Martha, but you must promise to behave yourself.' Eve looked out of the window. 'Now, the sun is shining and I would like some air. We will go out.'

'But what if the captain should come looking for you, Miss Eve?'

She put up her chin. 'Then he will not find me. Let him kick his heels and wait for *me*. Fetch my wrap, please Martha, and your own. We are going to explore the town, then we shall walk to the church and admire its fine architecture!'

Eve returned from her outing much refreshed and if she was disappointed to find that Nick was not waiting for her she would not admit it. It was still early and she sent Martha away to find out if it was possible for her to bathe before dinner. While the inn's servants built up the fire and toiled up the winding stairs with pails of water, Eve turned her attention to the clothes Martha was laying out for her.

'That is my cream polonaise, Martha. Have you nothing less…dashy?'

'No, ma'am, only the walking dress that you have been wearing all day.'

'But the cream gown is part of my trousseau.'

Martha gave her a sly look. 'Why so it is, mistress, and very romantical, too.'

Eve hunched a shoulder and turned away, knowing that any remonstrance would be wasted and would most likely lead to her own discomfiture. She allowed Martha to undress her and stepped into the hip bath to enjoy the hot scented water. It was very relaxing, but as the dinner hour approached her anxieties increased. When she had finished bathing she put on a clean chemise and allowed Martha to pin up her hair. Eve glanced at the creamy silk gown laid out on the bed. Its low neckline seemed to mock her.

As the maid picked up the linen stays she said, 'Lace me up tightly, Martha.'

'Very well, ma'am.'

The feel of the linen and whalebone enclosing her ribs brought to mind visions of knights in stiff, unyielding armour. Not unlike her own forthcoming meeting with her husband. 'Tighter,' she ordered, adding very quietly, 'I do not want to enjoy myself tonight.'

Martha helped her into the polonaise and arranged the folds of the skirt becomingly over the rose-coloured petticoat. It was not until the bodice was fastened that Eve realised the effect of the tight-lacing was not at all what she desired. She might feel restricted and unyielding, but the confining stays accentuated her tiny waist and pushed up her breasts so that they filled the gown's low neckline in a way that would draw any male eye. And Nick was most definitely male. Well, there was no time to ask Martha to undress her again now.

'Did you pack a kerchief for me, Martha?'

'Aye, ma'am, but—'

'Find it, if you please.'

Five minutes later Eve regarded with satisfaction the fine muslin kerchief that covered her bosom.

'There, that is much better.' Much safer. 'Now, Martha, if you will have dinner fetched up and make sure they remove the bath and all signs of my ablutions, you can take yourself off and join Richard Granby.'

* * *

Eve did not know whether she desired or dreaded Nick's appearance. She paced about the room as the hip bath, water and towels were carried away and the small table pulled out in readiness for dinner. Martha and the inn's servants moved quickly and efficiently, lighting the candles, drawing the curtains and building up the fire to ward off the slight chill of the evening. She watched them at work, reasoning that the longer they took over their tasks the more she could put off seeing Nick.

The hasty, booted footsteps outside the door told her she was mistaken.

Nick strode in, bringing with him a sense of urgency that had the servants hurrying through their tasks and scuttling away.

'Pray forgive the informality, madam.' He bowed to her. 'Will you allow me to dine with you in this attire?'

Eve's heart lurched as she looked at him. He was dressed as she had first seen him, in buckskins and topboots. His exquisitely-tailored riding jacket and the snow-white linen of his shirt and cravat signified the fashionable town beau, but his sun-browned face and the wicked twinkle in his blue eyes belonged to the adventurer. He spread his hands and said apologetically, 'I sent word to Monkhurst for my clothes to be brought here, but this is the best I can muster.'

She felt herself responding to his lazy smile. 'Then it shall suffice, sir.' She became aware that Martha was hovering by the door and waved her away. 'Yes, yes, you may go, Martha. I shall call for you if I need you.' She glanced at Nick, feeling awkward now they were alone. 'I believe she is dining with your man this evening, sir. I hope you do not object?'

'Not at all. He confided to me that he wants to make an honest woman of her, so I suggested he should wine and dine her in the coffee room tonight.'

'Oh. Is that why we must eat here?'

'No, sweetheart. We are eating here because it is more convenient.'

She observed his quick glance towards the bed and a little spurt of excitement flamed within her. Quickly she damped it down. He came closer, a faint crease between his brows.

'What is that thing round your neck?'

'What? O-oh, this.' She touched the muslin kerchief. 'It—um—seemed a little cool in here.'

'Well the fire is blazing well enough now, so you

won't need it any longer.' Before she realised what he was about he had grasped the kerchief and pulled it away. She felt the colour rush to her cheeks as his eyes fell on the full, rounded bosom. He put his hands on her shoulders, saying softly, 'Now why should you want to hide such beauty?'

He lowered his dark head and she felt his lips brush the soft skin just above the rim of her bodice. Immediately her breasts tightened. They seemed to want to push right out of their confinement, to offer themselves up to his waiting mouth. The breath caught in her throat. Dear Heaven, why did he affect her so?

'I…did not want to distract you,' she managed, her voice croaking pitifully. Another deep breath, another attempt to control her wayward senses. 'We have things to discuss, sir.'

He raised his head. 'Ah.'

A scratching at the door heralded the arrival of their dinner. As the two waiters set down their trays Nick escorted Eve to the table. His fingers burned through the silk sleeve of her dress. Heavens; a single touch and she was reduced to a quivering wreck! She looked at the food set out on the table; soup, a brace of pigeons, a dish of mushrooms, apple pie—her appetite had disappeared.

Nick took his seat at the table and watched Eve toying with her food. Something was amiss. She was upset; he could see it in her face, in the droop of her shoulders. She would tell him, before the night was out. Night. He wanted to pick her up now and carry her over to the bed and make love to her. Just the thought of it aroused him. She had been right to put that muslin about her shoulders; the sight of her soft round breasts pushing up from her gown was too damned distracting. He smiled, hoping he looked reassuring and not leering as he poured more wine into their glasses.

'I suggest we postpone our...talk, until we have eaten.'

He set to with a will, but he did not ignore her. He carved a few tasty slices of pigeon to tempt her appetite, spooned some of the mushrooms on to her plate and cut a sliver of the apple pie. She ate it dutifully, and he was relieved to see a little colour return to her cheeks.

The waiters brought in another set of dishes, including a ragout of mutton and a sweet pastry. Eve was once more in command of herself and they managed to talk of commonplace things until they were alone once again.

'So, is your investigation concluded now?' she asked him, nibbling on a pastry.

'Yes.' The tip of her tongue was running across her bottom lip in a most sensuous fashion. He dragged his eyes away. 'Yes,' he said again. 'I have made my reports. Captain George will escort the prisoners to London. I shall be obliged to go to town at some stage, but my work here is finished.'

She nodded. 'You will be anxious to return to your home, then. In Yorkshire.'

'There are matters there that require my attention, undoubtedly.' Now where was all this leading? 'Estate management can be tedious, I know, but it must be done.'

She was avoiding his eyes, looking into her wineglass as she murmured, 'You would much rather be at sea, I think.'

'Evelina—' He reached for her hand across the table, but she snatched it away. As the waiters returned at that moment he let the matter drop, but he waited with impatience for the table to be cleared.

'That will do,' he said at length. 'Leave the bottle and the glasses. You need not come back again.' He smiled again at Eve. 'Will you take a little more wine with me, madam? A toast to a job well done.'

'Very well, sir. But now I think we should—we must—talk.'

He rose from the table and held out his hand to her. 'Then shall we sit by the fire?'

He led her to one of the two armchairs placed on either side of the hearth. She sank down and spent a few moments rearranging her skirts. One dusky curl fell forwards and lay across the white skin of her shoulder. He resisted the temptation to reach out and touch it and instead sat down opposite her.

'Now, my love, what is it you want to say to me?'

She did not answer him, but kept her eyes lowered, her fingers smoothing the creases from her petticoats.

'Eve?'

She looked up then, her dark eyes fixed upon him. 'You said you must return to Yorkshire soon. I understand that. After all it is your home. I wondered if, perhaps, when you go north, you would allow me to remain at Monkhurst.'

Nick sat very still. He had the strangest sensation that his world was teetering, about to fall. Now, at last, when he knew what he wanted, was she about to snatch it all away from him? He said quietly, 'You regret our marriage.'

She looked up quickly. 'No! That is…' She sighed and waved one of her hands in a gesture of hopelessness. 'You married me to get Monkhurst. I know that, and I am not angry about it. I know that you did not intend to—to consummate the union. I believe you truly thought that if…if we did not suit, then the marriage could be annulled.' She gave a crooked little smile. 'It did not quite work out like that, did it? We are bound, now. Irrevocably.'

He shrugged. A cold hand was squeezing at his heart. 'We are man and wife, sweetheart. For better, for worse. Until death.'

Silently he cursed himself; he had not meant the words to sound so harsh. He saw the flicker of alarm cross her face. She jumped up from her chair and began to pace about the room.

'But that's so cruel, Nick. So unjust. We are too different. You crave adventure, excitement; catching smugglers, fighting for a cause, risking your life—it is what you do. I watched you, on board the yacht, dealing with the sailors. You are a natural leader, Nick. And—and when you were talking to Silas, about your life at sea, it all became clear to me. You miss it already.' She turned to him, her eyes dark and troubled. 'A life of quiet domesticity would not suit you, Nick. You would be miserable, and I do not want you to be miserable. You must be free to do as you wish. I know that, but I cannot bear the uncertainty of your life, knowing each time you ride off that you might not return. I would rather s-say goodbye now and live quietly at Monkhurst than have that recurring agony.'

Nick closed his eyes and breathed out slowly. The world was righting itself again. 'I thought we might go adventuring together.'

Eve put her hands over her face and shook her head. Why would he not listen? Why did he make it so difficult for her? She had to make him understand.

'No, no,' she said. 'Do you not see? I would be a hindrance to you.' Her hands dropped to her sides. 'This time you risked everything to rescue me. I know, I like to think, that you would do the same again.' She gave a sad little smile. 'But you will not always be able to save the world and to save me, too.'

He was out of his chair so quickly that she only had time to blink. He stood before her and put his hands on her shoulders. 'Is that what you think?' he asked her. 'That I cannot be happy unless I am courting danger? My sweet life, that may have been the case in the past, but not any more. My life changed when I met you; suddenly I had someone to live for.' He gazed down at her, his eyes more serious than she had ever seen them. 'Eve, when Bernard Shawcross put that bullet in me, I thought it better to let everyone think I was no longer alive. I thought we would round up Chelston and his gang and I could get back to you without you knowing anything about it. Then you wrote to tell me that your grandfather had died. That was the worst time of my life, sweetheart; I couldn't be with you to comfort you in your loss and, even worse, I had put you in danger. I vowed then that when this was all over I would never put you at risk again. And I mean it, Eve. I intend to be a model husband from now on.'

Eve blinked, trying to clear the hot tears that crowded her eyes and prickled her throat, making it difficult to speak.

'I would like to believe you, Nick, but I cannot. I heard what Silas said, about the sea. It never lets go…'

He caught her agitated hands and held them firm, his thumbs circling on the soft pads of her wrists, calming her. 'Silas is a sailor to his core, but I—' a sudden smile lit his eyes. 'I am more of an adventurer. I enjoyed the navy, but I can leave it for a new challenge and there are plenty of those to be had. We are living in exciting times, Evelina; in my native Yorkshire there are manufactories springing up for spinning and weaving, with the new canals ready to carry as much as can be produced to London or to the coast. England is changing, Eve, and we should be part of that. I do not need to leave you, sweetheart; there are more than enough challenges for a man here at home, especially one with a wife at his side.' He squeezed her fingers. 'Well, what do you say? I am offering you everything, Eve, my heart as well as my hand. I love you, you know. Will you throw in your lot with me?'

She stared into his face. There was no sign of the devil-may-care look now, only an anxious, earnest expression of a man awaiting his fate. That vulnerability was her undoing, it demolished the last of her defences.

'Yes,' she whispered, 'Oh, yes, Nick!'

Slowly the earnest expression disappeared, replaced by a mixture of love and triumph and happiness. He gathered her in his arms and she melted into him. His mouth slid over hers and he kissed her in a thorough, unhurried manner that had her senses reeling. She leaned against him, dizzy and breathless. She felt his hands on her shoulders.

'Open your eyes,' he murmured. 'I need you to stand up.'

He was unlacing her bodice, his long fingers drawing out the strings with a smooth, steady rhythm.

'What are you doing?'

The wicked glance he gave made her racing pulse even more erratic. 'This is a beautiful gown, sweetheart, but it is in my way.'

Heat pooled low in her belly. It was an effort to keep still while the laces whipped out of the remaining eyelets and he pushed the bodice away from her shoulders. The silk fell to the floor with a whisper and she felt herself blush. The thought flashed through her mind that her cheeks probably matched her rose-coloured petticoats. She began to unbutton Nick's waistcoat. 'Sauce for the goose, Captain Wyldfire,' she murmured, provoking a shadow of desire in his blue eyes.

Once she had helped him out of his jacket and waistcoat his hands slipped around her waist and stopped. He threw up his head, an arrested look on his face. 'What's this?' He squeezed the large pad of wadding tied to her back.

'It is a false rump.' She choked on a laugh. 'It is all the fashion.'

'Well, we can do without it,' he said, undoing the tapes and casting it aside. 'You have a perfect rump without it.' As if to prove his words he cupped her buttocks with his hands and pulled her to him. She gasped, feeling him hard and aroused against her belly. He lowered his head and trailed a line of butterfly kisses down her neck, causing her to moan softly. His hands moved up again to her waist. 'I've a mind to take a knife to these stays,' he muttered as his fingers tugged as the ribbons. 'This is layer upon layer of armour.'

She laughed, feeling her power over him. 'That is exactly it, to protect me from your wicked ways.'

Nick tilted up her chin and gazed at her. 'Do you *want* to be protected from me?'

Her insides had turned to water. Eve ran her tongue across her lower lip and shook her head. She did not think she could speak. His smouldering glance held her eyes while his fingers eased the ribbons loose. The friction vibrated against her body, sending ripples of pleasure through her limbs. Once the confining stays had been cast off he pushed aside her chemise and gathered her to him, pressing her flesh against his. For a heartbeat she remained frozen in pleasure, arching towards him, then the world exploded around them. Nick was kissing her neck, her face, trailing hot kisses over her eyelids. They were both gasping, eyes wild as the remainder of their clothes were discarded. With a growl Nick swung Eve into his arms and carried her to the bed. She clung to him, pulling him down on top of her, wrapping her legs around his waist as if to bind him to her for ever.

She drove her fingers through his hair, guiding his lips back to her own where she gave him back kiss for kiss. This was no gentle embrace, it was fierce, furious possession and Eve revelled in it. She ran her fingers down his back, exploring the contours, delighting in the iron muscles rippling under the skin. Nick's hands roamed her body, exploring and caressing, gently arousing her until she groaned, arching her back and thrusting her hips forward, inviting him in. He shifted his body, covering her, their bodies moving together, faster, harder until Eve could no longer control her own responses. She dug her nails into Nick's broad back, crying out as a spasm of pure pleasure rippled through her. She heard Nick shout out. He gave one last, final thrust and she felt herself falling, tumbling as if from a great height.

Nick rolled over and collapsed beside her on the

tangled bedsheets. He reached out and caught her hand, twining his fingers with hers.

'Well, madam, are you satisfied?'

She turned her head to look at him. His naked chest was rising and falling rapidly, his skin gleaming and golden in the candlelight. She smiled. 'For the moment.'

He raised himself on one elbow and gazed down at her. 'For the moment, hmm?' He drew one finger lightly across her breasts. They tightened immediately at his touch. 'You are going to be a challenge, Mrs Wylder.'

She rested her hands on her belly. 'I think we may have another challenge ahead of us, Nick. It is too early to be certain, but…'

He stared at her, a slight crease in his brows, then his eyes lit up and he gave a wide, unstoppable grin. 'Oh, lord, I never meant for *that* to happen.'

She sat up. 'Oh, you are not happy,' she said, dismayed.

'Happy?' He caught her to him. 'I think I must be the happiest man alive! Oh, but should you not be resting? Should I not even be kissing you, or…you know?'

She blushed at the thought of 'you know', her

toes curling up with pleasure. 'I do not believe we must give up our pleasures just yet, my love.'

He lowered her back down on to the bed and kissed her nose. 'Now that is a good thing. Because I have just realised that we have been apart for most of our married life. We have some time to make up.'

Eve allowed her glance to stray downwards. A tiny, mischievous smile curved her lips. 'Well, we have all night, my love…'

* * * * *

HISTORICAL

Large Print

THE VISCOUNT'S UNCONVENTIONAL BRIDE
Mary Nichols

As a member of the renowned Piccadilly Gentlemen's Club, Jonathan Leinster must ensure the return of a runaway. Spirited Louise has fled to her birthplace, hoping to find her family – but charming Jonathan stops her in her tracks! His task is simple: escort Louise promptly home. Yet all he wants to do is claim her as his own!

COMPROMISING MISS MILTON
Michelle Styles

Buttoned-up governess Daisy Milton buries dreams of marriage and family life in order to support her sister and orphaned niece. But Viscount Ravensworth shakes up Daisy's safe, stable existence. Could a tightly laced miss be convinced to forgo society's strict code of conduct…and come undone in the arms of a reformed rake?

FORBIDDEN LADY
Anne Herries

Sir Robert came in peace to claim his lady honourably. But Melissa denied their love and her father had him whipped from the house. Embittered, Rob sought his fortune in fighting. As the Wars of the Roses ravage England, Melissa falls into Rob's power. He should not trust her – but can he resist such vulnerable, innocent beauty?

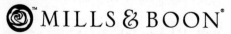 MILLS & BOON

HISTORICAL

Large Print

PRACTICAL WIDOW TO PASSIONATE MISTRESS
Louise Allen

Desperate to reunite with her sisters, Meg finds passage
to England as injured soldier Major Ross Brandon's
temporary housekeeper. Dangerously irresistible, Ross's
dark, searching eyes warn Meg that it would be wrong to
fall for him… But soon sensible Meg is tempted to move
from servants' quarters to the master's bedroom!

MAJOR WESTHAVEN'S UNWILLING WARD
Emily Bascom

Spirited Lily is horrified by her reaction to her new
guardian, Major Daniel Westhaven. He's insufferably
arrogant – yet she can't help longing for his touch! Brooding
Daniel intends to swiftly fulfil his promise and find troublesome Lily a husband. Yet she brings light into his dark
life – and into his even darker heart…

HER BANISHED LORD
Carol Townend

Hugh Duclair, Count de Freyncourt, has been accused of
sedition, stripped of his title and banished. Proud Hugh
vows to clear his name! Childhood friend Lady Aude de
Crèvecoeur offers her help – after all, turbulent times
call for passionate measures…

MILLS & BOON

HISTORICAL

Large Print

THE EARL'S RUNAWAY BRIDE
Sarah Mallory

Five years ago, Felicity's dashing husband disappeared into war-torn Spain. Discovering a dark secret, she had fled to England. Still haunted by memories of their passionate wedding night, Felicity is just about to come face to face with her commanding husband – back to claim his runaway bride!

THE WAYWARD DEBUTANTE
Sarah Elliott

Eleanor Sinclair loathes stuffy ballrooms packed with fretful mothers and husband-hunting girls. Craving escape, she dons a wig and disappears – *unchaperoned!* – to the theatre. There she catches the eye of James Bentley, a handsome devil. His game of seduction imperils Eleanor's disguise – and tempts her to forsake all honour…

THE LAIRD'S CAPTIVE WIFE
Joanna Fulford

Taken prisoner by Norman invaders, Lady Ashlynn's salvation takes an unexpected form. Scottish warlord Black Iain may be fierce, yet Ashlynn feels strangely safe in his arms… Iain wants only to be free of the rebellious, enticing Ashlynn. But then a decree from the King commands Iain to make his beautiful captive his *wife*!